KAITLYN BANKSON

The Dormant Age

First published by Kaitlyn Bankson 2025

Copyright © 2025 by Kaitlyn Bankson

This novel is entirely a work of fiction. The names, characters and incidents portrayed in it are the work of the author's imagination. Any resemblance to actual persons, living or dead, events or localities is entirely coincidental.

Second edition

ISBN (paperback): 979-8-9940905-0-3
ISBN (hardcover): 979-8-9940905-3-4

This book was professionally typeset on Reedsy.
Find out more at reedsy.com

To Mary, Megan, and Colleen, my three muses

Contents

I

PART ONE

CHAPTER I

What is wrong with a line? A line is a geometrical object that is straight and continues to go on infinitely in mathematics. To mimic a line, a person must be conscious of the movement being made to recreate the geometric object with precision. The hands must point in the opposite direction of the feet. Meanwhile, the feet are parallel to the floor, the torso runs in line with the rest of the line, and the chin is held up. Every single part of a person's body becomes involved in worshiping the line. A natural harmony is captured in gestures that any human being can read and understand. The symmetry of the positions and their movements allow for a pleasing experience for the viewer. Man's proportions allow for beautiful lines.

Until one day, the elbow bends, the knees buckle, and the torso slouches into itself. The person mutates into a rigid shell—no longer a human being. Curling the arms inward and approaching the floor to lie sprawled out on the stomach like a lizard, a person no longer feels like they are flying. Rather, a person forces himself into angular and low-lying postures that make him look as if he is falling. No longer does poise matter in a world made for the ugly. All grace is demolished when the line is no longer praised by people. The line lays dormant, forgotten in the dark ages of a past that once upheld reason and the beauty of mankind as law.

***

Chatter erupted among the girls as they ran up to see the cast list posted next to the door of the rehearsal studio.

"Danielle, can you believe I only made understudy?!"

"Jenny, look, look, I made it on the list! Finally!"

"No! Oh, no. I don't want to have to partner with Eric. He smells!"

Dawn Hayes pulled on the mangled black leggings she had used for two years now. The black was starting to turn gray from all the dirt and rosin she had picked up over the years from the studio floor. She did not even notice the state that her pointe shoes were in anymore. Pointe shoes were always seen in one of two ways: too shiny and new or dead. It was still hard for her to recognize when her shoes were just right for her to dance in.

Opening a bobby pin with her teeth, she tucked the final pin into her bun before heading into the crowd of girls. As she walked, her hip bones moved in her leotard sharply while her arms hung down loosely by her narrow sides. She was fifteen, but like many of the girls here, she had not yet grown breasts or wide hips. Her boyish figure was prized in class. At least in ballet class, standing in front of the wall mirrors, Dawn was not ashamed of her size. Perhaps someday her figure would properly fit a woman's leotard and tutu.

The piece of paper fluttered with the spin of each girl's head as she darted to the list and as quickly away from it again. After a week of auditions and then callbacks, the official cast list was out for this season's show: *Giselle*. Allard Ballet Academy chose *Giselle* as its opening season show for the students. The audition scene was one of Giselle's earlier variations, which Dawn had been practicing for months in advance. Her teacher was always snapping at her for sitting too much in her hips. As far as auditions went, Dawn felt confident that this year she would make it out of the *corps de ballet* of her class.

Reaching her hand out to steady the fluttering list, Dawn saw her name written next to the part of Myrtha or the Queen of the Wilis. Exhaling, Dawn drew away from the list with a smile on her face. She thought: Not only am I not a Wili this year, but I am their leader. Her sense of self-satisfaction made her mentally prepared for her upcoming class in ten minutes. She was the Queen, and she shared the role with no one else. It was delicious, glorious, and so right. Dawn grounded her muscles down into the dirt just so her fellow dancers could watch her in rehearsal. While her friends stretched out their sore calves in the obscure corners of the room, she was performing her solo variation. The choreographer's eyes followed her pointed toes and her extended arms circling round and round, casting a spell on all who dared to watch her. Even though this was not the lead role, it felt perfect for Dawn, who wanted this role with a vengeance.

"Hey, Dawn, I get to play Berthe!" said Bridgette.

"Giselle's mother? Good for you." Dawn smiled, moving none of her other facial features. Turning toward the door to the elevator, Dawn pushed the button to close the doors before any other girl could get in with her. She needed some time to herself outside. Down went the glass elevator and Dawn imagined herself with a crown and scepter standing above all of her sheep. As the elevator doors screeched open, she entered the lobby of her beloved theater. The theater was where she wanted to die—no cremation, no spreading her ashes to the open seas, and no grass. She wanted to be found either lying on her back on the wet red bricks leading to the theater after a heavy rainstorm, or she wanted to be found dead on the wooden floorboards that made up the original theater's stage. Her body would be cried over by all her Wilis as they moaned over her for several days and nights until, at last, they laid her down underneath her very own part of the stage. She could be shoved in a costume trunk for all she cared, simply as long as she never left the place that made her feel the most alive.

***

Dancing never meant a hobby for Dawn. In her head, every memory she ever had of dancing was serious and calculated in its attempt to show people what she could say with her body. She was ripe for change and growth. Her teachers were there to shape her into a proper dancer. She promised herself every day in class to beat her classmates in her movements. To her, there was no room for etiquette in the studio. The box all twenty of them lived in could not allow for anything but constant comparison. Stacy kept sickling her feet, David could not get his fingers to relax enough, Kaylee kept falling out of her *pirouettes*. These were all flaws Dawn picked out in her peers, and each failure made her own supporting leg a little stronger and her head a little higher. She felt grounded in other dancers' failures. Granted, she would never say so out loud…but in her head, it was the only thing she left room for, aside from the combination.

When Dawn was not spotting when doing her center work, she stared at the dancer closest to her. The music would start and her eyes would dart down to the other dancer's feet first. Catching a wobble rising up to *demi-pointe* gave her a thrill that made her knees shake. Her heart soared when she moved up to the dancer's legs, which were already beginning to shake at the barre. Tears formed in her eyes as she witnessed hips sunk on the left side and raised on the right, all while facing away from the barre. Dawn could barely breathe as she raised her eyes to the dancer's arms, starting to sink down into chicken wings. Finally, near to the point of fainting, Dawn bore into the dancer's skull as she watched the head tilted in the wrong direction as the dancer pointed their toes to the front. A blissful joy came from showing the other dancers what they were messing up. Dawn exaggerated the direction of her head, which reflected in the mirrors for all others to take note of. She watched other heads turn to match hers. She arched her toes to the point of pain just to watch as everyone else pushed their feet into a similar position. Playing the Queen was a daily job for Dawn as it was already, and no one was there to topple her reign.

Holding her hand gently on the barre, Dawn envisioned herself as Marie Taglioni wafting on the tiniest pointe shoes across the floor. As she rose up, her torso grew smaller and firmer. She worked herself up and over her supporting leg, reaching her hand down toward the floor into a *penché*. Lifting herself back up involved her abdomen and a bit of force, but Dawn always looked graceful pulling herself back up. If she did need some help, then a look in the mirror at another girl whose leg was not as high up as hers made her feel well enough to rise through the pain. Beautiful pain, Dawn often said to herself, sweet, beautiful pain have mercy on me.

Lifting herself up higher than before, she imagined herself in an ancient Greek tunic, waving around a sash of the finest silk, wrapping herself in its smooth embrace. The barre felt more like a man's hand than a piece of wood helping her to balance. It was smooth and sturdy for her to perch lightly on during class. Her muscles carried the rest of her into the air while restraining the very body parts she let soar. A tight smile made the ease of each position seem obvious as Dawn danced.

Dancing came into her life when she turned three years old and her mother brought her to the Allard Ballet Academy for the first lesson. Although she could not recall the day anymore from her memory, she relied now on pictures. In the old photographs, Dawn was in a pink leotard and tights with a short pink tutu and ballet flats on her feet. Her mother must have never read how to dress properly a little ballerina because pink everything was not correct. But on that first day, Dawn knew no better. Wearing the clothes given to her, she jumped with all her might over "newspaper puddles" laid out on the ground beneath her. She stretched her little hands out to the ceiling, hoping that they would spread like wings and carry her over the newspaper effortlessly. Unfortunately, she usually caught the very end of the newspaper with her foot. "Her legs must be stretched further apart," said the ballet teacher to Dawn's mother after her first class. So, yoga was implemented in the house every morning to help gain flexibility quickly. Time was never a friend of Dawn's. She had to be ready for a ballet career by sixteen, or die.

She recalled the pianist in the corner of the room laughing loudly before each class with the teacher. He always seemed to be ruffling through his sheet music for something he never could quite find.

When class started in the days of her early education, Dawn's feet heard the first note and drew themselves up into first position. Her hands looked as if they held a giant beach ball and her feet were like a slice of pizza. Her teacher taught her to raise her chin and lift herself as if held up by an invisible string. Every metaphor made Dawn a stronger dancer. When class felt slow on certain days, she even made up her own metaphors: her feet pulled by marionette strings, her eyes drawn by an artist's pencil, and her knees always over the feet as if they were stuck between two large walls with nowhere else to go.

There was room for imagination on mornings where barre remained the exact same combination. The dancer's body became imprinted on Dawn's figure through the daily habit of movement. First position came to be as inevitable as the sun rising in the morning. The physical demands needed to turn around or balance on one foot were guided and encouraged by the laws of physics. Dawn only observed. She listened.

***

Her teacher was a god. The studio was home. Dawn was a vessel. Being a dancer meant being a good follower in many ways. Her teacher knew how to execute each step, so why not obey her? When Dawn's leg turned out enough and she could see it shaking, she felt like she accomplished a new goal. Shaking meant stronger muscle tomorrow and a renewed stamina in class the day after for her. The system of strengthening—tear down, rebuild—gave Dawn a high she could not find in other activities.

During a rehearsal for a show when Dawn was seven, she watched the upper-level girls, who were just starting high school, dance. They had breasts underneath those chest-flattening leotards. They had hips that were wider than any of the other girls or boys in the school had. The girls were becoming women, and they filled out all of their costumes just like dolls or models. Dawn seethed. She wanted to hide away in shame until she could come out looking just as they did.

Dawn wanted breasts, a tiny waist that flowed out into wide hips, and lean legs that made pointe shoes look so much better. Finding the girls in her class too immature, Dawn began keeping to herself more. As rehearsals continued that year, she grew more obsessed with these young dancers, on the pre-professional track, who would soon become the butterflies she had always wanted to be.

The high school girls smiled without even seeming to notice how gorgeous they were now. Not only were their extensions nearly perfected at this stage, but they were also cast in the better, lead roles in all the school's performances. They never wore what other students their age wore either. The older girls never wore jeans, hoodies, or even T-shirts. They lived in leotards underneath their tights. They wore leggings nearly all year. They had hair that hung down to their bottoms, but no one would ever know because their hair was always in a bun before classes began. On many days, when the weather was even slightly chilly, all the high school girls would have trash bag pants on, big booties covering their feet, and a long-sleeved sweater over their leotards. Ballet dancers feared the cold more than anything else because cold meant tight muscles—tight muscles meant worse flexibility.

Even their entire composure differed from other high school girls. They walked with grace and utter control over their every muscle group. Like a flock of swans, the high school girls flew down into the studio to roost every day. Dawn begged time to speed up so that they could see her as more than just a girl.

In the dressing room before class, Dawn would eavesdrop

on the older girls.

"Did you hear about Bobby? Yeah, he got the part. I would love to partner with him if you know what I mean." The group of girls giggled profusely.

"Yeah, he's so hot. I want him so badly."

"I heard that he's not into girls."

"Hush! That's not true. It can't be!" All the girls wallowed in misery at hearing that Bobby might like none of them—no matter how hard they competed against each other to gain his attention in class.

Motivation for the high school girls came in the form of seducing the boys. At this age, they danced with their new figures to entrap the boys. They were like spiders, spinning a web around the room, only to have the boys stick to them. Dawn could see how their graceful moves would suddenly turn into sickening, lustful twists and undulations against their fresh catch. Dancing no longer was innocent for many of those girls. Still, Dawn wanted to be their leader someday.

Ballet to Dawn now, at the tender age of fifteen, still involved learning from the teacher. There was no real notation system for ballet. She could not read about the subject to get the combinations for *Giselle*, or *Swan Lake*, or *Don Quixote*. All of those dances were passed down from older dancers to younger dancers. Every single variation shown to a younger dancer was a gift. Dawn recognized the gift early on. In fact, she realized the gift was being shared with all the other students in the room, but she wanted the gift for herself. She desired to know all the parts, perfect them, and carry them to her makeshift grave underneath the theater stage.

To achieve this, her memory had to be reserved for dance notes only. She made a promise to herself to eat, sleep, and live only for dance. All the physically correct movements and expressions would live within her bones. Her muscles would hear the first notes to *Giselle*, and they would resemble her character, Myrtha, immediately in all their queenly glory.

The language of ballet was French, initially created in the seventeenth century, to describe the placement of body parts at any given moment. During the Renaissance, the rediscovery of ancient Greek texts made ballet an art raised to the stature of the classics. The god of music was Apollo. He is the ideal image of mankind and someone to be looked up to as a role model in the dance world.

When Dawn was younger, she thought that if she prayed to Apollo, asking for something better to happen to her feet or legs or arms, he would hear her and grant her wish. Sadly, the sudden improvements within one class never appeared. The splits came with time, the *pirouettes* came with time, and so did everything else Dawn was learning in class.

Ballet was conceived long before Dawn was born with the 1533 marriage between King Henri II and Florentine Catherine de Medici. Their marriage began the long-lasting story of ballet. The rebirth of culture leads to men caring about how mankind fits into the universe. How could we understand the world? God? Mathematical laws of nature? Dawn could not say which was correct in her ballet history classes, but she was supremely thankful for the creation of such an art form. There was nothing else for her to do in life than dance.

***

Her mind and body were constantly being molded and shaped according to what her teachers revealed to her. Their gifts were only given when she earned them. She drooled like a dog whenever her teachers would speak about a solo variation of a dance she had never learned before. When Dawn watched the boys work on their male variations, she stood back, imagining her thighs being just as strong and her shoulders just as wide as theirs. The boys could fly higher and longer than Dawn—just because she was born a female. Sometimes the physical limitations would get to her. She wondered: How could I be kept from doing it all? She desired to be better than everyone else in class. There must be some reason for my obsession with ballet, thought Dawn.

Louis XIV adored ballet. He was divinely dubbed king, so why not I dubbed the Queen of Ballet? wondered Dawn. I have spent my entire life perfecting myself for dance. I must be repaid soon with fame and glory and wealth. The time is almost here for when a company watches me dance and I prove myself the best prodigy of all time. Maybe one day, I will get to meet with "The Sun King" himself in his cloud up there, she thought. My cloud, of course, will be the largest in the entire place.

For now, Dawn continued to feed her habit. Her body was starting to take the shape of a young lady now. Although she had missed her moment to shine in front of the then-new high school girls who were, at present, either mothers or professional ballerinas with good ballet companies. They had moved beyond that moment where Dawn still saw them crystallized in life. Those older girls would always remain just as stunning and new as when she watched them dance at seven years old for the first time...and the envy for what they had enjoyed was still there.

Since her first class, Dawn had a competitive streak. She wanted to become the art form. No teacher was allowed to look at any other student in the room more than Dawn. Imaging herself of noble birth, she stomped her feet when she was little for the teacher to come over and correct her. Even having the teacher slap her wrist or correct her for a lack of composure was better than not being noticed.

To not stand out among the group of students with the same rib cages poking out of their leotards, with the same spindly legs bending awkwardly in their *pliés*, or with the same barely arched feet, was suffocating. Dawn could not stand being in a state of invisibility for more than a second.

Her tantrums from childhood were only slapped out of her. Today, they still erupted, but she kept them inside herself, which could be more deadly if she were to release all the previous tantrums from years of pushing them down. Dawn knew that her classmates would loathe her forever if they ever discovered how she thought of them and herself. Her classmates were amusing at times but always a threat.

A boy once said to her during partnering: "Why are you shaking so much? Don't worry, I'm strong." He continued digging his hands into her ribs because he could not even find her tiny hips.

Dawn shook harder. She was livid at having a partner who was inferior to herself. He took away her shine.

She only managed to jab her elbow a few times back into his ribs to see how he liked it. He never did understand what she was getting at. Her enemies did not need to know that she was watching.

The sense of competition has been shown to the outside world. It is nothing new to dancers. They sugarcoat their world on camera with "Oh, everyone is really nice" or "We make a great team." But Dawn promised herself never to say such things to the world. Her silence confirmed nothing. If she were to say anything out loud now, she would only hurt her chances of getting into a company.

People in this world like "nice" people. People who can be run over by anyone with half the skill they have. Dawn refused to be nice to anyone. What she would be is stern. Her focus remained solely on ballet and her name in all the top soloist roles. Nice people did not get those roles, only determined people. She did not bleed and sweat for twelve years of her life for nothing. Her gains were tied to her wealth, fame, and glory.

Ticking away, the clock in the studio reminded Dawn of her limited time left here in this studio she grew up in. The wood floor was one of her few friends. The floor could not be her enemy since she knew too much about it, like where every dip in the wood was or where it creaked the most. Her dancing orbited these places on the floor so that she never sounded too loud on landing her jumps or coming out of turns.

Her other friends were the mirrors, the barre, the uniform she wore, and her beloved pointe shoes. They never talked back or discouraged her. They just were, and Dawn worked with them to form her body and mind accordingly. The mirrors showed her all flaws she needed to fix immediately. The barre supported her in new combinations. The uniform of leotard and tights kept her focused on her habits. Her pointe shoes gave her the ability to soar.

Dawn wore out her friends in the studio over time. She had to continue buying new clothes and shoes. The spot she always stood at for barre was starting to rub down where her hand rested. The mirrors grew dusty and warped over time. The studio aged with Dawn, but she cleaned the studio as much as she could whenever she was not dancing. Her box to dance in gave her such pleasure to clean and polish because, with each wipe, she discovered a new angle or crack, as if she found a new piece of herself in the process.

CHAPTER II

A line of older women left the studio as Dawn was approaching for class today. The adult classes were taught before her final classes for the night. There was a beginner class and an "advanced/intermediate" class for the adults. They just love to play professional, Dawn thought. Why can't they find a hobby more for their age? Like knitting? She rolled her eyes as she saw one woman from the adult class walk past her right shoulder with her head held high. Dawn wondered, What in the world was there to feel good about after being in a class like that?

"Dawn, go! March into the studio so that I can get to my spot!" yelled Jeanne.

"I'm going! Calm down." Dawn lifted herself off her heels and walked into her home, which was sadly shared by buffoons. Ballet had too many baroque details for anyone over thirty to master. She knew she would master all the variations before she hit that dreadful number. After that, she could dance to her death like the Wilis or teach...and teaching was its own form of death for a dancer.

Stepping up beside her favorite spot at the barre, Dawn cracked her toes and moved her ankles in continuous circles. She warmed up her body in the same way before every class. It was the way she could tell time. After the third warm-up of the day, she knew it was the last. Her soft, warm bed was looming larger in mind. But she understood that the pre-professional exhaustion was nothing now compared to the professional life.

The pianist began to play, and silence spread across the room. Exhaling, Dawn prepared herself to obey her teacher's commands.

"Good evening, ladies and gentlemen! Tonight's class will be taught by someone new to the Academy. Please welcome, Madame Angulaire."

The students all clapped and bowed for the new instructor.

"Right! Students, please start out in first position. We'll do our normal *plié* combination, followed by a *cambré* forward. Then, switch to the other side."

The pianist struck his beginning cords and then Dawn followed suit. She stretched out her feet and arms symmetrically, as if attached to a single thread. Her head bowed forward while the top of her hand grazed the floor. She exhaled as she went down and inhaled on the way up. Nothing seemed out of order in her universe in those few moments of movement.

However, when center work began, class normalcy began to change.

"Now, we are going to practice some positions from *Giselle* in order to get you all thinking about your new roles. Eric, please step forward here. Good. Dawn, look at me, please step over there. Okay. Now, Michelle, please step back a bit. I want you three to get into position for *pirouettes*, but do *not* turn."

Eric, Dawn, and Michelle followed as they were told. All of them extended one leg and balanced on both in fourth position with their arms ready to turn.

"Excellent. Now, I want all of you to turn your feet in." Grabbing Dawn's foot, she pushed it inwards. Her feet, positioned this way, made her look like a broken doll. She scrunched up her face in horror, but then she exhaled with a laugh. Soon, the entire class was laughing.

"All right, silence. You've all had your giggles, but now is the time to improve your dancing tremendously. I am about to take you all into the modern age when dance is a *true* expression of the soul."

She shoved the other two exemplar dancers' feet inwards too. "Voila! Feet are inwards. Moving on to the arms. Please stick out your elbows as if they were trying to escape from your body." Taking Eric's arm, Madame Angulaire crooked his elbow out so much that he winced. The mirror showed a triad of scarecrows.

All the dancers watched in confusion. Their entire lives they had been told to turn their feet out and to round out their arms. Their movements were beautiful, while the opposite was ugly. The scarecrows before them now were ugly. Yet, the teacher wanted this. The teacher expected them to be ugly. They all laughed louder.

Dawn felt tears coming. She was trapped between crying for her ugliness and her joy at being freed. She could break and bend the rules now. She had been permitted by her own teacher.

"Please turn as you are now," said Madame Angulaire.

The ease with which Dawn turned became impossible. The physics were not there anymore to get herself around without falling. She tried two more times, but she had lost the ability to turn. Panicking, Dawn looked over at her other two colleagues.

19

They were also failing. "Look at them falling over themselves! We're just as bad as the adults tonight!" laughed Dawn.

"*Arrêtez!* Stop, that's enough! Did you notice what happened to you when I changed your positioning?"

"We couldn't balance," said Eric.

"We couldn't turn around," said Michelle.

"We couldn't even stand upright," said Dawn.

"Exactly. You looked like fools. But that is how a fool walks. That is how a fool on the street looks to others. What you felt is how a fool must feel throughout his day."

Dawn imagined the adult dancers looking as uncoordinated as they just did, but, for some reason, the image would not fully come. It disappointed her because she could not laugh at them again. Instead, she had to envision a monkey trying to dance or an elephant. She certainly felt tonight like an animal and nothing remotely human.

"I expect all of you to run through this exercise tonight in your dreams. In fact, I would like all the other dancers to come out from the corner and try to turn this way. If anyone manages to do it, then I'll give you ten dollars." The instructor giggled for the first time at her cunning. We all knew that there was no way to get around with turned-in feet and chicken wing arms. Yet, we all still tried over and over and over again to please Madame.

***

"Less poise, more unsightly! I will play some Stravinsky to show you the music that will expand your souls to the plight of human suffering."

Madame Angulaire gave the pianist a signal to stop playing as she turned up the volume on her phone. Stravinsky's famous *Rite of Spring* was playing through her tiny speakers, but it was enough sound to silence the class. The erratic volume and movement of the piece made certain students cringe. Timothy looked revolted, as did Stephanie; Michelle and Eric tried to turn to it in their newly fixed positions; Dawn stared at the floor, trying to follow a pattern. She could not find a pattern or story to the piece. All the music she heard before went along with a story and helped increase her musicality with its clear count.

"No longer are you dancing as angels would but as human beings in their darkest times. Look, here is another position that is very popular in other ballet schools today." Madame got down on her stomach and then rolled over while kicking her right leg up and out. Her arms lay there at her sides. She reminded the students of a clock telling time sped up. She swung her legs back and forth, mimicking a dying insect.

"Do as I do, class. Hurry!"

Everyone got down on the studio floor and rolled around as she did. They played themselves at their worst...

The music continued to play, the pianist picking at the hangnail on his finger, while the rest of the bodies covered the floor. Picking up other people's hair and dust from the floor, Dawn was thoroughly disgusted by the time she got back up on her feet. She wondered if she had rolled around like that when she was a baby and having tantrums. Maybe I was like that and ballet never expressed that type of babyish movement before. It still felt odd, though.

From birth, Dawn was told to grow up and mature into a beautiful young lady. Yet, here she was now in class, rolling around on the floor for her art. She could no longer envision herself as the Queen of the Wilis but only the court jester from long-forgotten history.

"This, class, is modern dance—modern ballet. It is a release from the aristocratic movement of the archaic world of the West. We are on a trajectory forward in showing how life *really* is and what the music of today *really* sounds like. Our bodies are finite, limited. It is okay to be afraid. We are all afraid in life. No one knows what they are doing from one moment to the next. You just have to go with what life's music sounds like in the moment." Madame Angulaire swayed on her feet to show life, taking her where it willed. She swung like a living pendulum, allowing what seemed like the air around her to move her to and fro. A few strands of hair swung from one side of her face, hitting her nose in the process, to the other.

Dawn watched her intently, absorbing everything she saw happening this evening during class. Rather than learning the parts of *Giselle* she had seen in videos, she was learning a new form entirely. The meaning of the entire ballet was beginning to shift in her mind. What was once the pinnacle of romantic ballet was shifting into a rebellious cry for revenge.

Revenge mixed with competition was a common emotion for Dawn. She watched her classmates turn and roll like insects. Their buns became antennas while their hands and legs crawled all over the studio floor. An urge to crush every single one of them cropped up in Dawn's soul. She wanted to soar in the air with *grand jetés* and land right on top of a head and then jump over to the next. The game she played included never touching the floor, and that was how she would maintain her control as Queen. She was Queen of the Insects.

To be a Queen of the Insects, Dawn committed herself to learning everything from Madame Angulaire. She walked up closer to the front of the studio, right beside her teacher.

Madame noticed Dawn, and she smiled. Her students

seemed to learn quickly. Soon her class would express every-thing that the modern world wanted to feel—true suffering. Akin to Christ on the cross, Madame committed her life to show what He felt like there dying for our sins. She wanted her dancers to show the blood trickling from their wounds. She knew they all must have them somewhere.

"Dawn, tell me about the worst pain you ever felt growing up," said Madame Angulaire.

Dawn froze. How could I answer that in front of the other dancers? she wondered. Dawn shifted from her left to her right foot before saying, "I'm not sure. My cat died a couple of years ago. That was sad." She gulped at her insignificant answer, hoping her instructor would accept that as her answer and move on.

Madame just nodded and said: "Timothy, what is the worst pain you ever felt growing up?"

She continued to question every student in the room during the last ten minutes of class. There was no movement that evening. The question lingered in everyone's heads long after class due to how many times Madame had to ask it over and over again: "What is the worst pain you ever felt growing up?" Dawn began to worry that perhaps the worst had not yet come. Her greatest immediate fear was not being able to dance her role in *Giselle*. Beyond that fear was, of course, the general fear of not being able to dance any role ever again.

Nausea rose inside of Dawn that night in bed, and she had to jump up and out of her room straight to the bathroom to breathe in the toilet water. Nothing came up besides the fear which made her gag. She felt her face grow pale and weary with the pain of suffering. She touched her cheek.

***

The next morning Dawn awoke a different person. Feeling much older and more tired, she foisted herself up on one arm to roll the rest of the way out of the bed. Her body felt bloated to the touch, and nothing in the atmosphere made her feel calm. Feet touching the cold floor, Dawn walked to the bathroom to get ready for the day's classes.

This morning's class would not be led by Madame Angulaire. Thankfully, none of us had to see her until the evening again, thought Dawn. The morning was left to the old regime. The way ballet used to be taught was safe. Every movement was already ingrained in her body—to *tendu* meant only one thing and not a dozen different things. A divide grew between her "old" body and her "new" body.

Madame Roberts was the most frequent instructor for Dawn's class level. She greeted every new day with *pliés* in first, second, fourth, and fifth positions. The music remained soft, allegro piano music. The pianist was just as relaxed in the mornings as the students.

Sunlight trickled into the studio and lit the floor. The rays moved their positions as class continued. Dawn grew higher in her pointe shoes when the sun chose to shine on her. When she was a younger dancer, she became mesmerized by the sunlight, making her pink tights shimmer. They were like little shiny scales that covered her legs. Allowing her eyes to go out of focus, she watched her tights shine. When her eyes focused again, Dawn began to recognize her own legs within the tights. Her legs were like two round balloons that were attached by strings by the time she got down to her feet. A ballerina's calves are extremely powerful while still maintaining delicate ankles and slender, arched feet.

Dawn leaped higher for joy when the sun chose her on those

days. She felt the sun was her first spotlight. Louis XIV must be up in the clouds, directing the sun to shine on her legs. The light made her feel so refreshed and whole. Standing there in the studio, in her ballet uniform, surrounded by light and music, made her soul sing. There was no other place she wanted to be in those moments.

Love must feel like that, thought Dawn, complete and utter bliss. She smiled as she placed her hand on the worn spot at the barre, which she claimed as her own. The wood of the barre felt slightly warm and welcoming. The music started off slow.

"Good morning, dancers. Please take your place at the barre. We will do our usual *plié* combination just to wake up those sleeping muscles. Also, it is a bit chilly out there today, so I fully expect to hear some cracks and pops!" Madame Roberts chuckled.

Class always started the same way and became a ritual for everyone in the room. Feeling relaxed in the morning was felt by all—it also showed through the movement of the dancers. A *plié* was no longer a physical movement but an act of scooping up water for your baby. A *frappé* was no longer a strike on the floor but lightning devastating your land. A *rond de jambe* was no longer a circle of the leg but a fish causing ripples in your water.

The repeated movements took on the emotional meaning of the dancer. Dawn gave her feet an extra striking power to the floor, and she imagined throwing lightning bolts down from the sky like Zeus. Smite the insects! thought Dawn. Her foot made the audible noise of hitting over and over again, hoping to make her jumps even more powerful in the center of the room later.

25

Madame Roberts looked pleased. "Very good! The musicality today is spot on. I really appreciate your effort to move in unison as well. Moving together makes for a better *corps de ballet*. Now, let's move on to some center work."

She led the flock of dancers into the middle of the room. The mother goose leading her babies all in a row. Dawn and the other dancers stopped just behind Madame Roberts to watch her every move. The combination given is deceptively simple, but Dawn was starting to feel a creeping sense of something being wrong. Should my feet really be turned out here? wondered Dawn. Or should my feet be turned in according to the music now? What about my arms? They could be crooked right now to convey the music's sorrowful sound. How can I show that more accurately with my body?

For the first time, Dawn felt paralyzed. She stopped in the middle of the combination, afraid to move.

"Are we stuck? Hello? What's wrong?" asked Madame Roberts.

Dawn violently shook her head. "No, sorry. I...I was just thinking about what Madame Angulaire taught us in last night's class."

"Which was what?"

"We were taught to turn our feet inwards and stick our elbows out," explained Dawn.

Madame Roberts cringed. "Do you think that is ballet?"

"I...I think so. She said it helps to express the music better if we match it with our bodies."

"What do you think we're doing here?"

"We're matching the music rhythmically but maybe not emotionally."

Madame Roberts bent forward, grazing her hand on the

floor, and then came up while singing a somber tune. "Is that not the most tragic thing you've seen?"

Dawn looked down. "Yes. But then why is Madame Angulaire so convinced that we are dancing all wrong?"

"Because Madame Angulaire has different theories on dance and choreography. Other than that, I cannot say." Madame Roberts waved her hand as if to throw away the question. Dawn saw her instructor's unease, and she could tell that she had more to say but refused to go any further with it.

The conversation ended there and class continued with Dawn in a haze. No longer did her movements feel as pure as they did before Madame Angulaire showed up yesterday evening. The world of dance for Dawn was shaken by her presence.

***

"Class, please give me some big jumps this morning. I feel like we need to release some tension." Madame Roberts eyed Dawn swiftly up and down before turning toward the rest of the dancers in the corner of the room.

The students leaped high up into the air. When it came to Dawn's turn, she felt like she lost several inches of her normal height. Her legs could no longer produce the strength needed to propel herself up into the air and beyond the studio walls. She felt too heavy for such flight anymore.

When she landed, Madame Roberts barely looked in her direction. Dawn's lips grew pale as her cheeks burned with shame. From the left corner of the room, Dawn watched the other dancers fly swiftly through the air. They seemed to have no trouble flying today after the arrival of Madame Angulaire.

Hunching her shoulders, Dawn watched her instructor give the left side variation over again. The dancers marked the steps out and jumped from the left. The left side was her weaker side, and she had anxiety over performing on that side. Her left leg stretched only as far as it seemed to dictate. Dawn worked for months with a stretchy band to pull her leg closer to the proper position, but her muscles were too tight. On this side, her jumps were just passing. But a professional company would never accept a dancer who had a noticeably weak side.

As she watched Michelle jump from the left corner, Dawn's eyes squinted. How could she have such clean lines? Dawn wondered. Why don't I have such a perfect split? I exercise more than her. I care about ballet more than her. She doesn't even know what she's doing with her body. An uncontrollable heat warmed Dawn's throat. Her immediate response was to run away, but instead, Dawn tore her face away from the other dancers and focused hard on her teacher.

Madame Roberts was showing the next combination. Dawn saw her perfectly arched feet wrapped in canvas flats. Her pink stockings were worn properly underneath her leotard, with her leotard covered by her flowing chemise skirt. The pink stockings were often covered by leggings, which were the shabbiest part of her attire. The knit parts around her heel were beginning to wear out as little strings stuck out from the hole. Her hair was kept in a chignon and sometimes a ballet bun. She had hazel eyes and brunette hair that probably came down to her bottom like all the rest of the female dancers. The most striking part of Madame Roberts was her pale skin. Every day she embodied Giselle with her Wilis. Her royal blue veins were clearly visible through her fair skin. She glowed, especially in contrast to her other darker features.

From underneath her leotard and tights, her body shined and spoke louder than any sound that came from her lips. She knew that her body was made for ballet. How lucky! thought Dawn. Madame is so lucky that she can look at herself in those huge mirrors and know that she is on the right path. Meanwhile, I look and all I feel is lost, like a sad imitator who should find another career.

Dawn peeked at herself in the mirror and saw a girl who was not thin enough. Her bones needed to be shaved down. Her hair was not coiffed enough. It needed to be thickened and hair sprayed into place. Her face was not sculpted with high cheekbones. That would require plastic surgery. She kept some of her baby fat in her cheeks and wisps of baby hairs blew across her forehead and neck. Her skin was fair but not glowing or haunting like Madame Roberts's. She also had a mole right above her lip, which in the eighteenth century would have been thought lovely, but not now. Even her feet, which meant everything in the ballet world, did not look as precise and graceful as Madame Roberts's slender feet.

Seething, Dawn turned her back on the incriminating mirrors toward the barre where she stretched out her calves. I cannot stand her! I cannot take being shown up every day by Madame. My teacher still gets to dance as a guest with the company of her dreams. She's made it already. She has nothing left to worry about. But I have everything to lose! I watch her perfectly execute steps I haven't mastered after two years of practice! She has it so easy because she was made for ballet. But I have to work like a dog to become acceptable. My body is just acceptable. It still has no curves to speak of and no glowing skin. I am no Giselle. I am a Queen of the Acceptable.

Choking back tears, Dawn raced through her *reverence* with her teacher, bowed, and ran off into the dark hallway of the Academy, hoping to be swallowed up in the blackness. Her home could never properly be here. Her body would never shape up like Madame Roberts's. There were only so many like her that mesmerized other people into watching them dance. Dawn could never rise to meet the high expectations of a company. Her weak side would never improve, her turns would stay at a minimum, her body would remain too wide for a ballerina, and her cheeks would never slim down.

Dawn worried the most about her feet. Ever since she watched the older girls put on their pointe shoes and dance together in unison, Dawn dreamed of being in their position. Her pointe shoes had to look graceful and ladylike, but that required her feet to be the correct size and shape. Of course, her feet required a pointe shoe that looked much bulkier than a normal dancer's shoes. Still, she was excited when she first started pointe class—believing that she would just simply force her feet to obey the shoes no matter what the cost.

CHAPTER III

The next morning, to prepare for *Giselle* rehearsals beginning, Dawn bought new pointe shoes. Buying new pointe shoes filled her with such joy as she looked down at the perfectly shiny, clean pair. Yet, she knew they would cause new blisters and sore feet until they were broken in like her old pair. Clicking the boxes together, the new shoes were always much too loud, and she knew they were too tight and slippery to be used for class now. That is why Dawn and every other girl *en pointe* prepared their pointe shoes for use. All the pre-professional ballerinas had heard that the professionals can go through one pair of new pointe shoes a day during a busy season. That is why they all had to have custom-made shoes made by the dozens for them just to make it the rest of the week.

With that knowledge in mind, Dawn created a process for preparing her pointe shoes soon after watching the older high school girls prep theirs. Some dancers only did a few things to their shoes before they felt confident using them, but Dawn did them all. She wanted her shoes to the point of death before even putting them on. Her feet were already covered in callouses and abnormal lumps protruded from areas where normal feet were smooth. Her feet required a shoe that fit

31

only them every time she danced.

The process went as follows: One, attack the shank of the shoes. The inner piece that keeps the feet foisted upright was keeping Dawn from arching into her best position. She gently pulled down the fabric, exposing the wooden shank of her right shoe. Then, she began pulling the shank away from the fabric of the shoe behind it. Taking out a box cutter, Dawn sliced a thin line across the shank and bent it forward and backward to break the firm piece even further. Finally, she took a pair of scissors and cut the end right off until it was three-quarters in length, and hit right where her arch was at its greatest bend. That way, her shoes would break up there and not down where her toes needed to be supported the most. Dawn made the shoes support her the way she required and not the other way around.

Two, shape the shank and glue it back together. Dawn used the box cutter to slice away the sharp bits left from where she had severed the shank. Then, she took out some glue and glued the fabric back over the exposed part of her shoe, where only a shadow of her shank was left.

Three, shave the wood on the bottom of the pointe shoes down. Flipping over her pointe shoes, Dawn took the box cutter and shaved off the side bits so that she would seamlessly balance on the floor. By shaving off the sharp curves of the shoe, her line would look better in certain positions and she would feel less wobbly.

Four, smack the shoes on the floor. Dawn lifted her shoes and smacked the bottoms down on the floor as hard as she could. The older girls always said that it made them sound quieter on the floor after landing from a jump when they prepared their shoes this way. Dawn had even watched

Michelle slam the tips of her shoes in between the door and the frame once.

Five, cover the shoes in rosin. Dawn took a paper towel dabbed in rosin and powdered her shoes until they had a matte finish. She always added extra crushed-up rosin to the base of her shoes so that it made her less likely to slip onstage.

Six, slice the bottom of the shoes some more for gripping slippery floors. A fear of falling onstage is very real for every dancer. Dawn obsessively cut even more lines on the bottom of her shoes where the wood is in order to grip the floor more easily. She never felt like there were too many lines underneath her shoes.

Seven, cut the satin off the top of the pointe shoes. The satin material was too slippery as well, so Dawn took her box cutter again to the top of her shoes and cut off the satin. Leaving a nice oval shape, she trimmed off any excess bits leftover.

Eight, spray water around the bunion area of the pointe shoes. Water softens the area where Dawn's feet need the most space to perform effectively. She spritzed her shoes until there was a wet line around each of them.

Nine, add shellac to toughen back up the area of the shoes that will weaken the fastest. Dawn took a cap half full of resin and poured it on the back of her shoes where she tended to break the shank quickly and another cap full of shellac and poured that down into the box of her pointe shoes to harden the bottom where her toes were working hard enough.

Ten, place the holes from the convertible tights over just the heels before putting on pointe shoes. Having skin contact with the pointe shoes prevented Dawn's heels from sliding out of the shoe.

After all of that prepping, it was time for her to sew her

elastic and ribbons on. As she was sewing, she also took the time to darn the outside rim of her pointe shoes. This further prevented slipping and promoted balance. Then, she taped her toes with toe tape to prevent her toes from rubbing together and causing even more blisters. Covering her toes with her tights, Dawn grew more and more excited about her customized pair of pointe shoes. She wanted to see her work in action. But first, she had to place her gel toe pads over her feet and finally slide on her shoes. Tying the ribbons around her ankle twice, she finished off the knot, ensuring to tuck in the little ends underneath her other satin ribbon. Dawn also dabbed rosin on the skin, showing from her heel being uncovered by the tights. The rosin made her skin blend in with the tights and would no longer be noticeable from the stage. Now, her pointe shoes were ready.

***

Sitting with her pointe shoes all ready on the floor, Dawn looked around the changing room. She felt sentimental as she often did lately. Ballet is only for the young, and every moment seemed precious to her. She gripped the pointe shoes in her hands more tightly, as if that gesture could keep her career from never ending. Death would be the only guest to come and rip her away from ballet. Dawn knew that she would never leave the dance world conscious.

The girl's changing room had a series of beige lockers and benches for the dancers to sit and dress on. The dull colors of the lockers and benches made the room appear poor, but the dancers filling it made it rich. When all the girls were dismissed from class, the changing room looked like a Degas painting with the amount of varied movement the girls were all in to change.

Some girls shed out of tutus, others repaired their newest blisters, and a few changed into street clothes. Dawn often took the time in between classes to prepare her pointe shoes or mend a rip in her tights. The changing room was Dawn's cocoon. Wrapping her soft insides up in tights and a leotard secured her form and the clothes on top made up her wings. Dawn emerged from the changing room into the studio, ready to fly.

Of course, that was before the new teacher arrived. The thought of Madame Angulaire reminded Dawn of her craving to discover more about her teacher's strange world. Dawn wondered, What allowed this woman to learn about ballet and then break all of its rules? What caused her to choose differently? Am I missing out?

Dawn pointed and flexed her feet a few times, watching them bend further than a non-dancer's feet ever would. A rush of pride kept her repeating the movement over and over again. Ballet molded her body. Could it move in any other way? Why was ballet the golden standard, anyway? Says who? Some dead aristocrats? She rolled her eyes and got up from her cozy corner of the changing room.

She decided to take a little walk around the theater before class would begin again in the afternoon. Perhaps the theater holds the answers to my questions, thought Dawn. Her investigation was about to start from the front doors.

Three sets of large oak doors stood divided by brick arches. Brown mixed with muddied red to create a warm connection with a past Dawn never knew. Yet, she saw the experiences of the past in the way the brick was weathered on the outside of the building and the worn-off area of the brass door handles to the inside.

The theater rose high up into the air, casting an imposing shadow on the onlookers below. There were large arched windows up the building's face to let abundant amounts of light in through its five floors.

At the top was a small triangular-shaped roof which was decorated with a beautiful circular window. The window contained a decorative ornament, much like the rose windows found in Gothic cathedrals. The smallest window of the bunch was the most beautiful and carefully constructed in the design of the theater.

Dawn knew that that was the very window her studio used. In the evening, the dancers could be seen out of the center window. Their dancing must look more like mimes and playthings to passersby from the street. They became nothing more than black silhouettes further ornamenting the face of the theater with their bodies. It was as if they were the figurines inside an automaton clock. When the clock struck five, then they all came out on a cold, winter night and danced for no one. Once the minute passed, they were sent back to the darkness of the clock's belly, only to come out again at the next important time of day.

Dancers were silent. Dawn could not shake the people at the foot of the theater and yell in their faces to watch her dance. She remained a silent facade of the building, like the ivy growing up a building for newcomers to comment on when they happen to notice.

Dawn ran her hand across the brick arches and felt the oak doors once again. She did not mind becoming a part of this building's frame. The music she heard daily and the movements she worshiped with her body would spread layer upon layer over the interior of the theater. The paint would be laced with her oils, her hair, and her sighs. The wooden floors could keep collecting her dead skin cells. Maybe one day, her layers would grow into a new dancer in the middle of the theater. That would remain the only way Dawn could imagine giving birth. It had to be born of the theater.

She slowly pulled open the doors to the theater and stepped over the entrance line, acknowledging her temple as she entered. Bowing her head down low, the smell of costumes and rosin entered her nose—home. This is the only smell she cared to inhale. She shut her eyes for a moment and held back her tears. Today, sorrow filled her soul for the loss of being able to fly purely, wholly anymore. Ballet was fleeting, and on many days Dawn awoke feeling like she had already lost her dream. The theater was too good to lose. Its goodness made her want to cry even harder. The goodness crushed her.

Backing up against the door, she slid down to the floor and sat there inhaling deeply, trying to slow her breathing, wiping the tears from her cheeks. Her angry hands tried smacking her cheeks until they felt hot. How can I feel so much sorrow without having lost anything yet? wondered Dawn. She pressed her ear up against the brick arches from the inside of the theater and she could feel the notes from the pianist reverberate through them. Whether or not the pianist was currently playing, Dawn knew the building held onto echoes of the music and movement of the day. All the creativity expressed within its walls never left.

***

The floor felt cool and solid underneath her heavy body. Dawn appreciated the closeness of the lobby where she sat. The walls narrowed in to direct its guests toward the main theater doors. Nothing stood out in the lobby, apart from the stars with donors' names above the theater doors and a thin red carpet leading toward the doors. The lobby was painted a dark beige color, which disappeared for the evening shows when guests came in and gossiped in the lobby until it was time for the performance.

Dawn rose up on her frail legs and took to her feet to walk up to the box office area where guests purchased their tickets. The box office window was made out of a large block of wood and some thin glass to keep the elderly coughs and sneezes from reaching the ticket master. Dawn felt like getting behind the box and imagining what life must be like for a normal adult. What must this job be like? wondered Dawn. A breeze, or perhaps tedious? Could this job be truly as freeing as she imagined it was compared to the militant rules of ballet life?

She ran her fingers around the wooden details of the box. Life seemed unfair in its division between the normal non-dancers and the abnormal dancers. Each side seemed to crave what the other side has. Jackie, the girl who tends to give out the tickets on ballet performance nights, looked at Dawn one night with sparkles in her eyes. Dawn knew that girl wished she could be in her position. Instead, Jackie got to sell tickets, share any backstage drama with the audience members, and wear shirts with the Academy's logo on them. Her life was all about the theater, but it was so far from the real work of the dancer.

Meanwhile, Dawn looked at Jackie on many performance nights when she was not running around for costume, makeup, or rehearsal fix-ups. Jackie never had to run anywhere. She got to stay all cozy in her box office area and watch the time pass. She could remain an observer all night rather than the performer. Her nights never felt like carrying a burden uphill, only to have it fall down again the next morning. There was no fretting about one bad performance night that might kill the rest of her career. No, thought Dawn, Jackie is free from such massive responsibility…how lucky.

The red carpet led up to the theater doors, which mimicked the exterior doors to the theater on a smaller scale. The wooden doors had handles that were worn down from all the use the theater had gone through over the years. Dawn gripped the handle in her right hand and used her entire body to push open the door to the theater. The bowels of the building lay here. The theater was the most intricate part of the entire building in its use of paint colors, fabrics, and architectural shapes. There were light blues and beiges and golds and deep reds. The curtain grandiosely hung high above the stage with its deep red color lined with golden arches. Mimicking the exterior and interior door shapes, there were three arches to make up the stage. The grand stage arch and two wing-side arches. The center arch was twice as large and contained the stage.

The stage lolled out of the backdrop curtain like a long, black tongue. There were still rehearsal ballet barres on it for the dancers to practice onstage. The floor was covered in rosin and dusty hairballs. Usually, the girls found bobby pins littering the stage as well.

The ceiling lights all faced in the direction of the stage and reflected off of the gold-colored paint that made the lines around the stage jump out. The seats were of red velvet and were set up as many theaters around the world were—in many little semicircles like ripples in water stretching all the way up to the balcony.

Each seat arm was gold-plated with the name of a donor

to keep the theater running throughout the years. The seat cushions were just as worn down as the handles on the doors of the theater. The soft, velvet fibers were more gray than red now and sunken in. The theater could only afford to replace things as they broke to the point of being completely unusable. There was no time to spend money on the more minor imperfections all over the theater.

Walking down the quiet theater hall, Dawn followed the carpet further into its bowels. The ceiling rose higher as she approached the stage. It had painted pictures of ballet shoes and drama masks by some of the local artists in the area. The stage was up high, so Dawn took a couple of little steps on one side of the stage. Her feet touched down on holy ground. The ground where new worlds were created and entered into even if they had been performed for centuries.

She got down on her knees and really looked at the floor. The stage had been painted black to reduce the shine from the stage lights but underneath was the same material as the dance studio: oak. Strong oak trees made up the interior of this brick exterior building. The oak floors aged with the dancer. No matter what color paint or sealer or varnish was used to cover up the wood, the oak floors remained. Over time, new creaks and cracks began to mask the girls' jumping and landing with their pointe shoes. The smacks against the floor of new toe boxes seemed softer on an old wood floor. The floor gave ever so slightly to help the dancer appear more like an angel. Over time, the wood became thinner in the areas where a dancer drilled holes with their feet the most. But the surface grew smoother with all of that movement and took on its own form of grace. The oak stage was an object to be envious of, thought Dawn, as she laid her body flat out on the stage, trying to take an impression of it with herself.

***

The stage was accommodating to the dancers' feet but not so much to their ribs, so Dawn arose with a wince from the hard surface. Placing her feet back firmly underneath herself, she looked around the empty stage and out into the theater. Being alone in the main part of the theater was as rewarding as the performance nights when curtain call occurred. Dawn could breathe in more deeply, alone there at center stage. Her lungs filled up with the musky air of the old oak surrounding her and the rosin being kicked up by her feet.

Turning around, she lurked backstage in the dark. The technical magic of the back never quite made sense to Dawn. She saw the drawstrings to the curtains and loads of black boxes with lights and other technical features hanging on walls. The key in the back of a puppet was what the backstage was for the exposed stage. Dawn knew that when she waited in the back, all the stressful, exciting energy wound her up so much that the relief of a *grand jeté* out onto the stage nearly became a necessity—a necessary release from the dancers around her.

There was so much for Dawn to explore and memorize in her ballet world. But there was no room to remember every detail of the theater. I must return again, she thought.

Exiting the theater, Dawn took the stairwell in the wings up to the other floors. On the fourth floor, the ballet rehearsal studio stood. It was the sparsest part of the intricate theater, which served the purpose of allowing the dancers to focus on their movement.

The stairs creaked and were tightly narrow, entangling each other in a kind of upward rectangle. The stairs brought people up closer to the chandelier that hung between the wrapped staircases. It had a far way to drop if it ever fell. The chandelier was one of the few light fixtures to light up the hallway to the studio. The dimness in ascending the staircases for evening classes gave off the feeling of coziness and warmth, especially when winter struck.

Although the building was old and it was drafty, so often the cold crept into the hallways and staircases of the theater. The girls, especially, all skin and bone, would clasp their arms and legs together until the studio doors opened to them and a gust of warm air greeted them all.

The teacher often opened the studio doors from the inside, which retained the heat from the previous class in it. The smell of sweat still clung to the air too, but no one cared about that when tight muscles were the primary concern.

Dawn opened the studio doors herself this time since there was no one here at this early time of day. Classes would not start up again until nine o'clock.

The oak floors greeted her in their great expanse, like a nicely made bed that a person would want to leap onto from afar. In a rush of excitement, Dawn ran straight ahead and then leaped up high with all her strength. Only when she looked in the mirror did she lose the momentum of her jump and it became little more than a skip. Dawn still had a problem to solve.

Instead of going high, she went low. Back on her knees, she felt and inspected the studio floors, which, like the stage, were of oak. But these pieces of wood were not covered up with paint. The oak came through clearly, even with the sealant over each board. She knew this floor well. It was her favorite because she could see its character up close and naked.

She crawled like a baby along the floor and looked up at

the row of rectangular windows. There were a total of nine separate windows in a row, with a tenth window being the rose-like one on top. That top window brought in the most light and beauty.

The walls of the studio were a yellowish tint and all the windows and trimmings were of wood. Any spots left bare were covered by framed pictures of ballet dancers during various performances: *Swan Lake*, *Coppélia*, *La Baydère*, and so on.

The barres were hung onto the walls, with most being right underneath the windows. Dawn always chose a spot by the windows. Looking out into the world while dancing made her feel like she could better communicate with the men and women who walked down below. She felt more able to shake them out of the reveries and into the music that she was feeling...at least that's what she imagined.

There was one more door linked to the studio on the other side—the changing room. The changing rooms were where Dawn grew up and ogled other girls since she was three years old. She watched the other girls stretch their tights over expanding hips. She eyed them, pulling their leotard over newly grown breasts. They had the tiny waists that fit into the costumes for the leading roles just right.

She hated them for it. Dawn was waiting all her life, and in many ways still was, to become the beautiful Aurora. She wanted to mesmerize the boys who were starting to notice their dance partners. She wanted them to look at her hips and chest. But, instead, she watched the other girls get the careful attention of the boys when they left the changing room.

The changing room had an ugly blue carpet and white walls. Alongside the benches and lockers were various pieces of clothing or costumes always hanging around: random ribbons from a pair of pointe shoes, torn tights, some baby powder, and sewing thread still attached to a new tutu.

Dawn felt she needed to remember all of it, as if this would be an important moment to her in her life later. She took in everything in that changing room as it helped keep the girls and boys in it alive in her memory as well. She turned toward her own locker and started to pull out her clothes for ballet class.

CHAPTER IV

Inside the changing rooms, the old costumes from the last time *Giselle* was performed were taken out into the daylight. The tutus needed some fluffing and the men's tops required some new beads to replace ones that had fallen off during the show last time. Having the costumes out gave a more definite feel that this was indeed the show coming up for the Allard Ballet Academy.

The rehearsals for *Giselle* began last week and the group of dancers was starting to learn their solos and the *corps de ballet* parts separately. After warm-up at the barre, Dawn was taken to one corner of the studio to watch Madame Angulaire go through the steps for Myrtha, the Queen of the Wilis.

"Right, when the music opens for your variation, Dawn, you start with those hopping *arabesques*."

Madame Angulaire hopped her way down to the studio from the corner they were in together. But Madame had her hair in a ponytail and little pieces of the tail were batting her in the eyes as she jumped. Her bones were sharply jutting out from her chest, arms, and legs. It seemed like all of that weight was kept off over the years by chain smoking. Her fingers were always scrubbed before class, but the odor still clung to her ballet clothes.

She had graying black hair and an upturned nose, which she turned in certain directions to dictate wordlessly her feelings on a subject. Moving her nose up and down meant yes, and moving it from side to side meant no to her students. The upturn also made her seem less friendly in general, like the all-knowing professor who will never think much of anyone else.

Watching her teacher jump at all made Dawn worry, since any pressure put on Madame looked like it would shatter her bones to pieces. The sweater and legwarmers around her body barely stayed on her. Clothes tended to fall straight off of Madame Angulaire's skeletal body. The dancers all knew that she was very proud to be in her forties and remain the skinniest person in the room by the way she eyed herself in the mirrors.

Dawn mimicked the hopping *arabesques* as her teacher displayed.

"Good. Now, in our version of *Giselle*, we are going to modernize it. Say goodbye to the romantic version of the evil queen. You are Myrtha, a woman of power and revenge. I want you real, raw, *ugly*. I don't want you to think about your role or your character. A good dancer does not think, a good dancer *does*. You follow the choreographer's vision of the ballet, in other words, me.

"I want to see you no longer running after beauty for beauty's sake, but calling all the ballet ghosts to help you feel inside yourself. Where is the dancer in you instinctually? All of your movements should be derived from the chemicals in your brain drumming out their own tune that you must listen to. Just move to your bloodstream.

"To be primitive again is something the dancer must recover, as an archaeologist would. How did our ancestors move? How did they dance before language began marring our purest of movements?"

At this point, Madame Angulaire pulled out of her bag a sheet that was made from some kind of stretchy material.

"Here," she ordered, "put this on."

Dawn took the sheet in her hands and stared down at it, confused. "How exactly?" she asked.

"However your gut tells you. This is test number one for getting into the role of Myrtha," said Madame Angulaire.

The sheet had a top and a bottom hole, with one side being a bit smaller than the other. Dawn decided to put it on like a dress over her head and figure it out from there. It appeared that there were no armholes for her to stick her hands through at the top.

"Hold it! shouted Madame. "That's perfect. Don't move... yet." She snatched her phone out of her bag and began playing a strange piano piece that had no melody. The music rose and fell just as sporadically as if there was no human mind behind the playing. There were bits and pieces of melody that Dawn tried to make a pattern out of, but could not.

Madame got Dawn a stool to sit on. "Please dance."

"But how—?"

"Ah, ah—just dance, don't think. You are a mime of emotions right now. Go."

The music played and Dawn felt constricted, almost claustrophobic, in the sheet. The material was getting hot and sticking to her skin. She felt the need to escape, so she started to writhe around to the spastic music. It was the noise that also kept her mind from connecting to what she should do to make a beautiful, straight line. Instead, she focused on her heart beating loudly from the fear of losing control. She felt untethered from reality. Dawn dragged the sheet over her elbows and head to further suffocate herself, believing that her teacher would not truly let her suffocate in the sheet.

Grasping and ungrasping her hands, twisting from one side to the other like a lopsided tree, Dawn moved aimlessly. Her whole approach to ballet was wiped clean—erased. Ballet was no longer about the beauty of a straight line or the nobility of grace. Now, ballet was about feeling, emotion, unabashed subjectivism—emotions shared by all people and not only by an elite set of dancers.

Dawn focused on her toes and wriggled them like worms trying to free themselves of the dirt weighing down on their sprawling bodies. Convulsing toes had another kind of erotic tone to them as Dawn remembered a male dancer who once sucked on her big toe for fun. She watched as they wriggled and she felt she had no more control over her own feet. Her mind was so far away from the lowly toes—how could they share the same body? It was a complete farce. Dawn began to laugh.

"Quiet!" said Madame Angulaire. "Remember, you are a mime. You do not speak! You listen to your soul."

Retreating further into the sheet, Dawn absorbed the hurt of her teacher's correction. Nothing within this sheet could reach the soft, fleshy meat of Dawn. She was untouchable in this state of emotional release. Her soul was being wrung out and nothing was being taken in.

Nothing could make her leave this cocoon. Dawn began to stick her arms out in the sheet and dig her knees into it just to create a form other than a round blob.

"Yes! Good, now you're starting to get it," said Madame. "I

want to see more odd angles: Jut out your chin, curl your toes, unlock your spine!"

Obeying immediately, Dawn nearly fell off the stool since she was moving so wildly. The music kept going and Dawn tried more things in her sheet. She touched her face and hands and thighs as if for the first time. It was like she could start a conversation with one of her own body parts and they would respond on their own. Her mind watched over the little legs and arms playing beneath it like a puppet on strings.

"Very good, Dawn! I knew you'd take to this form quickly, my little protégé. I want you to lose your composure and grace—go wild and raw. Contort your body into shapes other people never knew were possible before!"

Grabbing Dawn's calves, Madame Angulaire squeezed them tightly and foisted her up into higher jumps. "Higher! Use those athletic legs of yours to touch the ceiling before coming back down to the dirt."

Dawn was running out of breath and was still unsure about what this had to do with her *Giselle* rehearsal. Then again, she was taught to obey, and she jumped higher.

Madame Angulaire let go of Dawn's calves. She paced around her pliable student while thinking of the next task to get her closer to the version of Myrtha she really desired. Pausing, Madame took a step toward Dawn's chest and looked straight into her eyes. "You may take off the sheet, but never forget the feeling of being trapped by it."

Dawn slipped the sheet off over her head and dropped the claustrophobic-causing tube on the floor. She felt a cold tingle up her spine as she shed the warm cocoon. Dawn tried to hold on to the feeling to use in her dancing. Now she was feeling even closer to the dirt and further away from soaring more than any time before.

Dawn said, "I feel cold now." She looked down at her fleshly self, which seemed much weaker, and the skin on her legs tremored with any motion.

"Never forget that feeling. You are a worm caught out on the hot pavement of a rainy day. I want you to get down on the floor and squirm around like an uncomfortable worm in the name of art."

Obeying, Dawn got down on the floor and when Madame began the music she had played earlier with all its breaks and accelerations, she squirmed. Moving deep inside of herself, shutting her eyes, Dawn tried to listen to a voice coming from inside, but it remained black and silent.

"Pick up the pace! You are afraid of being stuck on the hot pavement. You want to crawl back into the dirt!" shouted Madame Angulaire.

To crawl within the sheet would mean moving like a worm, so Dawn picked up her frantic movement from the left to the right, throwing herself in fits from one side to the other. All of her weight being thrown on the floor gave Dawn new bruises and pulled muscles. The nerves in her fingers and toes ached every time she hit them on the floor. Jamming her knees into a floor that was soft, but not soft enough to cushion Dawn's knees as she dug in.

"More crooked angles! Lose yourself to the voice within. Don't even think about dancing, imagine that you are the worm!" Madame Angulaire was getting more excited watching her student throw herself with full force into the movements she expected to see: an elbow crooked underneath a knee, a back writhing in pain, and feet splayed in no similar direction at all.

Madame's pacing continued as she swarmed around her creation. The fascinating way her body could distort itself caused other students to come over and watch. These movements were never allowed in a ballet school. They were movements found in hospitals or sick people's homes. Dawn's convulsions were akin to an epileptic's fit or a poisoned person's last attack.

Meanwhile, all Dawn could feel were the eyes on her and the pain. She could not reach a safe place in her own mind or a voice calling out from the darkness of her soul. I must not be trying hard enough to find the voice, thought Dawn. I've never listened to it before, so it must take practice. She threw her weight to the left side when the music ceased playing and she naturally came to a close. Dawn's breathing was hard and raspy as she spit the dust and hair collected in her mouth out. The other students quickly walked away, almost embarrassed by what they had just seen, like witnessing an inappropriate sexual act in public.

However, Dawn did not have time to notice because Madame Angulaire was quickly lifting her up from the floor and smiling at her. Madame's smile was not typical; her smile included lipstick staining her teeth and pinched lips that disappeared over her teeth when she smiled, as if her lips could no longer cover the great expansive cave.

Madame's cheekbones stuck out whenever her smile dropped, and her cheeks sunk into her jaw. Her skin, in general, barely covered her face and one could assume it did not want to cover the rest of her body, either. She wiped off some lint on Dawn's leotard next to her bottom, while another tingle traveled down Dawn's back.

Dawn smiled back at Madame Angulaire, hoping to convince her she had indeed heard the muse and the inner voice while she was dancing. But after a moment, Dawn's face scrunched up, and she began to cry. "Oh, Madame, I didn't hear any voice telling me what to do in my head. Am I a bad dancer?" She then covered her face in her palms and turned away from her teacher.

Madame Angulaire touched her hands and smiled a wider smile.

"Of course not, dear. Not everyone can hear their inner voice on the first try. You must try again, persist!" said Madame, as she placed her skeleton fingers on Dawn's head. "Chin up! Perhaps it's just that your movements were not sharp enough or your head was not low enough to the ground to hear the muse...or maybe you're just thinking too much."

Dawn frowned. How can I learn to dance at this level if I am not allowed to think? she wondered. But it looked like Madame Angulaire was ready to move on.

"Okay then, you're uninspired? Is that it? Fine. Dawn, I want you to sit there on the floor and listen to the music of *Giselle* and just envision the story—your part. You are Myrtha, Queen of the Wilis. What role do you play in the story?"

Madame turned the music on for the Myrtha variation while Dawn sat on the oak floor of the studio, her eyes shut tightly.

"I play a woman who cannot forgive the scorn of her lover. She wants revenge, and she does it in the most reserved, cold way. The music pipes up at her arrival and allows her to mesmerize all her future victims in the night. Yet, even the music is afraid of angering her and so it follows behind her like a breath of wind. It gently unfolds as she does on the stage, awakening her band of ghostly maidens to join in her terror."

Dawn began to sway and move her hands to the part.

"Stop! No dancing. I want you to just listen to the music

and imagine the story. That's it. No dancing is allowed right now. This is another exercise for you in the ways of modern dance."

Afraid, Dawn folded her hands down between her knees and kept them shut up in there until her fingernails turned blue. Shutting her eyes again, Dawn envisioned the maidens in a band behind Myrtha, all gazing ahead with unhappy faces. They stalked the night and brought fear to anyone out in the darkness.

Just as soon as Dawn got lost in the story and the music, the music was shut off. Dawn opened her eyes and saw her teacher motioning for her to get up off the floor. Raising herself up, Madame positioned her in front of the far left side of the mirrors.

"Okay, next exercise. There will be no music this time, just the story in your mind and your dancing," said Madame Angulaire.

The idea of moving without music to an actual ballet struck Dawn as strange, but she had to obey.

Dawn hopped in *arabesque* like Madame had shown her at the beginning of class. She tried imaging the music playing in her head to get the beats right.

"No thinking about the music! Pretend there never was music for this piece. You are to dance purely based on the story," said Madame Angulaire.

Dawn came out of the *arabesque* and did not know the rest of the variation, so she had to invent the next steps based on the idea that Myrtha was the leader of these maidens and she was pointing out the next area to haunt. So Dawn turned and pointed her fingers in various directions. She slowly walked toward her destination in the studio in silence. She became a pantomimist.

Waving her arms around her head, she rushed from one corner to the other with little direction. Her solo was not really about forwarding the story but more about revealing herself to the audience. Myrtha, Queen of the Wilis, was just showing the audience her domain.

Taking that idea and moving with it, Dawn opened herself up to the audience with her chest facing out and her arms outstretched at her sides.

"Good! Now we're getting somewhere. Continue," said Madame Angulaire. Her character shoes clicked a bit as she moved out of the way to make more room for Dawn.

Dawn walked around more casually, as if she were at home showing friends her apartment. She stopped her graceful ballet walk and turned an imaginary doorknob in front of her.

"Better. Now, put yourself back in the sheet," said Madame.

Her body crumpled up and she could hear the thud of her knees hitting the floor. Images came to her of an entrapped Myrtha who is caught in a spider's web. Her own ghostly form cannot win against the physical strength of silk. Still, she struggled harder against the inevitable.

Dawn thrashed on the floor, trying to escape the web. Perhaps her maidens made the cobwebs to overthrow their leader. She imagined all the other dancers watching her during class and waiting for her to break a bone. All dancers were competitive. It was entirely possible Michelle or Sarah wanted her to fall out of the race to a ballet company.

Dawn was determined to win the coup and take her revenge on her own maidens once she escaped the web. Thrashing harder still, Dawn broke free and stumbled up from her violent movements into one of strength and power. She leaped, not high off the ground, but both legs had enough strength to split over one hundred eighty degrees. Like a demon, Dawn raced about in a circle and clawed at anything in her way. Some students actually moved away from her as she began taking up more of the studio space.

"Take up more space! That's it! And move any way that feels most natural," said Madame from the corner of the room to avoid getting scratched by her protégé.

Dawn slithered on the ground to find the little mice maidens, which she had yet to catch. She grew legs again and ran at nothing, only to splay open her legs and squat over the studio floors as if she were searching tall grasses for something she dropped. Her movements were becoming blurred with her graceful ballet poses and her natural gait. A wildness took over Dawn's appearance, which everyone else gaped at in the studio.

Dawn the pantomime, Dawn the animal, Dawn the modern dancer. She would now become known to her classmates as something "fresh" and "original." This lesson today would put Dawn on another track from her peers.

After a few more minutes of hogging the studio space, Madame Angulaire grew tired of watching her protégé writhe. She wanted to give her some relief.

"Halt! Stop! Okay, very nice, Dawn. You've done good work today. I hope you feel you've learned as much as I've seen in the past hour. Now, I will do the rest of the quick variation with you for *Giselle*, and then you are free to go for lunch."

Madame watched Dawn repeat the opening sequence with the hopping *arabesques*, but after a moment, she shouted: "Stop! I want that *arabesque* leg to turn into an *attitude* and those elbows to droop. You are meant to look like a broken scarecrow guiding your other broken bodies through the swamp."

Dawn did as she was told, but her posture began to slip and her thoughts grew darker as she looked at herself in the mirror. Why am I hopping around like an idiot? thought Dawn. I must not be doing this right. It doesn't look modern now; it just looks foolish. It doesn't even match the music.

Still, Dawn finished her introduction onstage as Myrtha and prepared for the next section.

Madame Angulaire gave a brief smile as she moved toward Dawn. "Good. The next part is a little ballet run to one side of the stage and then toward the back of the stage."

Dawn gave a little ballet run, which meant barely making a sound on *demi-pointe* using tiny, quick steps like chicks peeping out of their nest.

"Stop! I want you to remember who Myrtha is," said Madame Angulaire. "Who is she?"

"She is a woman who wants revenge."

"Correct. Are you running around like you want revenge?"

"No, I suppose not. But Hilarion, the unrequited lover of Giselle, does not always run with anger in his steps. He leaps and soars with power and emotion."

The protégé was quickly losing rank in Madame Angulaire's mind as she squinted her eyes at Dawn. "Ballet needs to come into the modern age and wake up to reality. Do men do *pirouettes* in the middle of a battlefield? Do women perform *grand jetés* when they are filing their divorce papers? No. That's ridiculous. They seethe; they shout; they bash their fists against things. That's what real life is about. The existentialists helped us get there, but I don't need to explain myself to a dancer. You will run like a scorned woman, a madwoman, a woman who is made to do harm."

Dawn felt uncomfortable as she began stomping her feet flat-footed onto the studio floor. She almost wanted to apologize to the oak floor for bashing her feet against its old exterior. It's not you; it's my teacher making me do this. Sorry, thought Dawn. Left, right, left, right went her feet as she trod across the studio, making a loud noise and a shaking floor creak with every step.

"Better," said Madame. Now that you are at the back of the stage, I want you to grab those two fake flowers on the floor in front of you. Take one in each hand and do the same hopping *arabesque* you did in the beginning...with my corrections, of course."

Dawn obeyed.

"The next part is to *pas de bourrée* in a circle still holding the flowers. Remember, you are not those flowers; you are death."

Dawn *bourréed* hard into the floor like a hammer hitting down nails into the oak. She made them loud and angry. Her *bourrées* were small but mean. Feeling herself getting angrier with each painful throb of her toes, Dawn continued to dance.

"Excellent. You're almost halfway! Now, form a slow *arabesque*, and when you come out of it, throw one flower offstage, run to the other side of the stage, and throw the other flower offstage," said Madame Angulaire.

Dawn formed a crooked, inelegant *arabesque*. Her back ached as she lifted her leg and curved it. Her arms drooped further down to chicken-like levels. When she ran, it was closer to stomping, and when she threw her flowers, it was with a violent jerk to the ground. A bead from the center of one flower broke off from the frenzied throw. Dawn watched it roll and shine from the lights of the studio. She imagined stepping on it later and the bead embedding itself underneath her skin the next time she stamped her way through the studio for rehearsal practice.

Madame Angulaire checked the wristwatch she had on that kept sliding farther down her skinny arm. "We're almost two-thirds of the way done, Dawn. Let's keep up that vengeful energy of yours, shall we? The next part is a *glissade*, *cabriole*, *glissade* with a *grand jeté* following, and it will go back and forth, three times for each. But, instead of light and airy, go for low to the ground and hunched. Please keep your knees bent and your landings loud. I want to go for asymmetry here. Go!"

Dawn launched up but not too far up. Her jumps felt weak and suffocating, as if she were still stuck in that awful sheet. But she fought through the claustrophobic feelings creeping in and jumped until her breathing grew heavier.

"Finally," said Madame, "you are to *bourrée* back and forth, shaking your fists to the sky rather than swaying like a graceful bird. You are stronger than a bird. The last steps are a series of three *chaînés*, *jetés*, one *tour jeté*, running back to position, *piqué* turns, *chaîné* turns, and your final pose with your hands in front of your chest. But, as with all of your dancing, your elbows and knees must be prominent and out of line with the rest of your figure. That is the touchstone of the modern ballet form."

Dawn obeyed.

CHAPTER V

A week passed as Dawn grew more alarmed at the rate of bruises cropping up on her body and the confusion she felt mulling over ballet in general. She wanted to join a company next year since for her there was no other option. Yet, there was no way she could enter one until she mastered the modern ballet that everyone else seemed to be dancing at the professional level.

Her very being hurt. She found it difficult to turn in her feet and cut the perfect bodily line. She wore the black-and-blue splotches from her writhing on the hardwood floors. This was a different hurt from the normal pain of ballet class and pointe shoes.

As Dawn reached the doors to the theater for class, she saw another student step onto the sidewalk and run toward her.

"Dawn, Dawn! Hold the door for me. I have to tell you something!"

Christina was short for a dancer and a bit too wide in the waist. Since she was built stocky though, she was better at jumps, threatening to attain similar heights to the male dancers in the studio. Like most of her classmates, Dawn did not really care for her much.

"Yes? What is it?" asked Dawn.

"I've just gotten my parents to agree to pay for my spot in this year's Prix de Danse competition! Isn't that exciting?" Christina almost fell over herself, jumping up and down in the lobby of the old theater.

"Really? Lucky you. I wish my parents would pay for me to enter competitions. As it is, they are just barely able to pay for my new shoes." Dawn closed up. Remaining impenetrable was the only way to keep herself from wanting to bite Christina's head off.

How dare she? thought Dawn. With her short, stupid legs and her waist that makes her look like a pancake? Her parents are just throwing money away on the poor, untalented thing.

Without saying much else, Dawn walked ahead of Christina toward the studio. Christina wrinkled her brows before realizing that she had made Dawn jealous. She felt almost bad, but that was just the start of her career in a competitive environment and she knew it.

***

Dawn had known Christina since they were toddlers in ballet class for the first time. They both wore the ugly pink tutus together and jumped over imaginary ponds together. Their teacher shouted unfamiliar words at them, as were their parents. New words were just a part of growing up in the world for the two young dancers, so they took it all with grace.

Their bodies were awkward and thin as they grew up in a ballet studio. Having tiny waists without form made all the little girls often indistinguishable from the little boys. Yet, their calves became tough little lumps and their arms grew into more rounded shapes as they aged.

Christina stopped growing much after her growth spurt at twelve, while Dawn kept going. Dawn's legs grew longer and leaner. Her parents often had to rub her legs at night to ease all the growing pains she had. Christina also seemed to stagnate in her ability to improve in ballet technique, while Dawn continued to excel. But here was the irony: one had wealthy parents who could throw money at their child, and the other one had poor parents who hoarded a small stash away for emergencies.

Dawn knew she would need scholarships, financial aid, patrons, and a job with a company to keep her ability to do ballet going. She had to feed her addiction on her own. It was either learn the combination or die; get a scholarship to competitions or die; dance for a company or die. There was no other alternative.

For Christina, she could always go back home and start afresh. She could always pay for competitions if she failed in the previous ones. Her ability to recreate herself into whatever she wanted was unlimited. She was free.

For Dawn, breathing dance was it for her. There was no life outside of the fishbowl. But her ability to improve in ballet and all of its modern forms depended on her success in getting into a company. The very word "company" was untouchable as it came sprawling out of her mouth. The thought of the goal was never meant to be much deeper because dwelling on it too long made Dawn desperate with longing.

She would listen and learn from Madame Angulaire more than Madame Roberts. Madame Angulaire knew about the state of the professional dance world *now*—in its modern form. Madame Roberts was from an era where classical was king. But now Dawn was Queen of the Wilis and all would be different in the realm of ballet. Modern dance was the new leader. It was the form that would show the wealthy parents who they should really spend their money on. The dancers who could adapt would survive and the others would become extinct.

Dawn recalled how, from toddler age until now, she was one of the few dancers to remain in the same ballet school. Her ambition had taken her to the top of the class, and she was constantly learning new techniques to add to her arsenal.

She would perform tricks *en pointe* to impress her peers and try to pull off more *pirouettes* than the boys. Dawn would learn how to contort her body again for dance. She would unwind her turnout, turn in her feet, hunch her back, lower her head, whatever she needed to do to get to where ballet belonged.

After all, her teachers who had traveled this path before must know where ballet is headed. They are its leaders who are birthing new variations on the old all the time. They must understand how ballet came to be and where it is going. The ballet teachers are the holders of what really is an oral history. There is no notation for dance. Our ancestors have tried and failed, and it is up to our teachers, and previous dancers, to share with us all they know. Dawn trusted in ballet and its teachers.

***

Reaching the studio far ahead of Christina, Dawn darted to her place at the barre, claiming her spot before anyone else arrived. She sat down underneath her wooden partner and grabbed her pointe shoes out of her dance bag. She put them on to give her the appearance of weightlessness, but she knew the truth—the shoes forced her down further into the oak. When dancing *en pointe*, Dawn knew that she was of this earth. Her pointe shoes reminded her she would someday be buried underneath the stage, below the boards, lying low in a costume box.

A chill made Dawn look up toward the door opening to the studio—it was Christina. She walked in without looking at Dawn and began stretching at the barre as far away from Dawn as possible. Staring from her peripherals, Dawn watched Christina pull her leg up close to her head. She saw her hamstrings bend and flex with almost as much ease as Dawn's did. But everyone knew that her body was meant to jump and not form a proper, flexible line. Christina was like a frog. She wound up with her bent knees and then threw herself up into the air with brute strength, only to land again elsewhere like a frog hopping to another lily pad.

Dawn could not stop observing her classmate. She had always been this way. Watching was her form of protection, since she could judge if her peers were getting better at dancing than her. Of course, most of the time they were not. Dawn could not tear herself away from using the mirrors as a monitor on everyone but herself. She, the Queen, had to watch over her Wilis. They required her leadership and guidance in ballet.

Today, she hoped to teach them what she learned from Madame Angulaire. Although it did not make much sense to her yet, every day was a search to find out what the meaning of ballet is and how it should be passed on down the generations. As a dancer, Dawn was told not to think, yet here she was curious about what her dancing really meant. She knew her other classmates were not thinking this way, but that must be why she was chosen as the Queen of the Wilis.

Madame Angulaire shouted at her not to think but to feel. Madame Roberts showed her to think about the structural rules and to follow those as gospel. Dawn ended up not really knowing what to do. So, she had been turning her mind "on" to learn the steps and then "off" to dance them. She tried to turn different body parts into the feelers of the soul. Her fingers stretched out as if trying to contain the music. Her stomach recoiled when offered anything but movement to eat. Her mind remained dormant as she strove to drink up perfection in dance.

To an audience, ballet dancers spin like ornaments on a string without ever changing. But just like movement in dance, the body is also moving on a micro-level. Yet, the dancer always tries to combat the sweat, the bruises, the blood, by wearing black leotards, bandaging toes before they dance, and fanning themselves between combinations. The result is a dancer who remains just as perfect upon entering the studio or stage as when they leave it. The dramatic bit that happens in between entering and leaving causes no scar on the dancer.

Dancers in that way are immortal. Dawn felt herself, especially before class or a performance, an abundance of energy. She had to be unwound to return to a peaceful state. Her arms and stomach and legs felt lean. No one could contain her.

Yet, there was Christina...and other dancers. They distracted and absorbed all of Dawn's pure power and energy. They all showed off too much. Christina stood there stretching her back at the barre, extending herself nearly into a backbend. She begged for attention constantly. Her parents were enamored with her, which is why they threw their money at her like a performing monkey.

Turning away from Christina, Dawn attempted to focus on herself again. But the mirrors always gave away what position the other dancers were in, no matter which direction Dawn was facing. Christina had the gall to use the mirrors to apply makeup to her face before morning classes. She circled her eyes with black, rouged up her mouth and cheeks, and even darkened her eyebrows. The face powder made her ghostly white with those dead, black eyes. Christina seemed to think she was the dead Giselle.

Dawn eyed Christina, pulling up her black, torn-up leggings over her muscular legs. Tights make everything look more solid, as did leotards, which made Christina appear thinner than she really was. But the leggings on top made her look even smaller since black blurred where her muscles started and her legwarmers began. It appeared that Christina understood what would make her look the best. Dawn felt it working as a cloud formed over her mind and she knew the rest of the day would be soured by her classmate looking better than her.

Dawn wore the mandatory leotard and tights, but she had been playing with different accessory items for years, trying to get it right. She wore her tights over the top of her leotard; she put on stage makeup for every class; she wore a loose-fitting, cut T-shirt and trash bag pants; she wore the long skirts with two different legwarmers underneath. But nothing made her feel like a professional ballet dancer as much as her other classmates appeared.

The fashion for a ballet dancer was as important as the musicality and technicality of dancing. A dancer was firstly selling their looks as much as the dancing. To be a professional, you had to have the body type and a beautiful face, or no one would even give you a chance at dancing for them. Dawn took note.

***

Dawn promised to continue trying to make herself look as

dancer-like as possible. Perhaps trying this modern dance style would be the key to making her appear more like the professionals. She stretched down to touch her toes and turned them inward on her way down. She saw her feet behaving in a way that still felt unnatural. Her big toes were not meant to ever meet the other. The way her heels separated was unheard of when they were meant to always be together.

Having come back up from her stretch, Dawn saw more students trickle in for the day's class: thin boys before their teenage growth spurts, wide-hipped girls who were not made for ballet any longer, tall boys, short girls, and vice versa. They all had their slight differences, which maybe were difficult to see from the audience, but in a room full of mirrors, it was obvious. Dawn knew not all of her classmates would make it into professional companies next year, and without actively dancing, there could be no visible dancer there.

Dawn picked Christina out of her context of the studio in her dance clothes and imagined her out on the street today. Would Dawn point and say to her friend, "Look, there goes a dancer?" No, thought Dawn, her entire existence would evaporate and be forgotten as soon as she left the theater.

She envisioned ballet just falling off a person like a lost shadow, left to drape itself in the corners of the theater. Ballet did not stick. It had no staying power on a person who chose not to live, breathe, and eat the art form. If you were deathly pale and thin, then perhaps someone would guess dancer out on the street, but otherwise, you were just labeled as homeless or anorexic by passersby.

Right before class was scheduled to begin officially, Christina snuck over to Dawn, her little baby wisps flying with each step.

Dawn threw her a savage look.

"Sorry, I didn't mean to upset you. I'm just thankful that my parents seem to believe I can still make it."

"Your parents shouldn't be the judge of whether or not you make it. They're not dancers."

Christina hunched out of her proper ballet posture for a moment. "I know. But so often our teachers correct everything and never give us a hint of us actually succeeding anywhere. It's just nice to have some cheerleaders in the world."

No one ever cheered Dawn on, and even if they did, she would not care. Her ambition to stay on this ballet journey would never waiver. She only relied on herself for direction and willpower. That is all she needed.

Now, Christina had glumly walked back to her barre as far away from Dawn as possible. She had not made a convincing apology, nor a new dance friend. Checking over her shoulder and then at the mirrors, Dawn followed Christina and her body. Christina went back to stretching, and during class, there was a sadness tinging her *tendus* and *port de bras*.

Dancers loved to play characters in their movements. Dawn was not easily fooled by Christina's movements. In fact, she thought, How dare she try to appeal to me through dance? Clearly, Christina knew Dawn would watch her during class, but Dawn refused to budge. Her movements at the barre were course flicks of the foot and speedy muscular shifts.

Ignoring her peers was impossible in a ballet studio. All the barres were lined up against the walls, so in a military sort of lineup, each dancer was constantly staring at the back of another dancer's head. If they were facing away from the barre, then no one escaped the eye of the mirrors, and if they were facing the barre, then peripheral vision got the best of them as they checked the nearest pointed toe toward them or the direction of the nearest head.

The space in between each dancer was tiny. They were an army of highly trained mimickers, and their instructor was their god. Madame Angulaire was the god of modern ballet and Madame Roberts was the god of classical ballet. In this new world of Dawn's, modern ballet was winning.

With that knowledge, Dawn ravenously followed Madame Angulaire's every recommendation, tip, or idea. If toes were to be pointed in, then Dawn followed. If hips were to be uneven rather than parallel to the floor, then so be it. Dawn was the perfect student, and she hoped that would translate into the perfect professional who takes orders with ease and grace.

After all, Dawn was made for nothing else; she had no money, no other passions, no hobbies, no wealthy relatives, no idea of a world outside of this theater right here and now. The future went as far as dancing with a company until death separated her from movement and laid her down beneath the stage.

Hopefully, it would end gently. Otherwise, she kept having dreams of her final ballet performance, and her heart only half shutting off. She dreamed of stumbling around violently onstage in front of a crowd, balancing on one foot and moving one arm while the other side of her heart shut down more slowly. She imagined following herself from three years old until a prima ballerina at forty in her mind as she fought against the inevitable failing inside herself. Her stomach leaped at the thought but going violently, fighting death to the end, seemed more of her personality than a sleeping beauty style of ending. Fighting to finish the performance, she would make everyone watch what a devil death is for us all, and at the end, she would fall to the ground with the curtain closing and the sound of applause filling the last of her hearing ears. The next day, her fellow dancers, including Madame Angulaire if she was still around, would lay her down below the place she worked and the only home she ever knew.

Ballet was all-consuming and there was no escape for a person like Dawn.

***

Class began with the pianist being late and Madame Roberts feeling flustered. Ballet was such a routine that sometimes we forgot to move our legs! thought Dawn. To make up for the missed minutes, the pacing of the class was much faster. By the time Dawn got to center work, she was already perspiring.

"And *relevé*, one, two, three, and back down. Other side," said Madame Roberts.

A cramp began creeping into Dawn's left foot. She kept trying to shake it out onto the floor, but she knew the only way for her cramp to loosen was to relax her muscles or dance through it. The pain was worsening as she raised herself onto the tips of her toes. Biting her lip, Dawn fought herself. Her classmates were not in pain like she was. They all looked relaxed, if not bored, as ever. Only here was Dawn, trying to combat the pain of a cramp which kept her from dancing gracefully.

In the center, Madame Roberts gave the longest *adagios*. The dancers all had to hold their frequently one-legged positions for more than a minute at a time to test their own balance. Not having a barre there or a physical partner made a dancer realize how much their body had to make micro-compensations for every position they were holding. Dawn watched as her right leg started to shake from being left so high for so long. More sweat poured from her face and trickled down into her leotard, which happily sucked up the liquid. There were dark sweat stains on all the dancers at this point. The smell of deodorant and cologne washing off the dancers' bodies revealed the other smell they were trying to prevent—sweat.

Sweat was a part of a dancer's life. It was always there in varying degrees. That made the physical aspects of ballet erotic in some ways. Young men and women with all of their chests heaving and the sweat pooling in one tight studio made for a very vulnerable setting. The shared visible sweat brought the dancers together in some way.

Dawn managed to blow a bit down her leotard and fan her face with her hand before the next combination in the center. Whenever she grew hot, her cheeks would burn red, and she looked like she wore a red mask across her face. The tinge made her eyes look wild.

"Dancers, I want you to push through the pain, don't think about it, and just focus on the steps. Push through the sweat and pain to reach out each muscle as you dance because that is the only way you will grow. I want you to express your souls through movement. You defy pain; you are immortal in the eyes of an audience. You defy sweat, cramps, and any other protests that your body may make to keep you from looking your best onstage and in class. You are dancers. You transcend all bodily pain and enter the spiritual world of the divine. All dancers will go to heaven." Madame Roberts finished her words of inspiration, just barely giving the dancers enough time to breathe, wipe off the sweat with the backs of their hands, and get ready to push themselves even further than before. "So, I want to do some small jumps now, and then we will head to the corner for waltz work," said Madame Roberts.

It was moments like this where the exhaustion beats out any other thoughts. All thoughts seemed to disappear behind a dizzying fog of the physical objects in the room and a dancer's relation to them. Spotting was staring at a picture of another dancer across the room and whipping their head around in a turn to focus back on that single spot. Granted, everyone still got dizzy, but as long as a dancer knew where the incoming object was and avoided it, then they were deemed successful.

Dawn thought that dancing to the point of exhaustion was the equivalent kind of escapism readers experienced when reading a good book. She lost herself to dancing. Her mind was no longer capable of having any other ideas outside of dance. So there she jumped up sharply and landed with efficient use of her bent knees to soften coming down. Her jumps were never as good as her waltz technique with its broad, sweeping steps and full use of the surrounding space.

"Good, dancers. Please travel now in groups of three to the combination. And one, and a two, and a three, next group!" Madame Roberts clapped along over the top of the pianist's music, which everyone knew he disliked. The pianist was an artist too. But the instructor was the leader of the group, and she chose to clap to the beat as they danced across the floor—the large mirrors revealing any flaws and some minor successes the dancers never paid as much attention to.

Madame Roberts's slender hands clapped more powerfully than anyone expected, and it awoke many of the dancers from their dizzying fog. They launched out into the middle of the floor and gave those jumps and turns every bit of energy they had left by the end of class. For a dancer, they are meant to take the ideas of the instructor and act on them immediately. There is no questioning the choreographer because dancers are just the performers, the wind-up toys of the playing child. But the choreographer is the visionary and puts all the little pawns in their places so that the creator can see them all as a whole.

Dawn committed herself daily to giving up her voice and her thoughts to her teachers. She only had control over her body and it had to obey the thinkers. She reminded herself that dancers were meant to be silent. Movement was their only form of communication. Dancers were all like standing buckets, waiting for the rain to fill them up.

CHAPTER VI

awn was waiting for more information about technique or musicality or acting. She would take anything and everything in as she neared the end of her precious time as a ballet student. Professionals had to learn about thirty new ballets in their first year as part of a company, and Dawn wished to make that transition as painless as possible.

"Dancers, it's time for *reverence*. Please follow me as we finish up class," said Madame Roberts.

Slowly walking back to the center of the room, Dawn echoed Madame Roberts's movements from her toes to the tips of her fingers.

The formalities of ballet class all made sense. Class began with a slow waking of the body, especially the feet and ankles. As Dawn focused on her individual muscle groups and her own form, the *pliés* were slow and low. The exercises at barre grew faster as class progressed, all leading up to center work where the real test of the ballet dancer began. The task was to balance alone with nothing to break a dancer's fall. The risk and responsibility lay with the dancer and their own control of their body. Then, class ended with following the teacher and thanking them for leading the class.

The name truly means giving reverence to the ballet teacher. The young are only capable of repaying the teacher with claps and bows upon exiting class. They are unable to give more until they, in turn, become the teachers. Ballet had this funny cyclical nature. The feeling of gratitude moved and changed hands as frequently as people grew another year older.

Yet, Dawn did not feel thankful this afternoon...or most days, really. She never left class satisfied. She left class today, as on many previous days, sweating with lowered eyes and a mouth that drooped with dissatisfaction. As she walked over the threshold separating the studio from the changing room, the adult ballet dancers gave them space and looked at Dawn and her classmates with awe. To the adults, the younger dancers were already like professionals. It made her cringe to be only adored by older, less capable beings than herself. All the adults were the age of her parents, so their praise felt like a given—all old people loved the young.

Dawn rolled her eyes after passing the adults while keeping her ballet posture a little taller to maintain her show of dignity and pride in front of them. Her sweat became her makeshift card of validation that she had worked hard to take off for a couple of hours. Their final class for the evening would resume after the adult ballet class ended.

"Welcome! Welcome, boy, I have missed you all!" announced Madame Roberts as she smiled and waved at the old people entering our studio.

Why would she miss those people? wondered Dawn. What was there to miss about bodies whose metabolism was slowing down? What was there to miss about gray hairs sprouting from the tops of balding heads? What was there to miss about trunk ankles and misshapen, bloated feet?

With each passing question, Dawn fumed more and more until the anger swung her around to peer back into the studio door's window. The adults were stretching while Madame Roberts collected her notes for class and found the appropriate music for the pianist to play that evening. Tears of laughter welled up in Dawn's eyes as she watched one of the adults squatting ungracefully and unable to get back up smoothly. His legs shook as he attempted to right himself. A baby could squat down more gracefully! Dawn thought. Then Dawn gagged when she saw one of the adult females in class without tights on. She only wore a black leotard under some baggy black shorts. What is this the gym?! Dawn thought. Her legs are going to be jiggling all over the place, and I must get out of here before she turns around! There was a good reason for ballet clothes being worn in their entirety. The tights and leotard buckled down the skin that was too soft for flight, even on the skinniest of dancers. The tights always shrunk back down to doll size when a dancer stripped them off, while the leotard armholes grew stretched from the battle of getting it over one shoulder and then the other before class. The shoes also contained the toes in a militaristic form that kept all of them aligned. Wearing a tight bun at the back of the head for the girls and gelled-back hair for the boys kept the hair away from the face. Anything flailing would lead to distraction and then to mistakes in every successive step—no properly executed jumps, turns, walks. Students at the Academy were never allowed to wear any jewelry or accessories for that reason, either. Talking before class was also frowned upon by the staff, as dancers should clear their minds before any dancing. A dancer had to enter a world of their own artistry in order to improve and create beautiful art.

75

Silence was something these adults did not have. They chatted and smiled cordially at each other while stretching. There was no concern about form and performance for these men and women. They did not live, breathe, and sleep with dance in their lives, thought Dawn. They must have jobs outside of the studio. Dull day jobs that keep them stationary at a desk all day, wasting away in front of a computer screen, and aimlessly awaiting their lunch break. The adults in the room not only showed their age but their food habits as well. One woman in the opposite corner of the studio had rolls poking out in her leotard, which it must have taken her *forever* to pack inside those shrunken tights, but at least she had tried to contain her fat. The men in the class just wore oversized shirts and longer shorts to hide themselves. Dawn knew what they hid, and she knew the mirrors could see just as clearly.

***

A mist of breath covered the window Dawn was peering through, and she wiped it off with too much force. Smudges and dirt cursed the pane she used to see these old people dance, which Dawn eventually came to accept as the only way to see these people—through a smutty fog.

The first *pliés* were attempted and even from where Dawn was standing, outside of the studio, she could hear the creaks and pops of bones abused over a lifetime. The woman over at the furthest barre into the studio arched her back like a fishing hook as she bent her knees. From the window, Dawn could even see the irregular veins wiggling through her skintight stockings. Upon coming up, her monstrous thighs shook and the muscles in her arm flexed as she pulled herself up by the barre. A simple bend took an entire old person's body to participate in the movement. Even after a full day of dress rehearsal for a show, I could never feel that tired, thought Dawn. My body has never known fatigue in the way these fools do. How can time be so cruel? If I devote all my energy to this consistently, why should time erase my efforts? Is it possible for me to look like those creatures?

In the *tendu* combination, the woman who bumped into Dawn before was at the center barre. Through her softened canvas ballet shoes, Dawn could tell that her toes were too buckled and weathered to point properly anymore. And her hands were too shriveled to look like delicate feathers. It seemed she was one of the brave dancers who actually just stuck to wearing a leotard and stockings, even though the leotard was navy blue. This old lady kept her auburn hair short, like a man's. Why did old people cut their hair short, anyway? wondered Dawn, as she kept her eyes on the woman at the center barre. Her face looked a little worn with wrinkles Dawn hoped she'd never personally experience. But her eyes were soft and kind looking, as soft as the little belly pouch she had where babies were probably pulled out of her. Dawn shivered at the thought. Condemned to life with a soft belly and a soft baby made her nauseous. In Dawn's mind, the hero is the firm, the beautiful was hard as a rock, and the graceful kept their straight lines no matter the pain.

Nothing could be soft and flimsy in the theater. Even the tender moments were built on a foundation of power. Dawn's breathing picked up and continued to mist up the window, but she did not care to wipe it off as she watched them all horrendously stumble through the *frappés*. A *frappé* should be executed with the top of the foot hitting the floor like a lightning bolt. There should be a bang! Instead, it was mostly quiet, with a few random swiping noises here and there, especially when the adults had to do the combination from behind. Not one foot struck the floor with enough force to even lift them off their heels, let alone into a potentially successful jump.

Did Madame Roberts see all of this? thought Dawn. She must know what blundering fools she took money from. How could she possibly stand spending her precious time in the studio teaching people who will go nowhere with their dancing? How could they pay money for something that was difficult and they would never succeed in?

The old man, an even rarer sight, at the barre closer to the window was stretching out his back, which no longer bent much further back than straight from all the days he sat in a chair. He moved at his own pace. When everyone was called into the center for *adagio*, he followed along halfway and slowly. He was unable to keep up with the tempo of even the slow music. But when the music would reach a crescendo, Dawn watched his eyes close. He was listening.

"Good class, you all moved to the music expressively. Now, to the corner!" pointed Madame Roberts.

The adults all looked at each other as their hearts sunk. The center meant no supporting barre to keep them upright; it meant no guidance from the person in front; it meant asking more from their already fatigued bodies. They all stumbled their way across the floor from the left to the right.

"I can see you are tired today, so let's try something a bit less rigorous. Please give me your best ballet walk. First from the right side, and then we'll move to the left. Go!" said Madame.

The lady in the navy leotard appeared to be one of the few who kept her head up through this seemingly sadistic part of the class. In fact, Dawn remembered her holding her head up high as she left her previous class too. Why? What does she have to be so proud of? thought Dawn. If any of these old people truly looked at themselves in the mirror, they wouldn't hold their heads up high. They'd crouch down ashamed and bitter that the gift they were given at birth—a body—had betrayed them so. Rage flowed up into Dawn's cheeks, giving them a red-hot glow. She felt like running into the class of stumbling frogs and beating them with her Queen of the Wilis scepter. Then she would throw it down and leap high into the air and show them her splits, her turns, and her young body. They would all leave the class painfully aware of what they could no longer do or be.

Then, the suffocating feeling rushed over Dawn once more. The feeling of the sleeve trapping her in a fabric cocoon. Her freedom was snatched away by the taut pull of the sheet and her flailing fragile wings were suppressed under the weight of each individual string. Clutching her own throat, Dawn felt closer to death than ever before. She looked out at the adults, who seemed so at peace even though they were closer to death than she was. Her thoughts raced, and she sat down on the cool, wooden floor panels to get a hold of herself. The ground was the only way to wake her from this nightmare of emotion.

***

Taking in a raspy and quaking breath, Dawn watched the final *reverence* part of the adult class. Madame Roberts led with her ghostly frame, her beautiful fingers stretching out to touch the hem of the divine. She gave the mirror, her audience, the most enticing look—begging the mirror imaginings to keep watching her and her body. Yet, behind her stood the infirm, the buckled, the worn. They stared at a mirror which, to Dawn, only showed them their hideous flaws. But no one in the class seemed to notice. The room was rather filled with the unified breath of people working to improve themselves. There was a certain grace and knowing emanating from their souls.

Squinting, Dawn attempted to see the invisible emotion filling the studio like a noxious gas. Instead, Madame Roberts turned around on her students to curtsy and wish them a fantastic rest of the day.

"*Au revoir, mes amis!* I hope to see you all in class next week," said Madame Roberts, as she turned back to her makeshift table with the students' checks and her sweater and water and whatever other random objects were found on the studio floor that day. Some of her students stayed after class to ask questions about improving their technique. How ridiculous! thought Dawn. They are over there asking the teacher things that only we would ask and could actually improve on! They will never really get in a pool and work on their *changement battu* or stretch every morning to get their middle splits! This is just a waste of time. This is why I would rather die before having to become a ballet teacher.

Disappointed at seeing Madame Roberts waste her valuable time, Dawn turned around and went downstairs to the changing room to look at the costumes being prepared for *Giselle*. Having reached the door's threshold, she saw the navy leotard woman gathering her things from the large wooden table. Her purse was smothering someone's performance tutu. Dawn restrained herself from backing up and immediately leaving the room once she had been spotted by the old lady.

Toying with her fingers, Dawn merely said, "Hello. Do you mind not squishing the costumes?"

The woman looked down and jumped to gather up her purse. "Oh! Dear, I'm so sorry. Is it yours? It is a lovely tutu." Her short hairs bobbed up and down on her head as she spoke.

"I don't think so. It's probably Jenny's since she is playing Giselle. Her costume is probably the first to be made by our seamstresses. I'm Myrtha, Queen of the Wilis."

"Well, nice to meet you, Myrtha. My name is Natalie Molchalin. I've been dancing my entire life—though not continuously. When I was your age, I remember thinking I wanted to devote myself to dance." A smile broke out across her face so that her crow's feet showed.

Dawn almost laughed at how ridiculous that sounded, looking at Natalie now with her crooked feet and her knobbly knees. She would not have had a chance even then of becoming a prima ballerina. "Hmmm, that's nice. What made you change your mind?"

Her eyes twinkled. "What do you think?"

"I don't know. An accident, school, weight… You tell me."

"A man. What else?"

Dawn's eyes widened. How could a man derail a woman from the most wonderful profession in the world? She bent forward slightly to better understand how much she should avoid the male eye.

"A man? A *man* took away your dream?"

"No, not exactly," Natalie chuckled. "You see, he was a man who I admired and wanted to spend all my time with. Ballet was so absorbing at that age that I felt like I could never see him unless he was a dancer too. I found his love and touch to bring a fire to my body that was greater than my desire to dance. At your age, I didn't think anything like that was possible. Eclipse dance? No.

"But he did, and two years later, we got married."

"You got married in your teens?"

81

"It wasn't so abnormal in my time," said Natalie. She gave a sigh then, which made Dawn shrink back in her own skin. "He's dead now. Aneurysm. Sudden. I've lived alone since then." Her face grew dim as the youthful memories disappeared into the darkness.

"Oh, I'm sorry." Dawn could not muster up enough to say anything else. She stood there awkwardly, floating in midair with her words because she had never really encountered death before. Of course, she knew the tragedy of *Giselle* and a bunch of tragic romance stories, but she had never come face-to-face with a widow. In a way, she could be a Wili…did that mean that Dawn could rule over someone older than herself? No, her parents still taught her to "respect her elders" no matter how silly they come off.

"That's all right, honey. It's been years now. I just wish I had had children with him before he passed. That way I could have held them to me like miniature hims. How I miss him so." Natalie looked down at the table, ashamed that she was revealing herself to a fifteen-year-old. But this chance at connection seemed right at the beginning of the conversation. Natalie felt a kind of kinship with Dawn. She could have been this child's mother, after all, she was only fifty-five.

Dawn began to feel the sheet of Madame Angulaire take hold of her again as time ticked on and she grew more uncomfortable. Why was this stranger placing such a burden on her fragile shoulders? thought Dawn. Why should she care? She was young and healthy, unattached to anything with wings and a bow in its hand. Why let other people bring her down? The world was open at her tiny feet and she was going to dance all over it before it seated itself down on top of her. She was not meant to be crushed…though the sleeve was suffocating.

"Well, anyway, it was nice meeting you, Natalie," said Dawn, as she turned around to slip out of the dressing room.

"Oh, lovely meeting you, dear. I will see you again tomorrow in between classes, I'm sure."

At this insistence on maintaining some sort of connection after today, Dawn became squeamish and attempted to walk faster in an effort to forget that last comment. Perhaps outrunning the vibrations that issued from her mouth could protect her mind from processing them. Her pace became hysterical at its walk-run speed that she may as well have run all the way back to her room at home.

But home was never really the place she wanted to be. Home, where mom and dad lived, was much less of a home than the studio had become. The dance studio at the Academy allowed Dawn to express fully herself. Only stretching and the methodical running through the steps were possible at home, with its shaggy carpet and cramped spaces.

As Dawn slowed back down to a walk, she heard a sound behind her. Turning, she saw Natalie not far behind waving something in her hand.

"Here! Here! I almost forgot to give you my phone number in case you ever need someone to pick you up or drop you off at class." Natalie handed her a perfumed piece of ratty old paper with the nice cursive hand of old.

Dawn grabbed the piece of paper carelessly and stuffed it inside one of her pointe shoes that were dangling over her shoulder. "Er, thanks. My mom usually is the one to drop me off, but maybe if she's sick or something…"

Natalie smiled as she clung to the hope of making a new, albeit unwilling, friend.

So both the younger dancer and the older dancer separated for the day, each lost in their thoughts about the other and how to respond to each other tomorrow.

There is no way I will call her, Dawn thought. I don't need her help. I'm perfectly capable of making it here on my own. Besides, my legs can walk great distances, unlike her bowed knees and wobbling stance. My legs were made to carry me great distances. They are powerful. And she continued to stomp home.

I hope she tries to call me, Natalie thought. It is refreshing to see a new life make its way onto the stage. Her story is just beginning to unfold. She has been sheltered thus far from the pain, corruption, and injustices that make up life. I wish she would never experience them. Natalie sighed. Oh well, at least I can be there for her if she falls…

The sun was moving lower in the sky and lent the world a golden hue. A radiant warmth washed over the town and landed on the backs of two people from different paths. It also encompassed both teachers who were fighting behind the scenes.

***

"I want this to be romantic and not all narcissistic!" raged Madame Roberts.

"I want the girls and boys to get a taste of what *real* romantic tragedy is. This is after all the twenty-first century, is it not?! Life is about pain and suffering and ultimately death. Giselle is fated to die miserably. She is not some go-lucky ball of sunshine! Why is that so hard for you to see?" Madame Angulaire seethed, her caved-in chest violently shaking with anger.

Madame Roberts took her slender wrist and shapely arm

and flung Madame Angulaire's choreography notes into her face. Watching the kettle boil over, Madame Roberts stepped back and folded her arms across her chest while Angulaire stooped to pick up and rearrange the pages.

"You, Madame, don't deserve to teach even a part of this ballet," said Madame Angulaire. "These students need to know that when and *if* they become professionals, they will have to know modern dance. Modern dance is taking over the culture. We are winning. The boring classics are the foundation they learn as children, but when they enter the real world, ha! Fairytale land has expired. The world is cutthroat and our system is not built for the good. Everyone is out there for herself—kill or be killed. They'll be lucky if someone doesn't sabotage their career by the time they reach thirty."

"You don't really believe that," said Madame Roberts.

"Of course I do! Look where we both ended up? Of course, I made it further in this game than you. I was with the top ballet company in this country, and I performed until my bones ground against each other. The pain got so bad that I would vomit after every warm-up class for the day. I was in no shape to continue. I had to retire and become a teacher. But you, my darling. You never had the drive or the body, if I may say so myself, to be a true prima ballerina. Your breasts are not flat enough and your bones are not visible enough under the unforgiving stage lights. You and I both know that...the mirrors know that. Now if you were to do modern dance, then perhaps the ballet world could have still used you. For, you see, modern dance allows for the imperfect, the ugly, the painful. Modern dance is a great equalizer in that way. You can move whatever and whichever way your heart longs to move and have it still be right. Principles of dance? Ha! There is only what's inside, your subjective feelings—your pain, your sorrow, your suffering."

"And what about my joy?" asked Madame Roberts. Her skin grew paler and paler.

"Your joy may be in spurts here and there, sure. You may leap up high in any way you'd like, but just remember that gravity brings you back down. You'll always come down, darling." Madame Angulaire smirked and left Madame Roberts pale and shivering. Death had fought for its place at the table. When the apostles ate for Apollo, they may very well have noticed the effects of the arsenic lacing every bite.

II

PART TWO

CHAPTER I

Dawn had spent the last two months preparing for her role in *Giselle*. Her preparation mimicked that of the professionals, from ice baths to Epsom salts to preparing her stage shoes to perfection. In the evenings at home, she spent hours listening to the music of the ballet and dancing discretely along with her steps. Everything became a prop on a stage. Even her parents played the same parts in her mind. Moments of losing herself in the music gave Dawn a melancholy demeanor throughout the months leading up to the performances. There was a glazed-over look in her eyes as she interacted with her surrounding world.

The inner world was full of fluid movements. She constantly walked with her turned-out feet like the older girls used to when she was younger and fresher to the scene. Bodily, she was always ready to jump onto her toes and transition into the next step seamlessly. Dreams involved roses and curtain calls that ended with waves of claps and bravos! The lights from the stage drenched her heaving body in sweat as she imagined curtsying and cradling her own beautiful bouquet of roses.

She envisioned her makeup caking on various parts of her face, some of it landing down on her chest and turning it a tanned color she had never been before. Her pointe shoes, as she had experienced before, would be dead by the end of the performances and she would thank them and add them to the pointe shoe Christmas tree she had started making at home.

Yes, the stage life was home. It was the beginning, middle, and end, which Dawn could experience over and over again. The end of a performance was a little death with all the efforts she expelled and no longer needed, like a snake shedding its skin. There was less of an amping up of energy and more of a downward spiral for the entire cast. In a unifying exhale, everyone threw their costumes back on the rack, massaged their weary bodies, and rested for days afterward.

This time would be no different, thought Dawn, as she gathered up her canvas shoes and slipped on her sneakers; she walked to class with her head held up high to emulate Myrtha. Each foot guides the other in a kind of flashy way. Her energy levels were high in the upcoming days before the first performance.

She reached the upper levels of the theater to the studio. Her first class, as usual, was with Madame Roberts, followed by the afternoon ones with Madame Angulaire. Both women were also buzzing with energy...and what appeared to be pent-up anger. The dancers all noticed the hostility but decided to not take sides, especially since the next ballet would be chosen by one of them and also the next cast chosen by one or both of them. Dancers would bow before anyone's feet who was the decider of roles. A choreographer could make or break a dancer's career and everyone in that room knew it—even if they were not professionals yet, this behavior made for good practice.

Christina still stayed away from Dawn, hoping to avoid any criticism from her that would harm her fragile ego before her performance. Meanwhile, Jenny's narcissism grew as she put her costume on for Giselle—her peasant clothes and then her beautiful, long, ghostly tutu were both things of beauty. Myrtha's costume was similar to Giselle's, but there was not the same amount of love from the seamstresses poured into it as Jenny's. Eric and Adam were practicing their acrobatic jumps that were meant to wow the audience. They both wanted to knock heads off with the strength of their leaps and have women crawling all over them for their feats. Dawn rolled her eyes as they landed on the window to the door of the studio. Through it, she could see Natalie watching her much in the same way she had stared into it when the adults were taking class. Goosebumps ran up and down her back since even her own parents had ceased coming to watch her dance now. When she was a toddler and everything she did was cute, her parents watched her in class and rehearsal. They clapped whenever she jumped over those newspaper puddles, but now that ballet followed her around with its cult-like aura, her parents stopped attending. They dropped her off and came for the first and last performance. Their little girl was lost to a world that they could not understand why anyone over toddler age would want to be involved in anymore. After all, there was not really a Myrtha in the world or a Giselle or the ghostly Wilis. It was all fake. It was all entertainment. It was adults trying to hold on to their lost childhoods. Dawn's parents could not see the life cycle of the theater or feel the way Dawn felt when she took the stage.

Madame Roberts was still not in the studio where all her students were stretching and waiting to be led. It was five minutes passed when class was supposed to start, and the students began poking their heads out of the doorway to check

91

for Madame. By the time another ten minutes passed, a noise came from the elevator that sounded like a muffled moan. The elevator doors opened and Madame Roberts could be heard sobbing on her phone.

"I don't understand! We can't afford to lose funding for this show now. It's about to go on *tomorrow*. I was told that we were following what the director of the theater wanted and what the current times were telling us. Don't talk to me—hey! Listen to me. Talk to Madame Angulaire. It's her damn fault!" Madame Roberts hung up, checked her coiffed hair in the mirror, and blew her nose with a tissue before turning to face her audience.

"Good morning, ladies and gentlemen. As you may have heard, one of the "Angel" donors has decided to pull their funding for the Allard Ballet Academy after watching one of our stage rehearsals yesterday. They thought that the whole thing was a despicable disgrace to the world of ballet and its history…and…and I must agree."

***

Madame Roberts looked down at the oak floors of the studio, pleading with them for comfort and understanding. Meanwhile, the students looked around at each other in confusion. Why should they concern themselves with funding? All dancers had room for was the art form and nothing else. So funding was cut? Who cares? It is not like dancers need much food to survive on, anyway. They would make it through all right. The sense in the studio was one of calm resignation and even apathy.

But Madame Roberts desired to explain herself further. She had tried this whole season to keep her mouth shut, but now that money was at stake and therefore her ability to continue teaching, she spoke up. Rolling back her shoulders and lifting her head like during warm-ups before class, Madame said: "Class, I hope for this performance you have felt a difference when you were dancing between my choreography and Madame Angulaire's. You see, I want you to dance classically with grace and poise and excellence in upholding this beautiful art. I want you to adhere with reverence and respect to the things my teachers taught me.

"My teachers taught me how to be stunning to watch move and humble in my words. They gave me memories I could never afford to pay for in their value. They brought harmony to my entire being as I moved throughout my long days, and even my nights were moved by the power of dance.

"I want you dancers to feel exultant in the knowledge of the five fundamental positions of dance and the cross-section that you live between. I want you all to go home on a cloud. I want you to feel above anything and everything that is not the best in humanity. I want you to dance classical ballet." The class watched as Madame grew taller in her spine with her dance shoes lifting her off her heels more and more and onto her toes. Her already slender torso grew smaller and appealingly showed off her chest and hips. Her collarbone stuck out in the morning sun coming through the windows. She was as ethereal as one of the Wilis.

"But, my dancers, when you dance with Madame Angulaire, forcing your bodies into odd shapes and sizes meant for clay and not the human form, you must feel hollow. You become these pliable, selfless things—grotesque in all your movements. There is no grace or precision to the heartfelt music. There is no more beautiful line. You turn into a bunch of acrobatic monkeys on a string! How could you not feel and see yourselves? You become a mockery of what ballet and the etiquette that it comes with represents. You lack respect for the art when under the spell of Madame Angulaire and her new wave of modern ballet. Modern ballet seeks to have you be a slave to your 'inner emotions' and the only way to revel in them is to throw your hands up and your feet out in all directions without purpose."

Madame Roberts looked up to see that her students were all staring at the floor now, whether or not they felt shame. Some understood that they had danced in an ugly manner for Madame Angulaire...almost as if their days were training in the pretty in the morning and the ugly in the evenings. They thought it made them well-rounded dancers to know what everything in between those two states created for their art. They felt like in the morning they were the aristocracy and by evening the lowest peasants. They felt wonderful and optimistic about life itself in the morning and depressed and horrified by it in the evening.

Lifting her head slightly when Madame Roberts paused, Dawn saw her knees shaking and her arms cradled closer to her sides, as if she was still stuck inside the sleeve of Madame Angulaire. Nausea made her too hot, while her body grew cold from understanding why she was feeling so much anxiety around the evening. Dawn frequently went home now exhausted, while having malevolent thoughts about harming Christina or the other students if they did not follow along with Madame Angulaire's orders well enough. Too many of them still turned out their feet or tried to point them when they were supposed to be turned in and stay flexed. They were fighting what society demanded of them—embrace this new form of dance. Use the brute strength of an animal to distort the body in ways that are hideous to the human eye. Not even animals put themselves in such positions because they know those movements will not attract a mate. The hostile moves could only scare off other predators if they even cared to look around rather than constantly inward. Inward where? Where a person's bowels are or their blood or thick layers of muscle? What was Dawn and everyone else supposed to be searching for in there? Did her liver have an answer or perhaps her kidneys? How about her lungs? Would they whisper how she must lift her right, lower leg into the crook of her inner thigh and hop on the standing leg to express loneliness? Would her heart tell her to jerk down suddenly and roll over on the floor to express deep suffering? Would her brain force her to lick the floor to show her humility in front of the audience? Is that what real art was about? Was it licking the floor for others to ogle or trying to guess what the dancers would do next? Is this called free will in motion?

Dawn shook her head. She knew it was all wrong but she could not understand why "society" wanted to see them perform in such a way. What kind of pleasure did they get out of this? Imagining sitting in an audience, Dawn ran through her *Giselle* solo in the manner that Madame Angulaire taught her and thought about seeing the poor, writhing creature on the ground. Perhaps the audience members enjoyed watching the suffering like when people viewed public executions. They made good stories.

***

When Madame Roberts paused and gazed out, looking up toward the rose-looking window, she could not help but believe there was a spirit up there who could help guide her and her dancers. A creator analyzed the anatomy of the human body and then made physics work with man, rather than against it. By analyzing reality, these inventors of ballet could shape it into something that looks magical—like it defied physics. Yet, Madame Roberts knew that it took an intellectual and elite class to form ballet into the best expression of the beauty of the human body imaginable. This was not a style of dancing for the primitive cultures but the industrialized ones.

She thought: When Russia began to Westernize itself with Peter the Great in the eighteenth century, it only had the peasants dancing mindlessly until a sense of importance for poetry and music combined with a need for a movement elegant enough to express those arts was brought to fruition. Ballet was more than just gymnastics meant to surprise and even disgust an audience. The movements became symbols for things like a living book. A *pirouette* could represent the circle of life, an *arabesque* could represent the will to stand alone, or a *grand jeté* could represent being able to chase after dreams. Men like Tchaikovsky helped to make *The Sleeping Beauty* the first real Russian ballet with a newfound depth that made ripples throughout the rest of ballet's history forevermore. Its scale was large and its music even larger and the dancer involved had to adapt—to rise to the occasion. A great responsibility fell on the ballet dancers' shoulders to maintain a level of excellence never to be seen before in human history. After that massive ballet came even more famous ones, like *The Nutcracker* and *Swan Lake*.

Today, due to important individuals in history, starting with Louis XIV, ballet is mostly seen as a Russian tradition since long gone are the days of the French and Italian dominance in ballet. The last remnants of classical ballet are maintaining the Russian elements from the time period—the grandioseness of it all. But a wave of modern nihilism is trying to attack ballet's core and its origin. Modern dance seeks to erase the rules, bring people back down from the lofty symbols they represented in ballet, and ignore the anatomy of the human body. It wants to dull the mind and sharpen the emotions, thereby allowing them to dictate what way our bodies move, regardless of the physical pain or injuries that occur from no longer understanding the way the body moves. The people who advocate modern dance want to lose themselves in another dimension, almost religiously, in a way that ignores what their minds are telling them. But they have to actively oppose their thoughts while dancing rather than being unified with them.

Classical ballet strives for unity between mind and body because a human being has and uses both—they are inseparable. When a dancer leads their foot from flat on the floor, to *demi-pointe*, and finally straight out on the front toes to form a *tendu*, they are telling their leg to move methodically. Their mind is focused on executing the correct form of a step and it takes up much of their focus, while in the background, they must also be focused on rhythm and character. The mind is used in ballet constantly, namely when a long or intricate combination is given and after a couple of modelings by the teacher, a quick memory must retain the combination and then execute it on both the left and the right—all the while still following the rhythm and character. The mind and body make for a ballet dancer with heart and soul, and the very best of them have gorgeously refined technique, strength, and an expressiveness that garners understanding of the story. They are empathetic individuals who bring their own stories into the provided steps. They bring their unique features to play in the hearts of their audience. The more captivatingly stunning the dancers are, the more symmetrical and, therefore, geometric their movements are. Only an excellent teacher can spot and bring those qualities out in a dancer.

But how to explain all of this knowledge to my students? wondered Madame Roberts. How can I possibly explain what they are up against in this anti-etiquette and anti-mind world? They will leave this Academy with a firm foundation, only to have parts forgotten in the dusty corners of their minds and the worst emotions teased out for all to witness. Dancers will take the stage stripped of their dignity. The grace which could have been theirs will be stomped out by the elders they used to trust to make them excellent in every way. The dancers will lose trust or follow their teachers into the ground and ballet will die and become a mere sideshow of the past. A forgotten art, lying in a dormant state until someone comes to bring it to a new light.

Madame Roberts said, "Please, class, it is what it is. But think today and in the future about how the different teachers and their choreography make you feel. I'm sure we will come back to this issue in the future. Now, if you will all place your left hands on the barre, we shall begin. And one, two, three, and one, two, three, yes, class, good."

Folding into a *port de bras devant*, Dawn said hello again to the blood rushing into her head and a mind that was overwhelmed with thoughts about her two teachers. She never really knew that ballet could be treated differently by other adults. She just thought that a *port de bras devant* was and always had been a *port de bras devant*. The steps were the steps in *Giselle*, and the dancers had the freedom to make different facial expressions appropriate to the character, but the steps were never changed.

She knew choreographers taught the ballets to their students, but she never knew that they could argue over whether Myrtha hopped in with her arms squished together or *bourréed* in with her arms out in a graceful curve.

Drawing her arms near her, Dawn allowed the music to guide her movements and bring her up rather than down. She focused on the girl in front of her, aligning her own body with the positions of the next, in tune with the rhythm. Time halted at the doors to the studio and sweat became the measurement of how long into the rehearsal day they all were.

"All right everyone, now we will go downstairs to the stage and run through the entire ballet. Let's go! Chop-chop!" ordered Madame Roberts. As the dancers all took the long, chandelier-lighted stairway down to the theater, Madame Angulaire had arrived. She walked straight into the theater, keeping her eyes on the stage, as if waiting for her own cue to begin her reign of control over the rehearsal.

"Ladies and gentlemen, please take your spots for the opening scene. Make Petipa proud," said Madame Roberts; to which Madame Angulaire said, "Ha! And make the unsung voices of the people today heard. The aristocrats have already had their time."

Madame Roberts shut her eyes to regain her composure, while Madame Angulaire took a seat and grinned.

The backstage hands pulled on the curtain's strings to reveal a German village backdrop and the orchestra's composer lifted up his arms to begin.

Dawn played as one of the vine gatherers among the village folk and watched from backstage as Eric playing Hilarion knocks on Giselle's cottage door.

Rehearsals took all day, so the students worked their weekends when they were not at school. Today was Saturday, and the rehearsal was going smoothly and racing toward Dawn's entrance solo as Myrtha.

Her entrance notes began and off she went to fulfill its calling. The sweetly melancholy music filled her ears as she *bourréed* across the stage once and then again. The pain emanating from her feet seemed so distant as she moved out into the dark stage, where Dawn's adrenaline was pumping through her veins—blue, as were the stage lights on her body.

In the blue darkness, her long tutu glowed like a phantom's in the night. Imagining the cold forest, where Giselle lies buried deep in the ground beneath her toes, Dawn felt more powerful and able to lead her Wilis through the night.

When the second part of her solo changed with the music, Dawn bounced through her *arabesques* just like Madame Angulaire taught her. Her right hand crooked out in front of her with her bouncing leg and her left foot back in the air to meet her angled left arm. Jumping, jumping, jumping up to the maximum that her calves allowed her, she came down, and then an ominous snap was heard throughout the theater.

Suddenly, Dawn could no longer jump or *tendu* or rise or walk. She looked around her to confirm that she was still standing and that the world had not turned upside down on her. But then the pain came, mixed with the shock of something not being right. As she caught her breath, she sunk onto the stage and screamed out.

Madame Roberts and Madame Angulaire hurried up to the stage and asked about what exactly Dawn felt. "Did it feel like a snap or a pop? Can you point your foot down or any way at all? Would you like us to call the ambulance?"

The frantic questions buzzed around Dawn's head like flies,

and she tried to swat them away. She just wanted to lie down to sleep for a while.

"May I…just…can I just…lay down here? I'm in so much pain," said Dawn.

Madame Roberts was on the phone with the ambulance while Madame Angulaire rushed to find some ice since she noticed the swelling around Dawn's right ankle.

"Can you stand up?" asked Madame Roberts, who squatted down to get Dawn to wrap her arms around her shoulders and foist her up. Dawn stood, but could not move her right foot at all.

"I can't move my right foot. Oh god, I can't move it. No, no, no…," she sobbed.

***

The ambulance came and took Dawn away to the nearest hospital. Watching all the other dancers with their hands over their mouths and some of them crying, Dawn knew they saw this as the end of her career. One that ended before she could even understand the full depth of her loss.

"The doctor said that you suffered an Achilles tendon rupture, which means that you won't be able to point your foot into *tendu* or rise onto *demi-pointe* or even really walk," said Madame Roberts, who mumbled out each word. "He said that it usually happens from jumping in dance and not having your muscles warm enough to take the stress yet. The rupture usually happens about two-and-a-half inches from where your Achilles attaches to your heel bone. This is a very common injury for dancers. I…I'm just sorry that you had to experience it today…now…before the performance." Her hands covered her forehead, overwhelmed with the running reel of watching Dawn land and hearing such a snap. She had always known that injuries like that were possible, but she had never heard a complete tear before—a total separation.

"In order to prevent it, you should have stretched and strengthened your calves more without bouncing, alternate your exercises for it, not jump as much, keep your muscles warm while dancing, and only dance or exercise on our wood floor that has a bit of a give to them. I told the doctor that we train all students to follow such steps, but they had been rehearsing for extra-long hours for this ballet. All he did was shake his head and patronize me. Besides, it's really Madame Angulaire's fault. She's the one who made you hop so high and suddenly turn your foot in which most likely twisted your ligament and snapped it in half." Madame Roberts looked up. "Sorry. I'm just frustrated with everything that woman has come in here and done to our Academy of dancers. They are getting hurt now from her incorrect and, dare I say, *evil* teachings." She patted Dawn on the head, rose from her seat next to the hospital bed, and looked out the window into the cool, mid-morning air.

CHAPTER II

Sedated by pain killers, Dawn craned her neck to look outside her hospital window with Madame Roberts. What would she do now? she wondered. Opening her mouth to ask the ultimate question, she closed it suddenly like a Venus flytrap. Struggling to use her vocal cords, Dawn finally exhaled a "Will I ever dance again?"

Madame Roberts looked over her shoulder to where Dawn lay with her ankle elevated by some ice—its swollen skin throbbing. She looked down at the floor. "Your Achilles will never be the same again and it may tear in the future. You may choose to strengthen it and fight for another chance on the stage...but...but you will never be a prima ballerina."

Dawn burst into tears and felt like throwing anything she could reach at Madame Roberts. In that moment of acute pain, her soul cracked and shattered into unknowable bits of feeling. She went simply numb.

"Michelle is your understudy and I will ask her to perform your part in tomorrow's show. With the state you're in, we will have to have her play Myrtha for this season's *Giselle*. I'm so sorry. The only thing I can do is comfort you by letting you know that the show will go on. You may choose to sit in the audience once you're out of the hospital." Madame Roberts squeezed Dawn's lifeless-feeling hand.

Dawn cried for hours, some of it alone and some of it in front of her teacher. When her parents arrived, she had cried herself to sleep. They both left the room to talk to the doctor, who walked them through what the next day would look like for Dawn.

"Well, we've already taken x-rays and an MRI of the injured right Achilles tendon. It was a clean tear. We are not going to allow her to eat or drink after midnight tonight so that we can perform the surgery tomorrow.

"Our orthopedic surgeon is highly skilled in fixing these ruptures and he should be able to do it within a couple of hours. The patient will likely be put completely to sleep, but the nurse will watch her vital signs the entire way through the surgery. Meanwhile, the surgeon will make an incision into the calf and insert a tiny camera and light to find the tendon. He may need to take out some of the damaged tendon, but that's usually unnecessary with a rupture like that, and then essentially he'll sew the ripped tendon back together and stitch up the muscle and skin around the calf.

"After the surgery itself is complete, we will place her ankle in a splint and monitor her until she wakes up. After that, we may have her fill out some paperwork, eat, and just make sure she's stable enough to leave within the same day. The patient will probably be able to leave by the late afternoon when we do the surgery in the morning.

"Now, she will have some pain within the first few days, so the nurses will provide her with a prescription for about eight hundred milligrams of ibuprofen. If she needs more, then call our office. Make sure she keeps that right leg elevated, okay? It will help reduce the pain due to swelling. Watch for any infection and we will also provide crutches for her to use for those first few days of essential healing.

"After about ten days, she'll need to come back so that we can remove the stitches put in and give her a proper cast. Keep it dry, please. The final step in this process will be physical therapy to get back to putting weight on that right leg and learning how to walk normally again. Any questions?"

Dawn's parents looked at each other and then her father asked: "Will she be able to continue dancing?"

The doctor gathered up his coat and inhaled deeply. "Well, with enough physical therapy, she may be able to resume dancing safely. But I'm not sure if she'll be able to reach the level that she was at in dancing before. For many ballerinas, this kind of injury can be a career-ending one. Sorry." He bowed out of the room and left the parents silently in tears.

The tears flowed and flowed. Dawn's mother remembered her little pink tutu and the newspaper puddles she had jumped over so courageously. Her little girl came out screaming and kicking. She never allowed the world before to hold her down. She knew she would not let the world hold her down now, but how long recovery would take she would never know.

Dawn's father seethed for his little baby girl, who looked up to him to protect her always. Why hadn't he protected her from what she loved? he wondered. Maybe because she loved it, he felt he had no right to intervene. Her love could not be trifled with, just like when she finds her first romantic love. As a parent, he felt no right to stop her from experiencing one of life's most thrilling aspects. Yet, guilt hit him hard in the gut. He should have reminded her to strengthen those calves or put on those leggings before going to class to keep her muscles warm.

Both of them felt immense pain at not having protected their child from this career-ending accident. And then the grief turned to anger at Dawn's teachers. Why didn't they see this coming? How come they did not ensure that their students were warmed up enough? Weren't they the experts? Dawn's mother's cheeks grew hot and her father's pale. Their hands shook and her father fled the room the doctor brought them to talk and into the room where his daughter lay broken…and where Madame Roberts stood bearing some of her pain.

"You! You should have known better. Why is my daughter here in the first place? We have trusted you with our daughter's physical health since she was three. What happened? How could you?!" he bellowed.

Madame Roberts stepped back from the window and looked Dawn's father in the eyes. "I *have* protected her since she was three. What about all those other performances? This is her first one where she has gotten seriously injured. Now, I know it's still inexcusable to you both because it is your daughter and her career, but this would have never happened if I was still her only teacher."

"What do you mean?" asked Dawn's mother.

"Madame Angulaire is to blame. She is teaching my students a form of dancing that is against everything they have learned growing up and it's hurting their bodies."

Dawn laid helplessly in her hospital bed, watching the volley back and forth between her parents and Madame Roberts. It seemed like hours watching her own cord of fate twist and threaten to snap, just like her Achilles. Would she make it out of this unscathed? Would she ever touch the stage again? Would she dance?

Entering the room, Madame Angulaire brought some flowers and a bottle of water for the hurt dancer. "I've brought you these. I'm so sorry, darling, about your ankle. But with enough exercise, it's something you can use in your art." She smiled brightly at Dawn, as if this was like a childbirth scenario. She smiled as though rupturing her Achilles would cause her to become a better dancer—like the pain and suffering only made her a better dancer.

Dawn wanted to scream. Madame Angulaire's skeleton arm reached out to touch her, and she tried to sink further back into her bed.

"Go away," threatened Dawn.

"What, darling? But I just got here," said Madame Angulaire.

"Get out."

Madame looked around at her parents and Madame Roberts, glared back at Dawn, and left the room. Dawn's father followed her outside the door and swiftly grabbed her by the throat. "You vile creature! You worm!" violently shaking her. Everyone in the room heard the commotion outside and Dawn's mother rushed out. "You stupid cow! You ogre! Why? What did you do to her?!" he cried.

Madame Angulaire gripped her hands around her throat and felt an awful feeling welling up inside of her neck when Dawn's mother pulled her father off. Breathing heavily and nausea controlling her thoughts, Madame Angulaire ran out of the hallway and down the stairs to the outside door of the building. She had to get away from a family that denied death. After all, we were all decomposing in our own ways as we age. She had made amends with death. Death did not scare her or the process by which she may succumb to all of its pain and injuries. Life was a series of injuries we accumulated over our lifetimes, both emotionally and physically. An injury that stopped a career was awful, but it could not have lasted forever, anyway. Dawn's timeline was just shorter than most girls. She was unlucky, but her unluckiness may prove to be her strength in modern dance. The person with the most experiences, including the painful ones, was bound to dance more beautifully.

A dancer must know sorrow. A dancer, or really any artist, should know pain, thought Madame Angulaire. They should be able to tap into that hurt, to prod and poke at it with scorching prongs from the fire. Prongs that burn and sizzle on the flesh. It is that kind of acute pain that makes us alive. Dawn should be thankful that she tore a part of her own body for dance. That kind of dedication to her art places her already over her peers. She is better than them and she knows it.

Although shaken by her father, Madame Angulaire turned around and walked back up to the hospital room door and turned the knob to let herself in. Before her father could launch at her again or Dawn could throw her out with her vehement words, she said: "You are Myrtha, Queen of the Wilis. Life betrayed her. Life always starts as this innocent promise, and Giselle took it. She dances lightly, so naively, in her little German village. But look at her, Dawn, she falls! Her heart breaks for a lover she cannot have! And Myrtha, Myrtha who knows her trials in life that brought her to haunt the living in death? Most of them were the victims of unrequited love. They danced with men until they died from exhaustion! *Giselle* is a ballet about *death*. It is a ballet about those innocent babes who come into life hopeful and leave vengeful. You could be different. You could learn early on to accept and embrace dying and go peacefully!"

"Madame Angulaire!" cried Madame Roberts, as she tightened up her jaw. Rage was nowhere near the fire that grew inside of her at this moment.

"Quiet! Let me talk some reason into the girl. Dawn, you have a gift now. *Use it*. Your Achilles tendon will never be as it was before. Use that in the fight for modern dance—the only kind of dance that makes sense in today's world. Everyone today is hurt in some form. Connect with them. Use your body to tell them the story we all must face in the end. Allow death to wash over you. Don't be a disgusting 'death-denier,' rather be a 'death-accepter.' Live like you won't rise tomorrow. Use your pain to show the world that humans are only humans through their collective suffering."

Dawn was crying now and clutching at the sheets beside her body. She had to ground herself quickly or else she would believe that this was all a bad dream that she could no longer control. Madame Angulaire was here in the room, telling her to accept death—give in—and she knew she could stop her. "Stop!" cried Dawn. "Just stop. I can't take it anymore. I don't want to die. I want to live on the stage, and once I've lived my life, only then will I lie beneath the stage. My ankle must heal. It *must!*"

***

Crossing the room, Madame Angulaire kneeled in front of Dawn and grabbed her hand with her tiny arm. "Dawn, darling, you must be brave like Nijinsky and dance for us all without fear or even emotion. You must heal to rise up again like a phoenix and show all of us what life really is—a long, hard preparation for death. Like the ancient Egyptians, we spend our lives building our tombs. I want you to forget about yourself now and think about *us*."

Madame Roberts had had enough. She said, "Dawn, don't

listen to her poison. You matter. You *must* matter to yourself. You will heal and you will work hard to get back to the dancer you were before this all happened." Tears rolled down her cheeks as she allowed herself to feel Dawn's own pain.

Her parents could not even make sense of what her teachers were bickering over. No one was going to die, and this whole fight for her soul was ridiculous. They knew that this kind of rupture has happened to others before and they learned to walk again…surely it wasn't such a stretch to imagine Dawn dancing again too.

Madame Angulaire still grasped Dawn's hand and said, "The rise of modern ballet all started with Nijinsky in *Le Sacre du printemps* by Stravinsky. That was all the way back in the early twentieth century! It has taken decades of time, teaching, and energy to instill the modern lifeblood into the culture. It's still why I have to convince you that this is the right way! Join the party of progressive thought and progressive movement, where dancing should allow you to go mad. Become feverish in your movement to show others that this is the way of the world. This is reality." Madame Angulaire shook Dawn's hand, her eyes bulging out of her skull.

Everyone in the room stayed silent. A void of silence opened, and the minutes passed without a single consciousness aware of it. A heavy blanket of depression covered the room, blocking out the light from the window.

"Are you finished, Madame Angulaire?" asked Madame Roberts. "I don't think you are wanted here anymore. Please leave."

"Dawn, would you like me to leave?" asked Madame Angulaire.

Dawn looked up at her teacher, still grasping her hand. "Yes, please. I will think about what you have told me today. Really, I will." She slid her hand out from her teacher's and looked away toward the window—trying to come up for air.

Leaving the room, Madame Angulaire left with her head held up high in honor of the collective she was fighting for.

Infuriating Madame Roberts, she walked away from her corner by the window and took the chair next to Dawn. "Dawn, please don't think too long and hard about what Madame Angulaire told you. You are an individual in the full meaning of the word. You are not to care about others' expectations of you. You are to work on yourself and *your* needs and not anyone else's. Classical ballet is about *you* and your body and mind. It should bring out the best in you as a unique person on this earth. The whole art form is based on forming gorgeous lines. That's why I also tell my dancers to focus on their lines—their legs and arms being the primary determinants. Look, when you dance with me in the morning at barre, don't you feel whole? Don't you feel so full? Your mind absorbs the combination I just demonstrated and your body executes each step with precision. Your soul flows freely through this form of creative expression. I know you feel it because I could see it in the way you pointed your toes, the way you held the barre, and the way even your eyes danced. You know that life is in dancing. You must *live* to dance.

"What Madame Angulaire is asking of you is to *die* for ballet. She wants you to break your bones, break your rhythmic movement, break your lines. Abruptly change over from a smooth, natural grace to a course, abstract vulgarity. She believes that fighting everything you know is the only way to progress. But tradition has lasted because people have felt how right it is because classical ballet was made for living beings. The first aristocrats and scientists of the day studied the human anatomy and brought us movements that pushed but did not break our bodies. We can work hard to achieve a kind of immortal beauty. Dawn, you must think over what I'm saying to you." Madame squeezed her arm hard so that it left the imprints of her hand on her arm.

"I...I'm so tired. I don't know what to think right now," said Dawn.

Growing desperate and frustrated, Madame Roberts said, "Can you hear that?"

"What?" asked Dawn.

"Can you hear Stravinsky's music playing in your head? The *Sacre* composition that Madame Angulaire mentioned?"

"I've only heard it a few times. But yes, I remember some of it. It is disturbing."

"I'm glad you said that. It is disturbing. The notes never resolve, and even the quieter parts are ominous. The audience is on edge the entire time and all they see onstage is group after group scurrying around like bugs. If your parents were to watch you in that ballet, they would never be able to pick out which dancer was you. You don't matter up there onstage. The composer and the choreographer are working to *annihilate* your existence, and in the least glamorous way. They want you to turn your feet in and shake your hands frantically about you, roll your head right off your shoulders—no thought, no mind, no reason left to mankind. To them, you turn into a bug without reason or soul. You just have a body that they can manipulate to work in tandem with a whole lot of other bodies. You are no longer *you*."

I am no longer me, thought Dawn. What must that mean? Her fatigue halted all further progress in thought as her eyelids began to droop and her mouth formed an O with a yawn.

"Oh, you must be tired after hearing us all try to make the decision for you. I'm sorry. We'll get out of here so that you can rest," said Madame Roberts, as she stood up and walked out of the room with her parents in tow.

Dawn lay there in bed and closed her eyes. She fell asleep for perhaps a few hours before slowly stirring in the late afternoon sun streaming in through her windows. She turned her head away from the sunny screens and breathed in as much as her pain would allow her.

I cannot understand how these grandiose ideas from each of my teachers affect them on a daily basis, thought Dawn. How could Madame Roberts always feel so uplifted since she believes she's dancing on the side of life? Whereas, Madame Angulaire always feels so depressed since she believes she's dancing on the side of death? Both ideas seem too abstract to really mean anything. Right?

Or it appears to be that Madame Roberts wants the status quo, like she is the conservative, while Madame Angulaire wants change, like a liberal. Which one is right? Is the way the West was better, or does it need to change? Was classical ballet in a better culture back then or now? And in terms of *Giselle*, a ballet that was made in the mid-nineteenth century, was this kind of romance still relevant today? Is a ballet made by the aristocracy as important for our culture today?

So many questions swirled around in Dawn's mind when the door to her hospital room opened and in walked Natalie.

"Natalie! What are you doing here?" asked Dawn.

"Oh, I didn't mean to startle you, honey. I heard what happened at the rehearsal today and I had to come over to see if my new little friend was okay."

Dawn didn't like being called "little" and she also didn't appreciate this old hag coming into her room. "Hey, are visiting hours for anyone at this hospital?"

Natalie winced. "Well, the nice lady at the front desk told me which room you were in after I told her I was your friend, so I guess so."

"Remind me to tell them to limit it to just family, then." Dawn stared her up and then down, noticing all the black spots, webbed veins, and wrinkles creasing in her legs and arms and face. She was a walking time bomb. Nothing could be unwound now that she agreed to let time wear her down. It looks like she never even tried to see a dermatologist and laser away her imperfections. Even her haircut was a sign that she had given up. What did she have now without her looks? She was probably a housewife her entire life, so she had no outside skills. She was just a simpleton—a nice, old fool with a pancake bottom.

"I...I can leave if that's what you want. I just wanted to make sure you were all right anyway, and it seems you are."

"Yes, I'm fine. You just missed the crazy lecturing that I got from my teachers."

"You mean Madame Roberts and Angulaire?"

"The very same."

"Okay, now I'm too curious to leave," said Natalie. "What did they say?"

"Madame Roberts talked about how dancing is meant to be beautiful and made for our bodies, and somehow that connects us to life. But Madame Angulaire said that the whole modern dance movement is about destroying the perfect lines and rigidity of ballet. She sees the future of dance revolving around truth, the truth that everyone dies and it should be depicted, basically. It's like Madame Roberts sees ballet as what people ought to be and not what people are in the worst ways. But I just can't see how these things affect each of them so deeply on a daily level. I can't understand the scale of their missions. All I could see was a distinct desperation in their eyes. Meanwhile, my parents were standing there, probably asking themselves the same questions that I was. They probably thought my teachers were even crazy! I don't know what to think..."

To Dawn, it seemed like Natalie's saggy eyes drooped as far down as her mouth. She took her shaking hand and placed it on Dawn's cheek. She could see the pulsing veins sticking out of shapeless skin and it made her ill. Turning away, Dawn's mind shifted to protecting her youth from this ogre. She promised herself repeatedly that she would never allow herself to get old—never, never, never.

"Honey, I want you to rest. I know that when you're young, everything moves very quickly and you have the urge to do everything at once. But once you get to my age and you realize how long life truly is, then all things will be accomplished over time. You don't really need to rush. I know that you only know such a brief span of life, but time is longer than you think."

What kind of woo-woo stuff was she telling me? wondered Dawn. Perhaps she knows something just based on her age, but she was not even around when *Sacre* came out. She did not witness the cultural change or the introduction of modern ballet to the culture. What does she know about time and history and how human life works? I dance every day. *I* feel the difference in my marrow. She knows nothing. She's just an old, silly lady who wants to make me feel better for some reason. Well, I cannot feel better because my career is over and my ankle hurts and now my parents and teachers have no reason to see me thrive. I am a hunk of meat left for dead now. Dawn's face contracted a bit at her own thoughts. Her realization was unsettling, and it made the pain that much harder to bear.

CHAPTER III

Dawn sat there watching Natalie warm up at the barre. She had had her surgery a week ago now and still wore a cast. It would be another five weeks or so until she could start walking again without it.

Today was her first day back in the studio, and she could not even participate. Instead, she peered through the curtained window of the door to watch others dancing but not her. With pleading eyes, she begged Madame Roberts to let her do something, *anything*, even if it was with the adults.

"No, Dawn. You can't start working on your form until you get that cast taken off. I will not be responsible for your not healing due to too much pressure on your ankle. I won't," said Madame Roberts after the adult class.

"Oh, please Madame, please! I can't stand watching other people dance and not me. It's not in my nature to just *watch*," said Dawn.

"I said no and I won't say it again. You can feel free to come inside and sit down to watch any class you'd like for the next few weeks. But you are to sit and put that leg up to promote healing."

Dawn stuck out her lower lip and turned her back on her teacher, only to see her peers watching her and her large cast. Ever since the *Giselle* performances began, the other dancers had avoided her, afraid and yet curious about what Dawn's next steps would be. Last weekend was the first two performances and the next weekend would be the final two for a total of four shows. And then it was all over. The show would disappear after next weekend and Dawn not only did not get to play Myrtha, but at this rate, she could not even dance in class. She fell from grace so quickly.

Dancers like Christina, especially, avoided Dawn because they knew she could and would bite back when hurt. Incapable of any outlet for her body's fury, everyone knew Dawn would verbally attack in new, creative ways. Still, Christina felt bad for her and she was sure that others underneath felt bad too.

I mean, who could be strong enough to let go of their career before it had even started? wondered Christina. Placing her leg up on the barre, she imagined her Achilles snapping right at that moment when she settled into her stretch and imagined in one movement how everything she had worked for had disappeared. Her eyes welled up with tears. She would rather die along with the snapping sound, as if the snapping was a vital string to her heart. Life would lose all meaning to her. Christina leaned forward to touch her nose to her knee and kissed it before coming back up and out of the stretch. Her body was the key to happiness, thought Christina.

When the class began center work, Madame Roberts started them all off from the left corner doing a waltz and *pirouette* combination. Dawn decided to sit in the studio for her classes, to remind everyone of the potential for losing it all. Her role became that of a Wili who was betrayed by her own two feet. Desiring to be as ugly as possible, she imagined embracing Madame Angulaire's call for a universal, collective soul, where each dancer became a tool for the mythical, revolutionary machine. All the choreography twisted and contorted the body and mind in the least human ways possible. Most of the dancers would not make it to the performance due to injuries like hers, but they would be forced to dance anyway. Like the Wilis' victims, Madame Angulaire would force everyone to dance to death. There would be no injury that could get them out of dancing. In fact, the more injured they were in this alternate reality, the more worthy they were to the cause. Perhaps that was the only path open now to the crippled, such as herself. Yes, thought Dawn, I will become a revolutionary ghost. I tried being the good girl, and it got me into this mess. I will come back with a vengeance and smite the others down with me.

Madame Roberts was finishing her *reverence* with the class when Dawn got up in an awkward, lopsided fashion from the chair in the room and moved in her own strange way. Dawn's arms bent out, one on either side, like that of a robot's. Her knees buckled inward, as did her feet. She appeared like a marionette doll or a broken toy. She let her knees bend and her arms move forward as she tilted down from the hip into an odd curtsy. By this time, the entire class stood watching her antics. She was losing the respect and clarity that so many expected from her during class. Now she shook her hands above her head, making tribal noises and gnashing her teeth together. Utterly distracting the class, Dawn emerged as the victor in her mind. *Reverence* was now overwhelmed by her new and strange movements.

When she had finished her dance, Madame Angulaire entered and was the only one clapping for Dawn. No one had ever looked as proud of Dawn as did Angulaire at that moment. They saw each other anew for the first time in the studio, as if no one else was there. Dawn limped on her cast over to Madame Angulaire, her thin specter calling her on another level. "Come here, my girl. I see you have made a decision, and I couldn't be happier with your choice," said Madame Angulaire. Cooing, she held Dawn by the shoulders, escorting her out of the quiet studio and into the chill air of the stairwell.

"Dawn, you have made me so proud today. Do you know that?" asked Madame Angulaire.

"Yes," whispered Dawn.

"I embrace you now as my first and greatest student. I will make you into the dancer you were meant to be. Trust me."

"I will."

***

A week before the cast would come off, Dawn practiced privately with Madame Angulaire. Madame allowed the practice before it came off so that she could jump right into dancing again. They focused on the arms and torso mainly, shaping them into the dancer they were always meant to be, according to Madame. Meanwhile, Madame Roberts refused to help Dawn practice. She would not allow her near class until her cast was off and she had completed physical therapy. She told Dawn repeatedly that she "would not put her own student at further risk of injury."

Recoiling further into herself, Dawn tried to embrace everything that the teacher who would let her dance, no matter what, taught. She pushed herself, no matter how much it hurt.

"Good morning, Dawn. Are you ready to begin?" asked Madame Angulaire. Today she was wearing one of her dusty rose leotards, and her ribs protruded prominently from it with every breath she took. The long bones made the shape of a cage for all her shriveled-up internal organs hiding away in there. She was always cold, so she normally began class in a sweater, but today she exposed herself to the chill.

It was extra early in the morning so that they could use the studio before anyone else got there. The sun was just beginning to peek out from behind the clouds and stream down into the rose-like window of the studio. It smelled crisp and those ritualistic smells of baby powder, sweat, and rosin made Dawn even more indulgent at this moment. Even the slight coffee aroma from Madame Angulaire's warm drink made her muscles warm enough to start free of pain.

"I am so ready to begin, Madame," said Dawn as she stretched out her back by the barre.

"Good, I'm ready to watch your full conversion!"

Madame turned on her speakers to reveal the cold, steely sound of industrialized music, an orchestra that was playing for the workers. Its blaring became the sound of the bell to keep working and its ominous wails were the sounds of the workers themselves, but not as separate voices, only one voice—the collective.

"Quick! *Vite, vite*! I want you to be a wheel. Fan your arms out and turn like you were a wheel. *Vite!*"

Initially paralyzed into believing this would make her look ridiculous, she shook her head and remembered that one is not meant to think in modern ballet—one must feel. Dawn swung her arms around her like a giant wheel or a clock that no longer told time. She swung like a propeller on a plane that would fight the ego. Her movements may have appeared silly to her in the mirror, but she knew it would look legitimate with a group of other people all moving at the same time. And

121

that is when Madame Angulaire had read her mind.

"Oh, don't you worry, darling. You won't be alone forever. I'll invite some of my other favorites one day to join you in performing the great *Le Pas d'acier*. The whole stage will be filled with wheels and levers and pulleys to show what everyone could achieve in an industrial age, but the whole thing only works if you're together. So be patient, my darling. Today is only day one."

Madame Angulaire turned on the music again, which startled Dawn into a jump.

"Good! Jump, if it's not too painful, otherwise just bend at the knees a bit to emulate jumping and swing your arms more," said Madame.

The pain from that miniature jump almost made Dawn lose consciousness, so she opted for bending at the knees, which made her feel particularly infantile. Her bobbing up and down reminded one of a toddler in a toy swing and not a prima ballerina, capable of so many wonderful and graceful movements. Instead, here she was throwing her limbs every which way to a sporadic, constant clanging of chimes and intensifying noise.

Don't think, don't think, don't think—just do, just do, just do, repeated Dawn to herself. She must become the wheel in the machine. She must honestly represent the wheel as an abstraction. This ballet is not about her thoughts or her emotions, no, it is about the wheel of progress.

"Madame, I am just supposed to be a wheel, right?" asked Dawn.

Madame Angulaire shut the music off. She turned on her heels and stared down at Dawn. "Just a wheel? *I* am? Ha! We have a lot to learn. Didn't I tell you not to think, you foolish girl? Stop that. You cannot question it because that means you are thinking about it. You are a wheel. There is not even a 'you' there! You wheel. *Wheel*. See? It's not that hard, but I need you to concentrate!"

"But…but Madame, how can I concentrate if I'm not supposed to think?"

And that's when Madame Angulaire slapped Dawn.

"What did I just say?"

Dawn held her hand to her cheek, embarrassed and growing hot from both. She started to tear up and wanted to hobble off and leave, but something deep within told her she deserved this and she stayed.

"What did I just say?" repeated Madame Angulaire.

Shaking, "You told me not to think or question," mumbled Dawn.

"Correct. Now, start again. Feel the music, feel the wheel. You wheel. *Wheel*."

She turned the music on again and this time Dawn obeyed. It was easier now that she had lost all dignity. Her self-esteem for the day was slapped out of her and she swung those arms around ruthlessly.

"Much better. See? It did not have to be so hard to get it out of you. Perhaps tomorrow you won't have to fight as much to get to this point of freedom. Can you feel how free you are at this moment? You are responsible for nothing since soon you will lean on your fellow man. Eventually, with more dancers, nothing you do will harm the production."

Dawn was not quite sure what she meant, so she asked: "What do you mean exactly?"

"Oh, well, if you get injured again, another dancer could take over in a heartbeat. You would not stop the performance from continuing without you," answered Madame Angulaire. "Isn't that beautiful?"

The music rose and so did Dawn. She carefully raised herself on her cast with the help of the *demi-pointe* position on her good foot, but she came back down again in agony. Relief came over her, knowing that she was not what made the ballet function...and yet. No, no thinking, scolded Dawn to herself. I have no right to own ballet anymore. I'm crippled, and I'm lucky they will even allow me to dance with the Academy anymore.

"Yes, I suppose it is beautiful," said Dawn, as she looked down at the oak wood floors that knew nothing of modern dance. The movements being made on it now were foreign and the floor could not support the dancer as it once did with the classical steps of ballet. Some parts of it rose up and sunk back down where *bourrées* had drilled down into the floor, or parts of it sunk where jumps were landed frequently, or rosin dust was wedged in between the boards from all the *pirouettes* executed over the same areas for generations.

Dawn drew solemn steps across the floor as she executed Madame Angulaire's next orders.

"Would you please follow along here with me?" Madame Angulaire took Dawn's hand, and they ran in an awkward circle that had no center, like they were running around a fire in a most primitive state, as if the light bulb had not yet been invented or the telephone or any electronic devices at all, really. Dawn could feel herself grow detached from her body, as it chose to do what it wanted in spite of her heart's desires.

Meanwhile, Madame's movements grew sharper as she pulled her along this aimless circle as if to say that she had no free will. They became the yin and yang symbol of the East, lighting themselves up in the fire.

Then, the two of them *pliéd* in place and ran in the opposite direction until Madame released her hand and threw her own up as if in despair. She did five *changements* and landed on the ground with all her weight. She was no angel; she was an ogre.

"Now you try," said Madame.

"But Madame, my ankle. I probably should not be jumping on it yet. I'm still in a lot of pain," said Dawn.

"Nonsense! We have banished the demons from your ankle and now you are free to dance! You could probably even take off that cast now and jump around this entire room."

Dawn's heart fluttered at the thought of being able to run and jump around freely. So, she bent her knees and put all faith in what Madame said. She jumped, and she landed with a scream.

Dawn fell straight down onto the floor, holding onto her ankle in enormous pain.

"Oh lord, get up," said Madame Angulaire.

"Get up? Get up?! What if I just tore my Achilles again?" cried Dawn.

"No, darling, there was no snap this time. You probably just stretched it a bit, and it is still sore."

"But you said my pain was gone. Poof! I was all healed without the demons?"

"Well, looks like you didn't believe me enough."

A blank look spread over Dawn's face because she could not understand how believing enough would heal her. Still, she closed her eyes and tried to erase all thoughts—negative *and* positive.

"Let's move on then. We can work on those jumps later if you are still struggling right now with them. I'm sure you'll come around soon enough, though. I want you to pretend for today, since we haven't ordered them yet, that you are holding onto a heavy mallet."

"A mallet?"

"Yes, now take it with both hands since it will look very heavy onstage and swing it forward with all of your might. Your strength is what helps your fellow man. Your wisdom is useless in this new world of ours. But, you don't have to have strength all over your body in the physical sense necessarily, just in the strength of your discipline and obedience. You must become the wheel and yield the mallet over and over again, daily, in order to accomplish anything for the group."

Dawn pretended to foist the mallet above her head like she was about to slaughter an ox with it.

"Good, very good, darling. Now, *penché* with it. The mallet is your new male partner. The tool is like you and you are equals now."

Dawn leaned over into a *penché* on her good foot with the imaginary mallet in hand. It felt like an extension of her own arm in the way she stretched out toward the floor with it. She had a long arm of pure power. An ecstatic fire flowed up her mallet arm and into her head. Thoughts suddenly grew silent, and the only thing holding her attention was the weight of the mallet in her hand.

The music grew more sporadic and chaotic, which made Madame Angulaire spin around and lose herself to the "free-ing" effects of the sound. She said, "Bash the ceiling with your fists like me, Dawn."

They threw their fists up to the ceiling and then clasped their hands together above their heads and leaned from one side to the other—without a spine. They both squatted down on the ground and pounded their fists down there, in unison, getting lost in following each other's flow within the noise. They only focused on each other, mimicking the other's movements until Madame Angulaire no longer had to speak to give the next combination. Dawn simply did as she saw, no more, and that is exactly the state that Madame desired her students to be in—complete and utter obedience. Madame's own sense of power secretly made her want to kiss Dawn on the forehead for giving up herself in such a way. She got Dawn to give her ego up to the altar of modern ballet.

***

"Wonderful! Dawn, can you feel it?" asked Madame Angulaire.

"Feel what?"

"Feel the music controlling your soul?"

Dawn moved back down through her spine and let it wiggle her around. "Yes, I...I think I do."

"Now, I want you to return to the beginning motions of the wheel. I will follow you."

Round and round went Dawn's arms, swinging in the direction of a clock that wanted to tick clockwise and counter-clockwise all at once.

"Listen," began Madame Angulaire, becoming breathless with her swinging arms, "we are going to create a ballet this season that represents 'socialist realism.' Do you know what that kind of art is?"

"No, I've never heard of it. But I'm not really into politics. That's one of the reasons I like ballet. It never seemed political to me," said Dawn, as her fingers pinched forward like a seal's flipper.

"Of course, ballet is political! Everything is. Socialist realism is using our art to show the gritty reality of the working class and its revolutionary spirit that only thrives on socialism, and, thereby, collectivism. Ballet is really a dance for the group, the group that really matters—people like you and me that make equality and access to all pleasures in life possible. We are the heroes. Do you see?"

Still swinging, Dawn brought down her hands like a mallet again and said, "We do dance all together…but what about the soloists? Aren't they unequal to us?"

"Yes, darling. That's why the socialist realist ballets do not concern themselves with 'soloists' or people who stand apart from the group. Everyone wears similar, if not exactly the same, clothes and participates together in the same combinations. We use our bodies to convey the fact that we are one, which can be much more powerful for an audience than reading or hearing about it in the papers. We desire nothing formal or aristocratic like fairies or princes or princesses, as in the old, outdated classical ballet. Everyone and anyone can take part in our auditions for this show. I'm opening them up to people outside of just the Allard Ballet Academy."

Dawn dropped her mallet position and stared at Madame Angulaire. "But I worked hard to get into this Academy to be able to perform…"

Madame Angulaire nearly slapped Dawn again at the sound of her protests, but instead, she breathed in and laughingly said: "Oh, my darling, you are no special snowflake in the eyes of progressive ballet. Besides, you're injured now, so get off your high horse."

A deep sense of shame and sadness overwhelmed Dawn as she bore holes into the oak floorboard. It is true that she was injured, but she was the best dancer in her class and always showed up, even when her whole body just wanted to sleep. Every day that she rose to go to the studio that beckoned her, she answered it. But to bring in an outsider who did not breathe, eat, and sleep in the dancer's inner world? It seemed much harder than a slap on the face. Outsiders, even the adult ballet students, were not welcome here, to Dawn. They did not belong, and yet here was her savior, telling her to open the doors wide open for just anyone to walk in and join the dance. Dawn wanted to rip her hair out.

Dawn could not answer Madame, so a time of complete silence passed between them before Madame said, "I know it will take time for you to rid yourself of your bourgeoisie ways, but it will get easier with time. I promise you that."

Madame Angulaire turned the music up a little higher to help drown out the thoughts weighing Dawn down at that moment. The music infiltrated her eardrums until all that was noticed was the pulsing in her head and the chaotic sounds coming from the speakers.

"Dance, Dawn, dance! Become the tool of the workers, be the wheel, forget yourself! Bend your body over the wheel like you were string cheese or an abandoned jump rope! Allow your spine to soften, your limbs to loosen, and your will to mold right into the shape you're emulating. Be the wheel, Dawn. Become the wheel, like this."

Sliding down to the floor, she rolled onto her stomach and bent herself backward, grabbing onto her toes from behind. She formed a crooked circle, but all Dawn thought about was how much her skeleton's hip bones must be screaming out in pain at being jabbed down into the floor like that. Like a pike, Madame stuck herself firmly onto the floor and into that backbreaking shape for several agonizingly long seconds.

Finally, Dawn could not take her teacher in that uncomfortable-looking position anymore, so she asked her to rest while she tried it. It hurt immensely and Dawn had a difficult time reaching back far enough behind to even touch her feet.

"Come on, of course, it hurts, *all* of ballet hurts. But that's why it's so grand. It is just another example of showing the genuine pain of the workers' struggles in life. Your pain is real. Embrace it. Give in to the pain, Dawn," said Madame Angulaire. Her eyes shined as she watched Dawn contort herself into the crooked circle of her teacher. Pushing herself back further and further to please her teacher made Madame's soul rise like a cat arching its back.

"That position was actually a very ancient one used in yoga called *Dhanurasana*, or the bow pose. Yoga is a very good way for dancers to stretch their tight muscles and also align with the belief that anyone can do these poses with their bodies. Yoga equalizes us. Here, try the *Urdhva Dhanurasana*, or wheel pose, with me, which I may even be able to fit into the ballet."

Madame Angulaire planted both feet onto the ground and her hands behind her head onto the floor, and hoisted herself up into a backbend. Dawn followed suit but could only get her head to touch the floor because she still had a spine to reckon with.

Laughing, Madame said, "Still have a spine, huh? Well, we'll fix that too. Tomorrow is another day, missy."

CHAPTER IV

D awn continued her training with Madame Angulaire in tow. They trained on forming her back into something akin to rubber or taffy in the way it could be stretched and pulled *en croix*. Her body formed itself into the shape of whatever Madame desired eventually, always giving in to the muscles that Madame pulled at with her arms or the combinations which demanded all of her utmost attention. Dawn gave in.

After class today, she ran into the incoming adult class and was caught looking at Natalie. Natalie just smiled and waved as she walked into the studio with her normal tights and leotard—nothing fancy. She never wore anything that made her stand out from the rest of the class. She followed the recommended protocol for dancewear and stuck with it week after week, year after year. Didn't she ever get tired of it all? wondered Dawn, as she gave a short upturned mouth and curt wave, exiting the studio as fast as her sore ankle would allow.

She hobbled down the stairs, knowing that there were only a few days left before her cast would come off and she could get back to being the dancer she wanted to be. At the bottom of the stairwell, she envisioned dancing in a group of the injured in Madame Angulaire's version of *Le Pas d'acier*. She had spent

131

much of her time outside of class reimagining ballet without soloists. Working through the pain of not being unique, Dawn fought to find pleasure in the dancing itself, regardless of what character she was. After all, she may as well have been a number for all the audience would care when watching her onstage. The only thing that mattered anymore was the group. Madame told her not even to enjoy herself because she said that was selfish and ungroup-like. But it was so hard…

As Dawn exited the theater, Natalie watched her out of the rose-like window from her spot at the barre. The morning sun was shining through, and she breathed deeply as she *pliéd* in second position. Madame Roberts gave them all slow combinations to allow for their muscles to get warm and reacquainted with the movements.

"Breathe in through the nose, hold, and out through the mouth. Good," said Madame Roberts. "Now, dancers, we are going to continue stretching here to wake ourselves up. If you hear any pops or cracks when you *plié*, don't be alarmed. You are all old enough to know your bodies, so please stop if you feel any sharp pains. Sharp pain is your body's way of telling you to stop immediately what you're doing. Discomfort or shakiness of the muscle is all fine and try to hold the position even if those things plague you. Just remember to breathe through the discomfort because that's the only way you'll get stronger and more flexible."

Madame Roberts smiled and turned around to cue the pianist to start the next combination's music. He touched the keys so softly and the music drifted in the air like a fairy, hanging on nothing while the adults moved with grace through each series of steps.

Natalie loved the warm-up exercises at the barre. They

were always the same, perhaps a tweak in the number of *pliés* or *cambrés* here and there, but the steps never changed. She craved that unalterability of the class. The progressive order from barre to center work made her feel like she could lose herself in the habit and focus on fixing those mistakes she made. Her mind could deep dive into focusing on one aspect to fix for the day, to improve herself on the whole as a dancer and a human being. Today, she may focus on the correct head position for each movement or the fluidity of her arms or the arch of her working foot. There were always things to improve in classical ballet because there was a standard by which to compare. Only the teacher and physics would tell you if you were on the right track. You were either performing the movement correctly or you were not. There was really no in-between in ballet, which saved Natalie from a *lot* of headaches. She knew that her flexibility had retracted a bit as she got older, so she came to expect as much as she could muster instead of perfection. She learned after what she called her "vanity years" to stop caring as much about how much higher she could lift her leg in the air than another dancer or how extreme her arch was as compared to others or how deep of a split she could attain. Her goal now was to maintain as much of her healthy body as possible and enjoy the process along the way.

Classical ballet was a form of meditation for Natalie. It was an hour of her day when everything else was forgotten for an art form that fueled her body and mind. It integrated her entire being into one, and she felt refreshed as soon as the class was over. Another day could not only be handled but conquered when she knew her body could do things like *penché* or hold an *arabesque*. The confidence given to her from ballet made life manageable and worthwhile.

"And one, two, three, switch!" said Madame Roberts.

Natalie turned to repeat the same combination on the other side. The addition to the ritual of evenly focusing on both the left and right sides of the body fulfilled her need to balance in life. When she was young, she always used to watch the boys play football and love the physical aspect of life, but when it came to attending class and working on their minds...well, they did not get very far. There was no balance between work and play. The same became true when Natalie got to quit her job at the supermarket. She was only eighteen then and just barely out of high school. She was just a girl...

***

Natalie's auburn hair glowed like fire in the studio as she adjusted her head to attain the correct postures. It was like she was swimming through to the next position with that kind of gravity-defying grace.

"The final combination on the barre today will be our *grand battements*," said Madame Roberts. "Please go only as high as your hips will allow you. I know it has been a while since our last class together, so remember not to push yourselves too hard. This class is for adults. You are not training to be professionals at this point and all we are focusing on is maintaining the health of your body, mind, and soul. I want you here at the Allard Ballet Academy to *thrive* in the outside world. The world beyond these studio walls, which so many of our students know nothing about. They are ignorant about the adult world and what happens outside of their homes or their classrooms or their studio. Those are the only places our students live in, but you all have other careers and other hobbies. Most of you know what it is like to sit at a desk job

134

from nine to five or give birth to a child or fight with a spouse. You are the worldly few who have found your way back to the foundations of classical ballet.

"Every single one of you gravitated to a world of ritual, method, and reason. You could not find it in this hectic world of ours, but you could find it in the exercises at the barre and the dancing in the center. Ballet gave you the refreshing and inspiring boost you all needed to go back out into the world and conquer it. You can act in a world that has classical ballet in it…some *good* left in it. Classical ballet hearkens back to the time of kings and queens and wealth and learning. It goes back to a time when people were discovering more about the human body and all the wonderful things it could do. This made dance a clinical kind of exercise, but it later become sheer drama onstage, the most profound way to express the finer emotions that mankind has. Ballet could be quiet and delicate or it could be loud and powerful, but it always brought humanity up—not down. Pointe shoes and *demi-pointe* positions made women and men more ethereal, showing the world how it ought to behave. The courtly etiquette from the 1600s in France grew to become a dance that everyone could join. There were even choreographers who tried to bring notation to ballet, like Jean-Étienne Despréaux in his 1815 manuscript codifying ballet positions, but it always ended up too complicated for others to follow. Dance is a form that seems to be able to be only passed down orally and physically. That is why my students and other ballet students around the world must uphold the classical components that came from a better time—a time where reason and its proper expression were allowed to bloom."

Madame Roberts looked all of her adult dancers in the eyes with a smile on her face and a light step. The class threw their working leg up as high as it could possibly go to show their appreciation for Madame's inspirational words for the day, while they grounded their standing leg deeper and deeper into the ground to help them balance. It was the only option that existed if they were to keep themselves from falling over and possibly injuring themselves. Physics made it so. Reality was their only guide.

Natalie came to class since she was a child whenever her parents, and then she, could afford it. For even when money was tight, her parents knew that ballet meant so much to Natalie that they always tried their best to send her to class when they could. If she had stuck with it, without falling in love with a man, she knew her parents were saving up for her professional dance career too. But what really kept her coming back year after year, life stage after life stage, were the teachers. Before Madame Roberts, her mother taught and had actually founded the Allard Ballet Academy. Her mother spoke the same way about ballet and its meaning. She even named the school *Allard* because it meant "noble" in French.

The idea of being a noble person in life attracted Natalie. It always did, even as a child when she watched in awe, and even envy, as the older girls danced in their pointe shoes with such grace and beauty. She wanted to become those girls. They were feminine and moral in the way they danced; for their movements taught her how to express herself in any situation. Perhaps she internalized the movements and sometimes they would come out in a touch or a glance.

Maybe that's how I found Charles and fell in love with him so quickly, thought Natalie. I touched him like I had found my duke, Albrecht. He made me feel like I was soaring in the most amazing *grand jeté*, only this feeling lasted forever.

Madame Roberts's mother also taught that dancing restrained people enough to express themselves civilly. It was never uncontrolled but clearly thought through like a robust debate between two opposing parties. Ballet could also bring people from various backgrounds together. There were also little Russian girls in her class when she was growing up who spoke very little English or little Spanish boys who would mime what they were going to do to achieve and correct their lines. And, of course, everyone was taught the French terminology for ballet. We all knew what *pirouette* meant and our bodies learned to, almost automatically, execute the step whenever it heard that series of sounds together. We all grew up to move like kings and queens from centuries ago.

Natalie truly believed that everyone could benefit from learning classical ballet. She came back even when Madame Roberts took over after her mother retired from teaching because Madame Roberts spoke of the same goals that a person learning dance can take from the classes. Everyone could walk with grace, and that was enough for Natalie.

***

Natalie continued to learn grace and etiquette at the Academy, and not only that, but she also learned balance. Balance saved her the most pain and money in life. She learned in class that maintaining each pose, especially those on one foot, required constant micro-adjustments of her foot and ankle. It was really necessary for her entire body to adjust itself to what the pose required. She molded herself into the shapes she desired. That is why even her pinky toes were needed to maintain stability and the strength of her calves kept her standing leg strong enough to stay there. Up close, she must look like a wiggly mess, but from far enough, she looked as graceful as an ethereal fairy, where every move was held and blended into the next one without a hiccup.

I still remember a few times in my life when I know ballet saved me, Natalie thought. I was only twelve when I stepped into a groundhog's hole in my parents' backyard. I had been walking along and down I went with my whole foot in the hole. In an instant, I stabilized myself as if that was my standing leg and balanced myself on top of that leg. I didn't fall over and break anything. I could keep my balance, put my working leg down on the ground next to the hole, bend down, and pull my foot out of the hole. Ballet gave me the readiness of habit to correct my body's movements in space. At twelve, I had more control over myself than an adult who had never danced. I avoided the hospital that day with a possibly rolled or broken ankle.

There was another time when I was older, shortly after Charles had passed. I was repainting the living room walls because they were this hideous yellow color and I wanted them to be white. I had climbed up the ladder with my roller and the ladder shook, nearly toppling over because I guess I had not opened it far enough. I caught hold of the sides of the ladder so quickly that I never fell off and had stabilized it before it could move to one side or the other to the point of tipping over. That kind of core stabilization and speedy reflexes came from the number of times I lost balance and had gripped the barre for help. My ability to react and balance myself that day saved me from a possible hurt back, a ruined paint job, and the cost of a hospital trip and the resulting tests.

Natalie dug up other memories of the way she walked and the way she stood in front of boys and the way she curtsied to her elders. All of these pieces of herself came from being taught classical ballet. Her teachers taught her the history of ballet too when she was younger. All the students were told to grab their ballet class notebooks and open them up to the next clean page. The dancers learned a new word every week. Usually, they were dance terms, but that day it was "Apollo."

"And what does Apollo represent, class?" asked Madame Roberts's mother.

Natalie raised her small hand and said, "Music!"

"Yes, very good. But he also represents civilization."

Natalie did not know what that meant, so she said, "What's that?"

"Well, civilization can mean many things—some people think it is where written records are kept and maintained, others think it is just a cultural group, some believe it has to do with technological development."

"Oh, like how we are all doing ballet in this room right now?" asked Natalie.

"Yes, we have all of our basic needs satisfied, like shelter, food, and water, so that now we have the time and energy to dance. We are civilized. I want you all to remember that. We are civilized, but it took a lot of work and suffering from our ancestors to get to this point. There is always a chance of losing it. Dancers must strive to be like Apollo, learn to be civilized, and you will remind us all of what we have and are working for." Madame Roberts's mother left her lesson on the name "Apollo" alone for the day, but Natalie went through the entire class with the name still percolating in her mind.

She focused as she imagined a goddess would. Her face became stoic and her lines were more rigid. All of her concentration went from her brain down through her legs, while her arms got any runoff with just enough energy to lighten up her fingers into a graceful arch with each finger on a different plane from the rest.

Every day began and even ended in first position. Natalie's teachers both taught that first position was like the sunrise and the sunset, the beginning and the end, the curtain rising and falling; and all the movement in between was essential to complete the dancer's day. The five "noble" positions in ballet were with the feet pointed outward, to that painful one hundred eighty degrees—as far away from pointing inward as possible. The Renaissance's thinkers taught their dancers that inward-facing feet were awkward, working against the body's natural line, and were, therefore, a sign of ill-breeding; feet facing inward were for the peasants.

One of the forefathers of codifying ballet was Feuillet, and he believed that the framework for each of the five positions dictated where all the ballet steps would be made from. It was within the reasoned confines of lines that ballet emerged. There were rules that had come from people's thinking about *civilized* man and what it means to be such in this world on earth. Therefore, it was a noble and even a spiritual endeavor that each dancer had to approach and come to terms with on their own. Understanding the full extent of classical ballet was a journey that Natalie was still on and endeavored to become better at it with each passing year.

***

As the day's class finished with its *reverence*, Natalie grew tall. Her arms raised and fell like a bird's wings and her torso lifted out of her hips, which made her legs look lengthier. She found her torso smaller and leaner in this upright pose, and she looked unabashedly at herself in the mirror. The mirror allowed her to admire things about herself that she would have forgotten. And if there was something to critique, then she looked at herself and worked toward improvement. At her age, nothing made her ashamed or gave her a good reason to be hard on herself. She gave herself enough space to improve continually. There was no more youthful competition like there used to be. Now, she was on her own time and that time was slower. There were no teachers in life guiding her toward "the right path." Natalie only had herself to take guidance from.

Natalie could remember those days when she would rehearse for a performance and the sweat would be pouring off of her. She recalled watching the soloists in awe of their ability, and she would later try to recreate some of the dances at home, only to make a fool out of herself. There was always a technical position that Natalie just could not get because she was not strong enough or balanced enough or flexible enough. The jaw-clenching frustration came from the days when she stretched deeply after class and *still* could not get all the way down into middle splits like some of the other dancers could with ease. She fumed with jealousy at the dancers, who could perfectly execute more than three *pirouettes*. It just seemed so unfair.

But what Natalie did have was an expressive face, and she used her emotions to express every movement imaginable. When the piano grew soft and gentle, her body became small and her fingers lighter than air. When the piano became all staccato and louder, Natalie threw out her chest and stretched her legs apart to reveal her openness to the music's brutal dictates. Listening to the rhythm that dance relied so heavily on, Natalie imagined herself as one of the vibrating strings inside. In making her body a part of the piano, her movements became much more responsive and available to meet the emotional demands of a piece.

Natalie would never forget Madame Roberts's mother saying, "Very nice, Natalie! Use your head more next time and you'll look like the pained Juliet. You certainly have the emotions there for it. Everyone's movements should show plainly the underlying human emotion, as Natalie here is showing. Please, class, take notice of her acting ability as you dance today. You may all learn something new."

So although she was a dancer who never had all the technical agility down, she had the emotional part. Perhaps finding the emotional veracity was actually more difficult for most dancers to find, but Natalie was still envious of those dancers who could make certain movements and combinations appear uncomplicated. As many dance students before her have done, Natalie also tried to strengthen her jumps in the pool on summer break or have her friends sit on her legs while she was stretching out her splits. She did idiotic things that now seem risky to an older adult, but back then, if you were at all serious about ballet, you just did it. Overstretching could have and did end up hurting many of the students before they even made it into a company, but, usually, the teachers caught us doing it and could stop us before we hurt ourselves. The teachers knew what to watch for in us young people. They understood more about how the body works than the students certainly did.

Natalie curtsied to Madame Roberts today, gave her a sparkly smile, and walked out of the studio with her feet still turned out like she always did as a child. She emulated the noblewomen before her, who exited the same studio in the past. There was an honor that came with being a student of ballet. You became a living representative of an entire culture that depended on *living* people to survive. It had no real written notation, and so its next generation had to learn the steps to teach to those below faithfully. Natalie took that job seriously and guarded the art form with everything she had in her.

On leaving the studio, Natalie saw Dawn still hobbling around in her cast.

"When do you get the cast taken off?" asked Natalie.

"Oh, in a couple of days," answered Dawn as she kept her eyes straight ahead of her on the doorknob to the studio. It bothered her greatly that anyone should even acknowledge her cast. Besides, Madame Angulaire believed her cast was her new strength. It was like it was there all along, according to her, only now that Dawn could recognize the wound could she optimize her strength.

"Oh, good, dear. I'm very happy to hear that," said Natalie.

Dawn finally peeled her eyes away from the doorknob and made herself look at Natalie—Natalie with her gray hairs sticking out, her crow's feet, her loose skin, and baggy arms. It made Dawn mad looking at her because she could not understand the aging process. Couldn't science just fix all of those problems now? Dawn wondered. There must be some blame for people who let themselves get old like that. But then she thought about the celebrities who just looked like fakes with all the injections placed in their skin... Why can't there be a natural way to reverse aging or stop it entirely? If there were a fountain of youth, I would be the *first* one to drench myself in it. There is no way I'm going to let myself grow old—never, never, *never*!

Finally, Dawn responded to Natalie's comment with a simple, forgetful, "Thanks."

Natalie could feel the thoughtless, cold sound of the word that fell from her lips but refused to believe that it was because of anything she did or said. The poor dear must be really upset about losing her dream career just before it had even begun, thought Natalie. I should invite her over for some tea.

CHAPTER V

"Oh, Dawn?" asked Natalie. "Would you like to come over for tea after your class this afternoon? I could pick you up if you'd like."

Dawn had difficulty keeping her eyes from rolling to the back of her head, but she did not have many friends from the Academy, so perhaps she would get along better with the older people. Ha! Who am I kidding? thought Dawn. She probably just wants to hear me babble to keep her company all afternoon.

Natalie picked up Dawn's hand saying, "Please? I can bake fresh cookies for you."

Why? So you can fatten me up and ruin my physique as you did yours? thought Dawn. Although cookies and tea do sound nice...

Dawn knew she would kick herself for this later, but she promised one cookie and one cup of tea and that was it. "Fine, yes, I'll come over. You don't live far from the studio, right? I can just walk myself there after class. No need to worry about me."

A pleased smile from Natalie confirmed the date between the two of them.

In the studio, Madame Angulaire introduced other students

to Dawn's studio practices. She made all of them dance together in groups and if any were out of step or lost their balance, she would slap them on the hand with a ruler. She believed that corporal punishment should have never left the educational establishment. On most days, Dawn's hands ached and had a blotchy red tone to them. Her parents never seemed to notice since they gave up trying to keep her from the Academy after what had happened. If she was going to ignore their wishes, they would ignore her.

In these special classes, Dawn was the center of attention and she *fed* on it. She kept her Queen of the Wilis status even after the performances were over. Although Madame Angulaire did not want Dawn to think she was the center, she could still tell when her teacher's eyes were on her and that she was pushed the hardest to develop herself into the dancer she was meant to be. Dawn liked to imagine herself as Madame's muse. Her injury made her special, and in return, Dawn rolled on the floor, covered in other dancers' hair and skin cells and lost bobby pins. She rolled in the dust and bent herself into postures made by the crippled few. Anything that Madame Angulaire willed of her muse, she got obediently.

By the end of class, Dawn picked up her belongings, stretched out her sore back, and walked over to Natalie's house. It was only a couple of blocks away in the more suburban portion of the area. She had a bit of room around her home but not enough to spread out and ignore the neighbors nearby. However, turning the corner made Dawn feel comforted. The beautiful tree branches swayed in the wind, everyone's grass was bright green and freshly cut, the intoxicating smell of watered flowers filled the breeze. It felt so wonderful here, like time slowed down as soon as she turned the corner.

Natalie's house was only one story, but its red bricks gave it a charm and cozy feeling. Knocking on the solid wood door, Natalie, followed by her cat, answered it.

"Oh, come on in, honey. I'm just about to take the loose leaf tea out of the cups. Did you know loose leaf has a much richer flavor than the bagged sort? I learned that from my neighbors to the right of me a few years back. They're a very sweet couple in their seventies," said Natalie. "Anyway, come, come. You can sit down right here." Natalie led Dawn to the living room, which was straight ahead. The couch sat before an untouched fireplace and the carpet felt so soft under her feet.

There was no television in the living room, which Dawn thought was strange. "What do you do in here when you're not in class? asked Dawn.

"I see you noticed I don't have a television. Well, I have a radio I listen to while I knit or crochet. I can go to the classical channel and do some ballet stretches before class. Also, I cook a lot, which is why my neighbors probably love me. I can never eat everything I make, so I'm always sharing with them. Let's see...I read. I especially love reading when there's rain. It just lets my mind wander more through the story. Anyway, enough about me. What do you like to do outside of ballet?" Natalie smiled, not even imaging what an insult she had given with such a question.

Dawn's jaw tightened. How dare she?! thought Dawn. How could she think I do anything but dance? If I am to even enter the professional world and be taken seriously, then she must know that I am wholly devoted like a nun to Christ to my art. Who does she think I am? A child? A nobody? Not the Queen of the Wilis?! I am going to make a name for myself or die.

Dance or death! Now, how could I possibly explain that to this simpleton?

Dawn shifted uncomfortably and her answer took too long to come out before Natalie got up from the lounge chair beside the couch and grabbed the two teas and cookies in the hopes of eradicating the uncomfortable atmosphere the girl was creating. Natalie knew how to bring comfort back into a situation. So she leaped up and made two trips with her delicate porcelain cups and saucers—one butterscotch cookie lay in the saucer, cuddled up next to the floral-painted cup with gold paint around its edges. Everything in the house was beautiful in its details. In fact, Dawn imagined this house being the uppermost floor of the brick theater, like a hidden room in the attic where Dawn could hide away from the challenging world of ballet.

Nibbling on her cookie, Dawn could loosen her jaw enough to say: "I am in love with dancing. That is all."

Allowing the words some room, Natalie stayed silent. She ate her cookie slowly and sipped her tea as she sat there smiling. She understood *exactly* that sentiment when she was Dawn's age. There was a fire in her stomach that was only quenched when she was dancing. The longer she stayed away from it, the more agonizing the flames became. She feared being burned up from the inside out if she did not dance frequently enough. Her passion back in those days was a wonderful curse. It would harm her mentally and physically if she did not obey—her passion was a cruel master. Having been so young, she had no grasp of time. She imagined life being so short as everyone said, especially for a ballerina, that she had to cram ballet into every day before it was too late. No one told her that by this age, life felt long. After all, it was long enough for her to find and lose the love of her life; it was long enough to find her career and lose that too. Natalie's life was long enough to change direction. Dawn just has not lived long enough yet to experience a great pivot, thought Natalie.

"Yes, my dear. I remember feeling just like you when I was fifteen. I wanted to sleep and eat in the theater before and after my classes, and I lived for the next performance when I was able to come alive again onstage. I lusted after lead roles. *If only*, I thought. My mind was only filled with questions concerning dance. Yes, it was both a wonderful and, in hindsight, destructive time for me."

Natalie's smile faded a bit as she took a peek at Dawn, who was focusing all of her energy on the blackened fireplace in front of her. She imagined that if she did not move, then maybe Natalie's old, addled mind would forget that she was even there. Why was she even there? wondered Dawn. What did this saggy bag of bones want with her, of all people? She wasn't anything special. Madame Angulaire told her that even as she watched her relentlessly through class.

"Look, what do you want?" asked Dawn, placing her empty saucer and cup down on the coffee table in front of her.

"What do I *want*?" asked Natalie, frowning now. "I don't want anything. I saw someone in the studio who had the same drive that I had for ballet. I just wanted to acknowledge it and get to know you…help you." Natalie curved her neck to connect with Dawn's eyes.

"I don't need any help."

"Maybe not. But I've seen how your teachers have been pulling all of their students apart. I'm not blind. I can see that lately you've been spending a lot more of your class time with that Madame Angulaire."

149

Dawn spun her head around to look at Natalie. Her eyes turned icy and her expression froze all the empathy it had tried to muster up while looking at this cozy hole.

"So what? At least she lets me dance, even when I'm injured. Madame Roberts doesn't care to see me overcome as Madame Angulaire does. But why am I even telling you?! You have nothing to share. Look at you! You're old. What do you know?"

Tears formed in Natalie's eyes as Dawn pulled her head down to her chest. She knew as soon as the words flew out that they were hurtful.

"I...I'm...sorry. I just—"

"Stop, please. I feared aging too then. But aging is just one of those things that creep up on you now and again, reminding you of what you look like now," said Natalie. She shifted in her chair and gave a light chuckle. "I remember looking in horror sometimes at Madame Roberts's mother when she was my teacher. She was a professional ballerina with a company and then she was just a skinny, bony, wrinkled version of the plump youth that used to grace the stage. Ah, but when she showed us a variation or a combination to follow, it was as if she became youthful again. It was like a magic trick. When dancing she lit up and moved like a teenager, but when she stopped, all the light left her body and it became the shrunken, wizened version of itself in the present. Dancing makes us older adults feel young again, Dawn. Allow us to feel that."

Dawn had never considered what dancing did for adults before. She figured if they could not do double beats in the air anymore or high leaps to the point of flying that they got nothing from it, except pain. She had never considered that the adults may have been at one point young ones who were capable of such things. She had never considered that a love for ballet could last so long in a person who could no longer keep control over every aspect of their form. For many women, she watched them grow up, fall in love, have babies, grow fat, and lose all that ballet had done for them. That's what she watched even some of her own classmates start doing. The first step was getting pregnant, or getting someone else pregnant, and dropping out of high school.

"I never knew that you were taught by Madame Roberts's mother. What was she like?"

"Oh, gorgeous, when she was dancing. She taught Madame Roberts everything that she had learned as a dancer. That's how it has always been—an oral tradition. Classical ballet still doesn't have a formal notation, though people in the past have tried. So, in much the way of an apprentice with a master, that's how ballet is still passed down from generation to generation."

Dawn envisioned a studio that was a little less worn, a teacher who looked similar to Madame Roberts, and a studio that brought in students very similar to herself. She wondered if they had had the same dreams and ambitions. Some of them must have felt the same way as she did. But how many of them wanted to die and be buried right there under that theater's stage? To preserve her own feelings, she imagined no one cared as much as she did...but this time she was not as convinced that was the case.

Dawn rose upon the realization that maybe there was already someone buried down there in the theater—in her spot.

"What? Leaving already?" asked Natalie.

"I...uh...yes. Yes, I have to leave now." Dawn's cheeks burned red. She grabbed her ballet bag and turned away from the fireplace and the couch inside the cozy home. With a pang of regret, Dawn began walking toward the door and she left without thanking Natalie for the cookies and tea.

Natalie wondered what she had said that disturbed Dawn so. The heavy wooden door was left open and Natalie looked out of it as Dawn quickly walked away from her home. Perhaps she had been hard with the child. She still did not yet understand that she would age too, nor did she internalize the fact that there was a history of ballet and she was just a minor piece of its continuance.

Dawn was only a part of the history, and although individual dancers contributed to its story and very existence, which made her important, she was not the beginning nor the end of ballet. There were young people before her who died or who are now old. There will be young people born and just joining companies when she is old.

Natalie closed the wooden door and her eyes as she ran her hand against the grain, imagining it as the floor of the stage. Ever since she was a little girl, she had loved the feeling of the wood beneath her feet. It was firm, but each piece was different, like a fingerprint; every piece of wood had its own story as she did hers.

Underneath her eyelids, she saw brief flashes of light and squiggly lines. Her doctor said that as people age, they can get more of these annoying pieces dancing around in their eyeballs. It was curiosities like this that made Natalie panic as she aged. When she was young, nothing ever hurt without obvious reason or went funny when a part of her moved too hastily or malfunctioned over time. Her body was this well-oiled machine that she had no idea how many parts were at play to make everything feel so...unfelt. She never noticed all the individual muscles, veins, bones, or tissue that made up her—Natalie.

Aging meant constantly feeling your body and putting things back together that became broken over time. Her well-oiled machine was beginning to rust. Natalie sniffed and held back tears. She thought, Let Dawn keep her youth and her freedom, even if that means she remains ignorant for a time. Only in youth can people truly feel invincible and static. Eventually, little things like gray hairs and crow's feet will wise her up all too quickly to the reality of living for a long time.

Living for a long time means gaining and losing in a linear fashion. She will attain the dance career she seeks if she wants it and then she will lose it. She will fall in love for the first time, and more likely than not, she will lose that too. But when Dawn is in the midst of it, entering her peak years, she may be blind to the others around her.

She lacks an empathy that only the wounded know. It does not even take much of a wound to humble a person—to bring them back down from the heavens to a world that can be real nice but not free from pain. Yet, the pain makes life much more precious and happiness that much more special when it is attained.

Natalie washed the saucers and cups slowly, thinking about Dawn and all the things she wished she knew as a child that she saw now. The suds enclosed her fingers and popped sporadically as she washed her dishes clean. The little house had wind chimes and a bird feeder by the kitchen window, so she watched the little birds sing their spring songs intertwined with the chimes. Breathing in deeply, she turned the faucet off and just listened. In these moments of slow gratitude, Natalie found peace. A peace she would have never found as a ballet student.

Maybe, thought Natalie, Dawn could incorporate some of my slower moments into her day. If I had even a taste of what it would be like once I accomplished my necessary life goals, I would have enjoyed my youth much more. Yes, that's what I'll do.

With a finality of thought before understanding exactly what she wanted to do to execute such a plan, Natalie smiled and laid down on the couch to read a book.

Meanwhile, Dawn walked the couple of blocks back to the theater and called her mother for a ride home.

"Okay, hun. Did you get out of class later than usual?"

"No, I went to visit Natalie, one of the adult ballet dancers. Remember? I had a cookie and some tea. But I just left and walked back to the theater."

Dawn's mother did vaguely recall her finding a new friend to hang out with, but she didn't realize she was another adult. She always did think her daughter had an "old soul," so maybe an older friend would be good for her.

Dawn's mother arrived and Dawn got into the car, feeling emotionally drained, with thoughts that kept hitting dead ends.

Her mind was spitting out blank receipts and maps without places. Nothing was computing and all she could do was sit paralyzed in the front seat next to her mother.

"Mom?"

"Yes, dear."

"When did you get your first gray hair?"

Dawn's mother laughed. "Gosh, I was in my mid-twenties, sorry, hun. You'll probably see some earlier than others. But it's a slow process. It's not like you wake up one morning and your entire head is gray. It's a single strand here, a couple there, a few more over here. Don't worry about it. You're only fifteen! Did your new friend scare you?"

"A little. I never thought that I would get those things…"

Dawn's mother ached with sympathy for her girl. "Awe, honey, you're just growing up. You're realizing that you will get old too one day. I think I was about your age when I truly realized that. You'll get used to that fact soon enough."

Dawn curled up into herself. She was feeling smaller than usual today.

***

At home, Dawn tried to shut out her afternoon with Natalie, attempting to forget all the warm visual cues that wrapped her in safety; otherwise, she may have decided to give in to Natalie's desires to understand her side better. No! thought Dawn, I will never understand why people have to get old and just give in. I would fight the wrinkles and the gray hairs. I would never let gravity win! With that, Dawn threw a pillow over her head in her bed and fell into an uneasy sleep.

By the time she roused herself out of bed, her hairs all askew, Dawn was moving her legs, one in front of the other, out the door to get to the Academy. She was supposed to have another earlier morning class with Madame Angulaire and the other students she now included.

The performance for the *Le Pas d'acier* was nearly ready with the curtains to rise next week. Dawn was finally getting her cast off tomorrow. She would be ready to dance without that clunky, ugly thing on her ankle.

Madame Angulaire watched as Dawn entered the studio. Her eyes went from the top of her head all the way down

155

to her toes and back up to her center. Even with the tight leotard keeping the flesh close to the body, she could tell when a dancer was gaining weight.

Indeed, Dawn had been feeling her ballet clothes getting harder to get on and off. She had felt swelling since her ankle injury in various parts of her body. Some more muscle grew in "unballerina-like" places where she had to compensate for not putting weight on her bad ankle.

But Dawn imagined she would immediately lose any water bloat she had gained when the cast came off. Madame Angulaire, however, believed differently. Her own skeletal frame survived injuries before, and she never puffed up the way Dawn was doing. It must be something that she is eating, thought Madame.

"Oh Dawn, can you come over here for a second?" Madame Angulaire waved Dawn over to the corner of the studio closest to the mirrors where the nearest restroom was. She grabbed her by the back of the neck, leaned her head forward, and whispered: "Next time, I will not be so private about this. Darling, you're gaining weight. We can't have that in our show. The workers are meant to look starving—not pig-like."

Dawn drew in her breath, trying not to cry or scream or produce a mixture of both. Her stomach clenched up as she attempted to suck in her bloated torso, but it ended up pushing out her ribs and giving her an even more unflattering look of trying too hard. This was the worst day of her life.

"I'm so sorry. Since the injury, I have not been able to move as much or work out as frequently. I'll try to limit my portion sizes more, Madame. I'm sorry." Tears were falling onto the oak floors, getting trapped in between the crevices where each plank was placed side-by-side when it was first created to serve the dancers on it.

Madame Angulaire tightened her grip on Dawn's neck and glared at her once more before releasing her bony fingers. Her hands were cold and her stare colder. Suddenly, Dawn no longer felt like her teacher's protégé. She had betrayed her teacher overnight with her body. Dawn displeased the one who believed in her and allowed her to dance.

Oh god! worried Dawn. My chance is gone. The only way she could maybe save herself before the performances were to starve herself and dance like a demon for Madame Angulaire. It must be done, or I am *doomed*, thought Dawn, as she heard the first few bars of music for the ballet start up again.

This ballet was mechanical. There was no actual plot. It was meant to have the steps of the workers be continuous, like a machine where there was no room or space to breathe. Akin to a machine, there was no thought—only the doing that made it function around the clock, and the music matched in a blaring kind of way where every waking moment was a climax. *Le Pas d'acier* lacked, on purpose, the sophistication of a culture or human civility. All it produced was noise and its rats who were turning the great wheel. For what end? The end stopped with Madame Angulaire, or at least it did for Dawn. Dawn could either be an injured dancer with Madame or quit. And quitting, for Dawn, was a death sentence.

The music blared and woke Dawn up. She waved her hands about like a clock, while her male peers performed some *changements* and then mimed the dancer's movements next to him. There were so many frivolous jumps in this production that, by the end, the workers were exhausted. There was no room to think while dancing or after dancing, which stood as a relief for Dawn because she did not want to think any longer—not about Natalie, not about Madame Roberts, and certainly not about Madame Angulaire.

So, she danced without thinking.

Madame Angulaire noticed she had abandoned herself to the muscle memory accumulated over the past few weeks. She felt keen anger well up inside of her breast because as she watched her student dance irrationally, she also saw the minor jiggle come from her midsection as she landed one of the many jumps. Her own student had betrayed *everything* she had given to her by becoming a *lazy* worker. A lazy worker, thought Madame, was no good to anyone. They brought down the entire group. Everyone else is the same size and they all are wearing the same costumes next week, but this ungrateful swine will look different. How dare she! Enraged, Madame refused to look in Dawn's direction for the rest of class. By the end of it, she had moved Dawn back further into the group, so the audience would not even see her face—just her legs moving to the music. Her status as Queen of the Wilis had been officially ended by Madame Angulaire.

CHAPTER VI

The day came and went and soon Dawn found herself back at the doctor's office to get her cast off.

"Am I finally going to be able to walk on the foot, Doctor?"

The doctor looked at her like she had exposed herself in front of him. After re-collecting himself, he chuckled a bit and said, "No dear, this is the beginning of a very lengthy process. Now, you get a walking boot and physical therapy for the next six weeks, at least."

"No!" screamed Dawn. I thought the cast was it and I could perform next week…just without putting a lot of pressure on my ankle! How could this happen?!" Dawn wanted to chop her leg clean off to make it more obvious to herself that she would *never* dance again. She could not take this teetering-on-edge kind of healing.

"I'm sorry. Really. In about six months, you should be able to walk gently on it without any help. But you realistically will not recover to the maximum you can achieve until a year passes, on average. And even then, everyone heals differently. Some might jump back and feel fine within that year, and others might never be 'back to normal' again. It is a waiting game. I can't make it go any faster for you."

Dawn crawled up on the medical table, hugging her legs into her stomach. She was sure to gain more weight with a boot on for another several weeks. Every day, she could feel the lag of her technique and skill falling behind her other classmates. I should just give up now and save face, she thought. That way, no one can say I was not being realistic in my goals. I'm a cripple and a no-good dancer now. I should stop holding everyone else back.

The doctor's nurse brought in the trap to bury her damaged foot in after the doctor examined its healing process.

"Well, Dawn, it looks like it's healing just fine. I'll get you scheduled for another appointment after six weeks, and you should start your physical therapy this week. Okay?"

"Yes, Doctor." Dawn slid off the table and landed on her unhurt foot. There was no energy left in her today to fight. She was a slave to her body. Her mother saw her pain and stayed silent the entire car ride home, secretly relieved that her daughter may leave ballet in her childhood and pick up a career that would actually make her money.

Later in the day, Dawn was scheduled for a rehearsal with Madame Angulaire and the group since opening night was fast approaching. Madame Angulaire contemplated calling her parents and requesting that she stay home and out of the performance entirely. She was no longer needed unless she got her pig-eating habits under control. With thoughts and decisions running around in her head, Madame spent much of her morning scratching out Dawn's name from the playbills and posters and anything else that included her in it. Luckily, the poster for the play had the group, and Dawn was caught in a dark shadow, so no one would recognize her. The wheel and the steel items on the stage sparkled right off the poster more than the bland-looking group of workers on the stage. This was the revolution that Madame was seeking, an image of the workers' products for the state or, in this case, the Academy.

What must survive is the Allard Ballet Academy. The little rats who fuel the place are replaceable, but not this school in this theater right here and now. There is no way to replicate the magic that comes from this stage. Everyone gives up their power to Madame Angulaire so that she can keep the wheels of the theater running. After all, thought Madame, who takes care of the bills now? Me. Who takes care of the majority of the choreography now? Me. Who teaches the students what real ballet is all about? Me. Once this performance gains enough success, I'll buy this place right out from under Madame Roberts's nose. She is too old and dusty to keep the reins of this place any longer. Her nepotism is the only thing that got her here anyway, not her ingenuity or her artistic vision.

I am going to bring this Academy into a new age. The modern era into the postmodern one and beyond. There will be no plots, no mimes, only abstract movements divorced from thought. We will move in such a way that would baffle even the plants and animals that have instincts! And I will never, *ever* let myself choose favorites again. Dawn must be eliminated from the cause, thought Madame Angulaire. But how to get rid of her?

How am I to stop her from fattening up my flock of starving mes? How can I stop her from shoving their mouths with dreams of food and other lies? There is only dance! The only thing these insects are allowed to believe is that dancing is their source of life—their fuel. Anything else is merely archaic, bourgeoisie "needs" that are taught by the previous generation to be good for a living organism. Well, *my* organisms don't need sun, food, air, shelter, water, *nothing*! None of those things give the Academy and its leader, me, the ability to thrive and continue on.

We, the Academy, require an obedient wave of energy to move the thoughts of a culture toward our views. We desire Dawn *gone* because she has taken advantage of her crippled state to forget herself. She no longer thinks only of dancing to feed her, but she thinks about pie and bread and chicken and engorging herself with things other than the airiness needed of a true dancer. Her focus has become of *this* world, in the mud, and not to a world built in the sky, in the air. She has allowed fat to control her fate and not her own teacher. Her choice has been made and now we'll make her lie in it.

***

Madame Angulaire welcomed Dawn into the class that evening without any reservations. Her sudden attention disturbed Dawn after all the mental anguish she had experienced over the last couple of days. Yet, here was her teacher, keen on watching her again in class during their last rehearsal before the performances.

Dawn no longer had her large cast on, but there was still a walking boot on that continued to make her dancing awkward and clunky. Madame noticed it immediately and her nostrils slightly flared at the sight of it.

"Dawn, I thought we were getting that cast off yesterday at the doctor's?"

"Uh, yes, Madame. Apparently, I am stuck in this boot and physical therapy for at least another six weeks."

Walking straight up to Dawn, Madame merely opened up her arms to hug her for several uncomfortable minutes.

As Dawn's head rested there on her chest, she could hear Madame's heart beating loudly and heavily. In such a thin frame, the noise seemed to fill up Madame's entire body with an angry beat, enough to frighten Dawn right off of her chest.

"Is everything all right, my darling?" asked Madame in the most sickeningly sweet way.

"Yes...yes, everything is fine. We should probably get rehearsal going though, right?" said Dawn, backing up into the center of the studio to assume her position, now further in the back with the others.

The music began blaring and everyone moved through the steps most mechanically from having gone over the whole ballet so many times. This state of habit over passion is an aspect that Madame Angulaire did not want to shake out of her dancers, unlike Madame Roberts. She drilled them so hard that they were dancing on fumes through the fatigue she caused them. The death-like movements, draped in sleepiness, made the steel around them much more shiny and believable. Madame preferred her students to serve as the props as opposed to the surrounding machinery. They were simply the wheels of the great machine.

Class ended when they practiced their final curtain calls in the studio. Tomorrow, they would rehearse onstage, and that evening was scheduled to be the first performance of the four scheduled ones. Dawn found that balancing school and ballet was more difficult than anything she had ever experienced when performance time came around. She had no energy left to learn about math and reading and geography. There was really no more space when Madame Angulaire was in charge of the show. She worked her students down to nothingness, like the diminishing eraser on the tip of a pencil.

As Dawn began picking up her belongings, Madame called her over.

"Hey Dawn, I would like to see you run through some of the steps for me out on the theater stage before you go to make sure your boot doesn't slip on the floor. We may need to add rosin to parts of it. Hopefully, your doctor won't mind," said Madame.

"Oh, sure. I didn't even really think about that. That's very kind of you to consider," said Dawn.

Madame Angulaire gave a cheap sort of smile and led the way down the stairwell with the chandeliers to the backstage area of the theater. The lights were already shut off by maintenance, who had left the building by five. Being a little after that time and with everyone else gone, the theater was free to make its own sounds heard, like the creaky stage floor when people walked backstage or the squeaky door hinges whenever the wind outside blew. The sounds set a new mood in the theater, and it made Dawn nervous for the first time to be there alone with Madame Angulaire.

"Madame, what would you like me to do first? I should probably call my mother and tell her I'll be a little late tonight if you want me to do multiple combinations." Dawn walked out onto the stage, ignoring the creaks and squeaks answering her.

Meanwhile, Madame had turned out the stage lights and followed Dawn out onto the stage. The clicks of her dance heels sounded like shots fired. The bullets were all aimed at Dawn as Madame said, "No need to call your mother. I won't keep you long." Madame began loudly humming the music and clapping her hands to the beat. "Dawn, I want you to start with the opening scene and go until I tell you to stop."

Dawn moved into her first position before Madame hummed the opening bars for the group's entrance onto the stage. In Dawn came with the little energy she had left, while Madame eyed an open costume trunk in the corner of the side wings, invisible to the audience. Madame made her way to the other side of the stage, still humming and clapping all the while. Once Dawn drew closer to Madame, her skeleton body jumped out and threw Dawn into the large trunk. In one fell swoop, surprised and overtaken by her hidden power, Dawn was thrown into a small box and she watched as Madame threw the heavy lid down right over her head. Madame quickly sat her entire weight on top of the box, looking for the key to the lock. She shimmied herself around on top of the box while she continued to hum loudly and clap her hands in order to drown out the screams coming from inside the costume trunk. Finally, she spotted the large ring of keys hanging up beside the curtain's ropes.

Still holding a foot on top of the trunk, Madame lifted herself up, grabbed the key set, and shoved every key in the lock until she found the right one—an antique turnkey that must have come with this original trunk when the theater was brand new. From inside the darkness, Dawn could hear the deadly click of the key turning in the trunk, and she stopped her pounding fists and scrunched kicks against the confines of the box. At this point, to conserve her energy, Dawn had to beg.

"Please, Madame Angulaire, please...I know I gained some weight, but I was—am still injured. I promise to do better. Just please don't leave me alone in this box!" Dawn pounded her fist against the lid once more, then growing quiet to hear a response, *anything* just to know that she was still there.

"Sorry, Dawn, but you betrayed me, your team, the Academy,

and dance itself. You chose *food* over dance. You chose to let your injury win rather than conquer your troubles by relying on the group. You are lucky I'm not filling this box with water or rats or something worse!"

Dawn screamed. She could think of nothing else to do than scream.

"Shut up!" shouted an enraged Madame Angulaire, kicking the box with the tip of her character shoes. Her breathing came in gasps as her heart raced inside the cage that held her upright and somehow still alive. The thin flesh moved over her bones as she breathed and the shadows danced under the spotlights that remained on. Sweat rolled down her chest and soaked into her leotard as she thought about what to do next. Should I leave her here overnight? wondered Madame Angulaire. How long must she serve her punishment? Who could hear her screaming from beyond the theater's closed doors? They were thick enough that she knew performances could never be heard from outside the building. An entire orchestra could be playing, and there would only be the faintest noise from outside. Pacing, Madame began to think she should sleep on it and check on her in the morning before classes. The little rat was bound to scream and alert someone once students came in for class the next day. So, it was somewhat determined that Dawn would have to stay at least overnight in the trunk.

"Madame? Madame, please. I can't breathe very well in here. It's dark and I'm frightened! Let me out so that we can talk about how I can mend these sins!" Dawn's face was puffy and soft from all the tears. She knew that her mother would worry and come look for her. "My mother will find me soon, and then you'll be fired immediately!"

Madame really had not thought about the sound problem

and the fact that her mother was probably waiting outside in the car for her. Swiftly turning the key and opening the lid to the trunk, Madame took one of the silk neckerchiefs lying in the box next to Dawn and tied it around her mouth as a gag. She also took a pair of pants and a blouse from underneath her bottom to tie her arms and legs together. At least that would muffle any sounds she made, thought Madame Angulaire.

With as much energy as she had left, Dawn fought Madame Angulaire, but it was not easy to maneuver around with a hurt ankle in a boot. The thing had gotten wrapped up in the costumes below and it slowed her movements enough to be predictable to Madame. The lid was back on and locked before she had time to think of another way to hit her teacher.

A deep sense of fear paralyzed Dawn now that she could no longer speak or move freely. The feelings only grew worse when she felt Madame Angulaire wiggling the box.

Madame found a dolly backstage, behind some of the equipment and props for the performance tomorrow. She shifted the costume trunk onto the dolly, rolled it backstage, and out the door that led to the stairwell. Carefully, clunking the trunk down each step, Madame went all the way down to the basement door, which she opened.

She rolled the tied-up Dawn underneath the stage in the basement area. It was all made of limestone, so the floors were covered in dirt and spiders ruled this underworld. There was a chill down there and everything was a gray, sooty color with the dim light that only came from the stairwell lights. Madame Angulaire groped her way around in the dark and found the one string connected to a pitiful-looking light bulb on the ceiling. It was only placed there in the mid-twentieth century after candles became a historical fixture and not a practical one any longer. Electricity lit the theater up and took the romantic element of candlelight with it. Now, the little buzz from the bulb and the rustling sound of Dawn squirming around was the only thing that could be heard in that room.

Dawn attempted to scream and Madame had been waiting for her to make as much noise as she could before she could leave the theater more at ease. It was certainly not loud enough to alert anyone. Plus, she had placed the trunk down in a corner and covered it over with an old sheet, so it looked untouched for many decades. No one would realize that any living person was down here, thought Madame. Quickly, she kicked the trunk again and ran upstairs to the lobby to see if she could hear any of Dawn's pathetic screams. Nothing.

Madame Angulaire hurried back downstairs to the basement, shut off the single light bulb, and shouted toward the trunk, "See you in the morning, darling!" Sneaking out the back door, Madame avoided running into Dawn's mother who was indeed in her car waiting for Dawn to emerge late as usual.

Madame set out on a hurried, *demi-pointe* run toward her car and drove away. Serves that girl right messing up my entire show, thought Madame. She should just curl up and die with at least some dignity for our group!

Meanwhile, Dawn had heard her teacher's last words and the successive silence coming from her absence. She contemplated being trapped in cold water in the trunk or having rats scurry and run all over her body in this confined space. Yes, those could be much worse. But being confined there to darkness and a certain timelessness that comes with losing track of that precious measurement, she felt afraid anyway. She knew she had wished to die and be buried under the stage, but she did not mean being buried while she was still young and very much alive. There was no comfort or peace here either, as she had fantasized there might be. That night she lay with the ghosts of the theater.

***

Dawn opened her eyes a few times after she had fallen asleep. There was no indication of the time without light or noise. She could have fallen asleep for hours...or only several minutes. Unsure, Dawn screamed as loud as she could through the fabric covering her mouth. There was no one outside to receive her cries based on the utter silence that followed.

Her stomach grumbled, and her bladder was full. Time passing was becoming more consequential the longer Dawn stayed trapped. Turning her head every which way, she tried to see an opening or even just a tiny hole to show perhaps a weakened spot that she could work out from. What would happen if I shifted all of my weight to one side of the trunk and it fell over? wondered Dawn. Would I be able to escape from there, or would I be just as trapped, only more uncomfortable by tipping it over? What if more fabric fell on top of my head and I suffocated to death?

Dawn's heart palpitated hard in her chest as it resisted the thought of suffocating, which it was already trying to battle with the little air in the costume trunk as there already was. She knew, though, that her mother must be taking some sort of action by now. She *must* be...

Dawn's mother had waited there in the car for fifteen minutes until her fury levels brought her out of the car, aiming to drag her daughter out of that theater. All she could think about was the dinner getting lukewarm, or worse cold, on the table. Stomping her way up the steps, she grabbed ahold of the knobs and foisted open the heavy wooden doors, which to her shock opened up to a completely dark theater. Running now up the stairwell, she ran into the dressing room first, which was dark, and the studio second, which was also dark and locked for the night. Panic froze her as she began thinking of where her daughter could be. Where was she? Where was her teacher?

Picking up the phone, Dawn's mother called her father: "Dear, I can't find Dawn. I waited for fifteen minutes outside for her before going in to get her and it was all dark. Help me!"

"Okay, calm down. Did she message you at all about being late or visiting a friend?"

"No! I would have remembered...I think. Let me check again." Dawn's mother looked at her phone's messages and the calls listed and there was nothing there since two o'clock that day. "Oh no, no, no, this can't be happening—not to me—not to us!" Tears and muddled words are the only things that made it across the phone at this point.

"Okay, calm down, sweetie. We'll find her. She can't have gone far in fifteen minutes. We can even call the police to file a missing person report when you get home. Okay? I'm sure she's around somewhere. Come home."

"I'm going to *kill* that rotten teacher when I get my baby back," said Dawn's mother, after which she ran out of the theater, into her car, and headed straight home.

Dawn heard nothing. The large brick-and-wood-built theater masked sounds too well. In her mind, there was no one looking for her yet. She just lay there in the trunk, wondering how she got there and how to ignore the growing hunger in her stomach.

The police began a search that night and all the neighbors

on the block helped Dawn's family examine the immediate area for her. An Amber Alert was sent out several hours later describing what Dawn looked like and what she was last seen wearing.

Natalie was sitting on her couch at home, in the early morning hours, reading a book under the lamplight, when she heard emergency vehicles and received the alert. Her heart plummeted when she saw the name in the message and she joined the neighbors looking for her as well.

That spring morning was chilly, and Natalie held her sweater up close around her neck. The folds of skin sagging were lifted with the weight of her hands. She knew Dawn would never be far from that theater; she headed over there without haste.

It was six in the morning by the time Natalie reached the theater—still a few hours before morning classes were to start at the Academy—still enough time to search from top to bottom to see where Dawn was hidden. The attic of the theater had costumes and props from past performances. After the *Le Pas d'acier* performance, there was to be another modern piece over the summer that involved a poem read at the beginning and the little booklets for it were in a dusty box up there. Madame Angulaire was set to choreograph the next one, and she wanted masks without faces, asymmetrical and opposing movements, and costumes that matched the chaotic theme. Madame Roberts was to be the director next season of the annual *Nutcracker* ballet. The Sugar Plum Fairy's costume was the most beautiful of all and it was a shame to be getting all dirty up here, thought Natalie, as she peeked around corners and lifted random box lids filled with music and smaller props and accessories. There was no one in this attic, so she systematically went down to the next level and the next and the next and the next until she reached the basement.

In the basement, Natalie did not know where the single light bulb was and was blinded by the sudden darkness of the cave. Groping around, with only a bit of the stairwell lights she had turned back on to guide her way, she bumped into the string hanging down from the ceiling, and down she pulled until the entire cave lit up. Down here there were other props and things, but they were much larger in general: backdrops, wooden swords, sets that were not painted yet, and other objects for cutting and sanding wood. A large costume trunk sat in a far-off corner, and Natalie walked toward it.

Dawn could finally hear footsteps, and she screamed again with all the energy she could muster out of the great fire from hunger and fatigue that was ravaging her body.

III

PART THREE

CHAPTER I

Natalie jumped back from the fright. "D-d-d-awn, my dear, is that you?"

"Help me! Yes, it's Dawn. Get me out of this trunk!"

Natalie ran over to the trunk and realized that it was locked with some sort of key. Frantically looking around, she figured that the monster who had put her in here must have gotten rid of the key, so she switched to searching for some kind of wrench to pry the lock open.

"Dawn, don't you worry! I've just got to get this lock off. It's Natalie!"

Dawn's face grew wet with tears again at this luck—her stomach, by this point, was cramping up badly.

There was a pile of tools beside one of the unfinished wood projects. The only thing Natalie could think to use on the lock was the handsaw lying there. Picking it up, she tried with all of her strength to saw through the metal, but nothing really came from grinding away on it for a few minutes. Natalie needed to find someone with the proper tools.

Pulling her phone from her sweater pocket, Natalie called 911, and within five minutes, the lock had been cut off with a pair of bolt cutters.

Dawn was pale and sweaty, her hair was a mess, and Natalie had to untie all the fabric that was wrapped around her before she could successfully escape the trunk.

A policeman said, "We had been looking for you for the last few hours. I'm glad your friend here knew where to look or else it could have taken us much longer. Who did this to you?" He flipped open his notepad, and Dawn told them how she was fooled by Madame Angulaire.

Other police headed to Madame's home, only to find that she had fled—all of her most important belongings were missing from the house.

"Thank you, Natalie. How did you know where to look?" asked Dawn, who was wrapped in a blanket and given a tiny amount of lukewarm broth in a thermos to drink.

"Well, I knew you would never go anywhere far from this theater. I assumed this was the most obvious place to look thoroughly for you. Not to mention, I told you I had seen the arguments between your two teachers. Anywhere the conflict is, the trouble is," said Natalie.

Dawn looked up at her savior in admiration for the first time. This woman was so down-to-earth in the way she thought and behaved. It was like nothing in life could really scare her or knock her down. When problems arose, she shined. Like in combing through the theater, she knew Dawn loved...and perhaps even Natalie loved. This fiasco was not the theater's fault. It was the people who filled it that could betray such a beautiful building.

Sharing in that love brought Dawn back and Natalie peace this early morning. There was still an hour left before students would start to come in, so once the police had all the information they could collect at the moment, Dawn and Natalie left the theater. Dawn went back home with her parents and spent the rest of the day in bed, nursing her aching muscles and stomach after all of that excitement. The performance was that evening and Dawn had *no* intention of going back.

Natalie visited Dawn later that day, after she had taken a nap and settled her nerves. She had had her cup of tea and breakfast and slept in her sweater on the couch in front of the empty fireplace of her tiny, cozy home. That poor girl will be traumatized forever by this teacher, thought Natalie. What can I do to help that girl? I could bake her a cake, or read to her, or write a soothing poem for her to carry around. "What do you think, Mister Kitty?" The cat meowed for its food. "Well, that's not very helpful at all." She got up to feed the cat and then headed over to Dawn's house, taking some extra homemade cookies along with her.

Meanwhile, Dawn was reviewing every step of that awful evening in her head: from Madame Angulaire asking her to stay after class to her moving from one side of the stage to the other to the dark silence that filled her ears for hours with only her stomach's cries for food reminding her she was alive.

How could a dance teacher do such a heinous thing to another dancer? wondered Dawn. What did she do to deserve such a response? Yes, she had gained a little bit of weight—did that really mean she had to starve in a costume trunk for her sins? Madame Roberts never did such a thing to her...

In fact, when Madame Roberts heard the news, she rushed right over to Dawn's house in tears. "Dawn! Oh, my girl, I'm so sorry! How could she do that to you? It's not your fault you're still healing!"

Dawn tried to raise herself on her elbows to get some air

over Madame Roberts's tight squeeze. "I've been trying to figure that out myself. She initially told me that my injury would be my strength as a dancer, and I'm not even sure she was upset about me still needing to wear a boot...I think she was more upset that I gained weight. For some reason, that fact set her off. She wants her dancers to look starving for the performance to show how tirelessly the working dancers work for the Academy and the people. I told her I would lose the weight as soon as I could, but the next thing I see is the lid of the trunk being slammed in my face."

"Oh, Dawn, if I had known she was this crazy, I would have never allowed her to teach at my Academy! I'm so, so, so sorry."

"That's okay, at least I know now who to trust. I'm sorry I was angry with you for just wanting me to heal. I just thought that if I didn't make ballet my career that I would die. I still feel that way...but...well, maybe I'll need to find something else." Dawn's body shook as the drops fell heavy on her arms. She had never considered letting ballet go until now; now that it was scared out of her, now that she had faced the possibility of starving to death in a box under the theater. Had she been dancing for death or life this whole time?

**

Perhaps she had never really thought about where ballet came from and what she was doing it for. There was simply a drive, a push by the dancers around her to move forward on this ride toward prima-ballerina-hood. She trained like a knight who would be armed for combat when the hard times came in her ballet career. There was an utter faith in her teachers that they would be the keys to her success. She never questioned their backgrounds or why they chose to devote their lives to dance. She obeyed orders like all the good little students.

It was only when Madame Angulaire came Dawn began to think about the meaning of ballet. What was ballet meant to convey? wondered Dawn. Was it just meant to entertain people or teach them a lesson or both? Madame Roberts's classes always felt like they had a purpose to them. You had to straighten your legs to create a straight line because straight lines on a human body were beautiful. She taught combinations meant for the human body or for prepared choreography for a performance that followed a story. There was a beginning, middle, and an end to every class and every performance.

But Madame Angulaire's classes had no purpose to them nor a beginning, middle, or end. There was no story or meaning. It was a combination of movements driven by emotions from creatures without a mind—without *reason*. The movements may entertain an audience, but they must leave a foul taste in their mouths afterward if they were honest. No one wants to imagine themselves with no direction or purpose, writhing in the dirt of the earth, like a worm in the sun. There were also no straight lines, only peculiar angles and opposing movements that boggled the reasoning mind and confounded the soul.

One class left Dawn feeling inspired and ready for the world, while the other left her feeling hopeless and unwilling to rise from bed the next morning. Dawn imagined that an audience must come away from a ballet with the same messages—one that wanted them to continue living and one that wanted them to die.

Dawn had never seen her teachers before in such a clear way. It had taken a near-death experience to enlighten her, and she was almost thankful for it. Today, Dawn learned an invaluable lesson, and she wanted to share it with someone…with Natalie.

After Madame Roberts finished her apologies and left, Dawn called out for her mother.

"Mom! Can you come here? I need something!" said Dawn.

Her mother came swiftly, hoping to ease any of Dawn's suffering in the hopes of mitigating it, as all good mothers do. "What is it you need, sweetheart?"

"Can you ask for Natalie to come over? I want to talk to her."

"Sure. I'll go give her a call right away. I'm sure she'd love to see you. She seems like a nice lady."

"She is, she is, Mom."

Dawn's mother got a hold of Natalie, and she came over faster than either of them expected, perhaps wishing to mimic the motherly sentiment. "What is it, dear? What do you need?" asked Natalie with her hair sloppily done up and her makeup not finished.

"I just wanted to tell you I think I get it. I think I know why my teachers are fighting. It's like a deep battle between them of life and death."

Natalie squeezed Dawn's shoulders and smiled.

"No, I mean it."

"I know you do! I wasn't laughing at you. I'm just glad you are putting the pieces together at such a young age; I suppose an event like the one you just went through will age a person. So, tell me about what you have learned."

"Well, Madame Roberts is teaching classical ballet that wants people to live, and Madame Angulaire is teaching modern ballet that wants people to die."

"A very stark, yet astute, observation, my dear. Tell me more." Natalie continued rubbing Dawn's shoulders.

"I always felt different after each teacher's class, but I could never put words to it before. I even thought that Madame Angulaire's teaching style was more freeing and expressive than Madame Roberts's. How foolish I was! Every time I danced with Madame Roberts I felt good and with the other teacher I felt bad, almost *guilty*..."

"You know, I observed Madame Angulaire teach her first few classes here from the studio window, and I also had to figure out for myself why her coming here felt like such a violation. Why did I feel so violently disgusted by what she was teaching these young, impressionable dancers? I sat on that couch you were on before for many nights thinking and reading and researching until I remembered encountering that same feeling before when I was a young student in school." Natalie settled into a chair by Dawn's bedside in her room. "I hope you don't mind if I tell you a bit of a long story, my dear."

Dawn shook her head. "No, I don't plan on doing much for the next week—no school, no ballet classes. Everyone heard what happened and my teachers all understand. A girl from my class is going to be bringing me my homework so that's good, I guess. Go on. Tell me how you figured it out."

"Well, I hadn't felt that kind of disgust in years. The last time I could remember was when I was in high school, which was back in the '80s! I had a teacher named Mr. Glendale. Now, my school was somewhat religious when I was growing up, but it had never been crammed down my throat before. But Mr. Glendale was the first teacher to tell me I had original sin and that I was privileged to be at that school. He taught English and we read books about the poor, the tired, and the sick.

"Mr. Glendale felt that none of us had given enough to

those underprivileged people. He felt we had no right to complain ever, and he even snuck the ruler punishments back in when he didn't think he would be caught by any higher-ups who frowned upon the practice—not that it was illegal or anything at that time—just frowned upon if there were other alternatives for the teachers to discipline the student with.

"Anyway, my teacher also talked about how we never did enough for our fellow imperfect man. We read a story, in particular, about a little boy from rural Iowa whose parents were drug addicts and he was hungry. The only thing left in the fridge was a packet of ketchup from some fast food place. Well, one day the parents came home from buying more drinks at the liquor store with what little welfare money they had left for the month and found their son dead on the living room floor. They chose to spend the extra money they had on their alcohol rather than on food for their son.

"And you want to know what my teacher thought we all should take from that lesson? It was not that the parents were scum and they are responsible for him, instead it was that the village did not look out for its people. Other people are to blame for the parents being on welfare and hooked on drugs. It was *other* people who killed an innocent boy. My teacher said that the boy only gave in to the true desires of his parents— they did not really want him, so he got rid of the problem.

"I left the class feeling rotten and out of control over my own life. It was like Mr. Glendale had discarded all of my free will and placed it in the hands of this anonymous outside group. I had no control over my actions or the way my life was going. I had to trust 'my village,' which I had to respect and always stay obedient to because I was bound to need them at some point. There were no equal trades in Mr. Glendale's mind, only sacrifices to be made at the expense of others.

"Of course, I could never articulate it this well until many years later, when I discovered I could get up without an alarm clock and there was no more homework or school to attend. Once I entered adulthood, I was the only one in charge of how my days were spent. I was often plagued by the question: 'Why am I doing this?' The answers that automatically came up for me were: 'Well, because other people need your help.' But then, those automatic responses faded, and I thought more and more about how these jobs had made me feel.

"Today, I work for myself. I take responsibility for my life and the outcomes that stem from it. Now, I'm not naive. I know I cannot completely control illness or accidents, but I can eat healthily, get enough sleep, and exercise safely to minimize the risks. *I* am in charge and no one else. You must realize this for yourself, Dawn."

Natalie's eyes were fiery like they were prepared to do battle, and it made her face so much younger. Dawn could see the glow emanating from her skin, which made the wrinkles fade. Her loose neck skin appeared less noticeable because she lifted her head up so much higher as she spoke. Natalie used to be beautiful when she was young. Dawn felt closer to her now.

"Natalie, I feel like these past few days have been a slap in the face to me that not all adults are right. They are not infallible as I believed they were before. But when I was dancing for Madame Angulaire, I feel like she made me express dark and nihilistic ideas much more powerfully than with Madame Roberts. Can those darker emotions be portrayed better in classical ballet than modern?" asked Dawn.

"Why, yes. By having control over your own life, you still may encounter tragedy. Like when my husband died suddenly.

I lost the love of my life, but the rest of my life would be colored by how I dealt with the situation. Just like in ballet, Giselle is heartbroken by Albrecht for not being who she thought he was. Now, in the story, she dies as a result of this discovery, which is the ultimate tragedy one can suffer. But the movements have her falling gracefully to the floor, always conscious of her lines and the angles she is creating with her body. The audience watches her get back up again and run toward her lover and then turn away with her head in her hands. We watch her mood change from emotionally broken to sheer madness until her heart gives out. But she is always dancing with delicate fingers and soft, turned-out feet. She is always in control of her mind, even when she is showing the audience the height of madness. Ballet is an integrated system of mind and body. It never betrays that connection or else it will lose the honest audience.

"Today's audience, like much of the world at large, is mixed. It's full of people who are confused about whether to use their minds or shut them off for fear of betrayal. It's full of people who are told by philosophers not to trust themselves and politicians who second that notion. The village of no names controls your life just in case your mind decides to power off. Just in case you decide to shoot someone or rob someone or harm yourself without reason. As a result, our world has become smaller, sicklier, and weak in the confines of what sometimes feels like one big psychiatric hospital. There must be rules in place to keep all of us in line."

It was at this time that Dawn was feeling nauseous. She never realized how set up and stuck everyone was in this confusing mire of ideas. People do not know what to think. All she could say was, "What a shame…"

Natalie nodded sadly. "Yes. And our culture is just an outcome of all those beliefs mixed together. Let's look at ballet again. We have a culture of ballet that now has a smattering of the classical and then a smattering of the modern. It reflects all of us attempting to separate our minds from our bodies, as if we were preparing to leave the body and just input the mind into a chip. But would that hold anything that was us? Truly us? We require both mind and body. We need to touch and feel this world, but only our brains process those sensations and make sense of them. Ballet without a head is ugly; ballet with a head is beautiful. Next time you watch a ballet class or a ballet performance, monitor your emotional reactions. It is usually your subconscious that gives you that first inkling of something being off or something being right. When a dancer lifts their leg into a split, a perfect one hundred eighty degrees, does that make you feel satisfied? When a dancer collapses on the floor like they are actually having a seizure, does that make you feel uneasy? Watch each movement and analyze it."

"I will," said Dawn. "I promise."

Natalie smiled as she gripped Dawn's hand in hers. She knew this was her moment to have a daughter of her own—a daughter of dance—that she would teach how to enjoy and appreciate dance. It was a gift that she was given as a child and now she wanted Dawn to share in it too.

"But, Natalie, I'm ashamed to say it, but…well, how can people your age…older people still enjoy ballet? I thought it was only for the young? And even for the young and most fit, it still is near impossible to be perfect at it."

"It's all right," Natalie laughed. "I understand. I thought old people were all useless too when I was your age. Although when you get older, fifty-five won't seem so old to you

185

anymore."

Impossible, thought Dawn.

"It's true. But anyway, to your question, older people are not the focus of classical ballet, that's true. And I venture to say that most of the adults in the adult ballet classes learned mainly when they were children. They just have the muscle memory and flexibility from childhood to guide them through an adult class naturally. It's difficult to teach adults new tricks when their bodies are already matured. However, that doesn't mean that we cannot work on new things repeatedly and improve slowly over time." Natalie sat up in her chair by Dawn's bed. She bent forward to show Dawn more of herself.

"Look, I know I have wrinkles around my eyes and mouth. I know my lips are becoming puckered. I can see the veins on my legs popping out more than before. I am not as tall as I used to be any longer. I have new moles and bumps and lumps of various kinds all the time. I am aging. It happens to everyone. I am not holding out on doctors reversing it all anytime soon. 'Old people' are not oblivious to the changes, though there are things we do in life that make us forget, sure. When I dance in class, I revert to the smooth-skinned, thinner version of myself."

"But...the mirrors everywhere?" asked Dawn.

"Eh! My eyesight is not powerful enough to see all the wrinkles from across the room. I look and feel much younger in a leotard and tights, dancing in a room filled with mirrors, than I am showering in my own home. I hope that someday, when the culture is better, we will have a classical ballet that is not just for professionals or students who will be future professionals. I do wish my classes were slower."

Dawn sat up a bit more, curious about ballet becoming

something different. She asked, "Slower how?"

"Well, all the teachers tend to teach classes the same way, including center work. But for adults who still want to learn something new, I envision the center work, after all the warming-up work at the barre, to be focused on one, single movement or combination. The rest of class, maybe thirty minutes or so, could be focused on, let's say, how to raise and lower the arms. Another class could be just a series of *pas de chats* back and forth across the floor. But the teacher would have much more time to describe and explain the muscles doing the work and the meaning of the words and the total execution of the step. The more information is provided for the adults, the more refined their steps will be. Now, that's not to say that we do not have to practice and work on it repeatedly, but it is to say that running through center work and expecting the adults to improve is mistaken. I have been with Madame Roberts and her mother since childhood up to the present and I still cannot do *double pirouettes*. Maybe my body was just not made to turn, but if I had had someone slow down and really make me practice one piece of the movement at a time, then maybe I would have been able to do it eventually."

"Adults don't seem to practice enough on their own though," said Dawn.

"That's very true, honey. I agree, and that's why maybe the center work should also be simpler—more based around graceful walking and curtsying or simple waltzes. Just because we lost our splits doesn't mean that we cannot feel the same way about ballet. Dancing still makes me feel graceful and beautiful, regardless of whether my leg is almost up to my ear. The young can strive toward pushing their bodies, but the old should focus on maintaining and appreciating the grace they have gained both in and out of the studio."

CHAPTER II

Dawn carefully observed Natalie describing the gifts she got from dancing, and a slight glow in her soul made Dawn want to explore the perspective that Natalie had of the world. Being only fifteen, she found it too hard to separate herself from her life of ballet from the beginning to the present. It all still seemed so fresh, so new, so feverish. Still being "in" the dance world, Dawn could not look back on her days with enough distance like Natalie.

"Natalie, you mentioned before that you were sort of 'in and out' of ballet classes. What did that mean?" asked Dawn.

"It means that there would be a year or two in between ballet classes, sometimes even more. I once went six years without it in my life as an adult, and I truly came to miss it so much that I would find myself dancing around the kitchen as I was making my meals. I knew that that meant I had to go back to fill that craving. I bet you know what that dance bug is like," smiled Natalie.

"Oh, of course. Except the bug for me barely lets me take a day away from ballet classes. I'm thankful my parents always scraped up enough for me to take classes every season." Dawn squeezed her fingers together to lessen the guilt erupting from her last statement. Her parents may not like her obsession, but they always allowed her to follow it.

"Yes, you are lucky in that way. I was not so lucky. Ballet class and all that came with it was a luxury for me. But now that I'm an adult and can choose where to put my money, I always find a spot for a class with Madame Roberts."

Pressing her fingers now into her legs, Dawn sighed and said, "I think maybe I need a year to think all of this over. I don't know, maybe to gain some distance. It seems like an impossible task, but I feel so mixed up right now with how I feel about dance. Now in class, I am overcome by the deepest sorrow, the bitterest jealousy, and yet the truest depths of inspiration. I constantly compare myself to the other dancers in the room, beating myself or the others up for flaws. I envy those girls with better extensions than me or more perfect turns or jumps or whatever we are reviewing that day. I absolutely despise the adult classes I watch because I thought they were too old to waste Madame Roberts's time…" Dawn paused and peeked quickly up at Natalie's face, trying to gauge its expression. She looked stone-faced.

"Go on," said Natalie.

"Well, and yet when I do get back to focusing on myself, I am always in awe of what my body remembered about corrections and tricky combinations. I am inspired to see my kicks swing up in the air the way they do. I am proud of how much work my one leg can support, and I just love feeling the weightlessness that ballet can give you. I am flying every class. And I just want to feel that more, not less, with the way things have been going lately."

Natalie could see where she was going with this and was heartbroken by the thought. "So…so you won't be going back there for a while then, will you?"

"No, I don't think I will," said Dawn. "I need to heal this dumb ankle to the best of my ability, like Madame Roberts wanted. I'm sure I'll lose a lot of my technique and muscle mass, but I'd rather be back prepared to fight than be unprepared and hurt."

"I think that's a very mature decision for a young woman, such as yourself, to make."

"Thank you. Will you still be seeing Madame Roberts?"

"Yes, would you like me to tell her you're focusing on your health for now and will not be back for a while?"

"Oh, would you? I can't even look at her right now. I feel so ashamed, like the biggest failure at that Academy for not going on with my class and auditioning for companies. I still can't believe I won't die for going against this path. What did I work so hard for if not to get into a company soon?" Swiftly hiding her face in her hands, Dawn cried.

A soothing back rub kept Dawn grounded as Natalie told her about what life could be like outside of ballet classes. "You know, most adults get up in the morning, they have their breakfasts, kiss their children goodbye on the way to school, and go to work until the evening when dinner and social time begin. In the adult world, things are chaotic while the children are small and become slower as they grow up. But it is certainly not as packed full of stress as the professional dancer's schedule is. You can ease into and out of your day beside the one you love and the rest all falls in between those heavenly moments. A life is a series of actions fit into a day, followed by another day, followed by another. The amount of change you decide to implement is up to you. Isn't that powerful?"

Dawn nodded. "I never had time to even think of boys when

191

I was dancing. There was no room for anyone else. I just wanted one thing. Do adults just want one thing?"

Natalie chuckled. "No, most adults are expert jugglers. For them, a happy life comprises a strong relationship and family life, which is bolstered by friends and pets and food and work and things, and, especially, love. They are well-rounded and love in many varying ways. In a way, the balanced life is one where everything that happens in a day brings some kind of joy—even if that joy takes work to earn it, like washing the laundry to get clean clothes."

Joy—that word is one that Dawn wanted but had not gotten yet in life. She wanted to feel a constant sense of joy. "I mean to 'defect' then from modern ballet. I renounce it and someday, when I sort myself out, I hope to rejoin the world of classical ballet...if it will accept me back."

"I'm sure it will," said Natalie, as she gave Dawn a hug.

***

The next morning, Dawn woke up feeling empty and afraid. Without ballet as her primary focus, she felt like she had lost the shell that protected and kept her safe. Today would be her first day back at school without ballet classes before and afterward. She was going to be normal, like the other students. A tiny whirl of exhilaration lit up her stomach at the thought of coming home when it was still light out and just taking a walk outside or relaxing in front of the television, leisurely working on her homework, instead of being in a mad rush she usually was in to get everything done in her day.

For the first time, Dawn sat in class, considering all of her subjects and how they made her feel. What did she love, if not ballet? What were her strengths and what were her weaknesses? Ballet is an art, so maybe I should stick to that

192

field, thought Dawn. I really like my biology class, but I'm not very good with math and all the scientific vocabulary that comes with it. I do like my English class and my history class, although sometimes I get a bad gut feeling about what they are teaching me...kind of like how Natalie felt with Mr. Glendale. But if I could just read and evaluate the books myself, then perhaps I'd love those subjects without the bad gut feeling. Her recent interest in her studies would surely bring her grades up too so that a good college would take her even if she didn't pursue dance as a major.

Coming home from her first day back, Dawn found her mother in the kitchen. She was turning on some quiet piano music and tying an apron around her when Dawn came in.

"Hi, sweetie," said her mother. "How was school?"

"Good! Did you know *Hamlet* is Shakespeare's longest play?"

"No, I did not know that."

"Did you also know that the Louisiana Purchase was made in 1803 for only four cents an acre?"

"Boy, you're absorbing things like a sponge, I see. I'm very glad," smiled Dawn's mother.

"Yup, I spent my day trying to envision myself in another career, or at least another area of study for college. I think I'm strongest in the arts and humanities, though I like science too, and even math and physics are interesting, but I'm no good at them."

"I used to like the same subjects when I was your age. I loved English. I remember each book I got being like a piece of candy I got to enjoy. Do you remember when I took you to the library all the time as a baby up until you started to think libraries were not the 'cool places' to be?"

Blushing, Dawn said, "Yes, I remember some of my earliest

memories in the school and public library, where I'd find the smallest little corners to hide myself in with a book. The carpets were always so colorful and soft. I can still feel the warm glow of the darkened library and its wooden shelves. I can recall the little ruler-like sticks to put in between the books, so we wouldn't mess up the library's system. I was always very careful to put the stick in gently and pull it out when I was done."

Closing her eyes, Dawn also recalled watching movies on the moon landing and other historical documentaries on the projector screen in the library, and it was so magical. Everyone around her knew things, and all of it was so new and fresh. It seemed like she learned something new all day long.

It seemed like bliss to be learning all day and not having to worry about how much you were making for a living. Frequently, Dawn was given the opportunity, like on the weekends, to just sit down and read for hours on end, getting lost in a different world from her own. She missed the escape that only ballet used to bring her.

"Hey, I'm just starting to cook dinner and it will take a couple of hours. Do you mind helping me or do you have a lot of homework to do today? If you do, then that's fine, I understand." Dawn's mother pulled out some large bowls and measuring spoons from one of the upper cabinets.

"Sure, Mom. I'd like that."

Dawn reached for another apron and began pulling it over her head, trying carefully not to pull her bobby pins out of her hair. "What are we cooking?"

"Tonight, we are making chicken, potatoes, and asparagus. Does that sound good to you?"

"Oh, yes. All of those things sound delicious!"

"Good, I'm glad because that is what you're getting tonight whether you all like it or not!" she laughed. "Now go turn the oven on to four hundred twenty-five degrees, while I rinse and chop up the asparagus."

"Yes, Mom. Then do you want me to peel and rinse the potatoes?"

"Yes, please."

They stood at the island of their kitchen, the marble counter held out all the excess juices and water until a paper towel absorbed them into its puffy skin.

"Okay, now heat up one tablespoon of that olive oil over there, while I put foil over the baking sheet and season the chicken."

Dawn simply followed her mother's orders. She forgot how much she sometimes just enjoyed being her little yellow-tufted duckling, waddling around trying to pick up bread crumbs. She still felt small compared to her all-knowing mother. It was comforting to still cling to her and her certainty about reality and the way life worked.

"Okay, I browned both sides of the chicken already for about two minutes on each side on the stovetop. Now, we can take the chicken and place it in the oven with the potatoes and asparagus for about five minutes on each side. Sometimes the vegetables will need a bit more time than the chicken, but we'll keep our eyes on it. Okay?"

"Yes, Mom," said Dawn. "Someday I hope I'm as good a cook as you."

Her mother smiled and tried not to cry. It had been a while since her daughter had really wanted her for anything. When she was first born, she needed something *constantly*, but by the time she could walk and talk, that all dwindled. She was a full-time mother for so short a time.

Sighing, Dawn's mother turned to the oven to finish up the dinner, while Dawn daydreamed about a new life with time and family and love in it. She imagined a life without the gnawing competition that caused her stress and such emotional pain. She no longer had to engage with herself in the mirror anymore—facing every imperfection she saw and then comparing herself to the others. No longer would she care about where everyone else was in line to become the next good meat sold to the ballet companies. She was free! Free to laze around and feel the sun's rays tickle her face, free to dance when her body and soul needed it most, free to enjoy every moment of every day! Dawn paced around the living room all giddy and that night after a delicious dinner, she could not fall asleep for hours.

By the next morning, Dawn felt exhausted. She rolled out of bed and the energy rush she experienced yesterday was missing in action. It was Saturday, so there was no school and she did all of her homework on Friday night already.

I think I should visit Natalie and tell her all about my dreams, thought Dawn. After all, she is the one who said she would help me onto this novel path.

Natalie was at home, still in her nightgown, which she was a bit ashamed about when she opened the door to let Dawn in.

"Oh, hello! I was not expecting you to come over so soon," Natalie said as she combed back her hair with her fingers. "Let me just get into something more appropriate and then we can catch up, okay?"

"You don't have to dress up for me," said Dawn.

"Oh, it's more for me, dear, than you. Take a seat on the couch and I'll be right there. Please feel free to get yourself a glass of water or let me know if you would like any tea. Did you eat breakfast already?"

"Yes, I'm fine. I'll just get a glass of water." Dawn walked to the kitchen and took her time enjoying how at home she felt there. She could see herself calling Natalie her children's godmother and having them play on the floor with their toys, while the two of them caught up on the latest news. Dawn could envision for the first time Natalie, old though she already was, sitting on the comfy chair next to her knitting and listening to her baby woes, like a fountain full of wisdom rather than youth. Granted, if Dawn could keep herself from aging, she still would. But she saw Natalie in a much more kindly light after seeing her take a role in her life.

"Natalie, do you think a person can ever be happy being a professional ballet dancer?"

Natalie walked out of her room in a dress that accentuated her hips and minimized her torso. She looked very feminine.

"I do, but it takes a lot of hard work and even pain to get to a place, I think, where you are happy with yourself. Why?"

"I just never seemed to be happy in class."

"Now, even I don't believe that. You must have had moments of happiness, otherwise, you would never have continued as long as you did...unless you're a masochist," chuckled Natalie. "My guess is, and you have every right to feel this way, that you started to hate ballet by the end because you were no longer dancing for yourself anymore. I'm sure Madame Angulaire told you to snuff yourself out and dance for the group. Didn't she?"

"How did you know that?"

"Once you are my age, you can tell a lot about people and their beliefs just by seeing the way they interact with others. I

197

watched her scold you and menace you with her facial features. I can't say I saw her hit you—"

"She did."

"Well, then, that just further proves my point," said Natalie. "That teacher ruined the purity and strength you found ballet gives you. Without dancing for yourself and your own enjoyment, then what is the point? Bandaging up your blistered toes and icing your legs every night is *not* worth it if you are doing it for others."

Nodding her head up and down in silence, Dawn was putting together the pieces she had been missing before. Ballet was not inherently bad but the teachers could be.

"Hey, I've got an idea. Do you want to paint our nails while we talk?" asked Dawn. This spontaneous desire struck Dawn after it came out of her mouth as childish and she blushed.

Natalie caught the emotion and said, "Of course! Let me go get the few colors that I have. They're mostly pastels, I'm afraid. I hope you like those." Nearly jumping up from the couch, almost like a sprightly girl herself, Natalie got the nail polish.

The powerful odor, for some strange reason, gave Dawn the confidence to push through the hard knot she was trying to unwind.

"But Natalie, why do I feel such a thrill at not having to do ballet anymore now?"

"Ah, well, you were too stressed out with the whole situation that it was no longer fun anymore, nor was it worth the struggle to get in and out of tights and a leotard. The hard work that you put in does not hold you back from your passion, but it takes a much greater effort if you don't like what you're doing anymore. Does that make sense, deary?"

There was a long pause before Dawn could say: "She made me crawl around on the floor like I was nothing."

Both women began crying: Dawn for herself and the way she felt with her teacher, and Natalie for Dawn's suffering at the hands of an adult, like herself.

"I'm so sorry, Dawn. Ballet is not about putting you down, it should be all about lifting you up and your audience, then taking away the same message." She blotted a tissue under her eyes and then wiped Dawn's own tears away with it. "Someday, you will find your way back to ballet. I don't know how long it will take, but there will be an aching in your heart which nothing can fill but the movement of your own body in the confines of classical ballet."

"I know. I still can't envision my life without being in that studio every day, let alone leaving and coming back after a break."

"I don't mean to keep coming back to my own tragedy, but it is the only real parallel I can draw to how you may be feeling now. When my husband died, I thought I would never fall in love again. He was my soul mate and the only one I could envision myself being with in this life. I felt the most enormous hole inside of me when he died because we had been living together as a couple for years. It was just long enough for me to forget what living alone was like or even living with roommates. I was united and utterly attached to another human being, like vines intertwined around a tree. We did a dance together of love and living.

"To me, there was no one else who matched me so well. But I had no choice when I lost him but to accept the hole and minimize the pain when I could. I actually plugged the hole with the cork of the drink for a while."

"Really?" Dawn looked at this sweet old woman with astonishment.

"Yes. Going to and from work, exhausted, hungry, and feeling unloved daily, left me to reach for what I imagined was my only friend. It took me a long time to heal and discover that the bottle didn't return the feeling. I started therapy as so many others do and cried over and over again for my loss. They were deep bitter tears, but they had to come in order for me to continue breathing...for the both of us.

"I did eventually go back to dating for a while when an ache came back for simply holding another person close at night. Still being alive and having needs, I missed warm kisses and the attention of someone other than my cat." Natalie glanced over at her old cat and said, "Sorry."

Dawn could not help but giggle as she sat there, feeling the same kind of hole in *her* heart that Natalie was describing concerning her husband. It was nice to know that at least other people can feel similarly and as deeply, thought Dawn. But how did she survive it? Especially growing old alone?

"Natalie?"

"Yes, dear?"

Dawn wrapped the blanket she draped over herself around her hand. She looked like a large boulder all squished up on the couch like that. She cleared her throat, preparing herself to ask another personal question: "Do you think your husband ever tried contacting you on earth?"

The answer was already clear on Natalie's blank face. "Sadly, no. I still talk to him and have dreams about him, but those are all just to make *me* feel better. I just think he's gone, which is why it took me a long time to heal and then to make sure I continued to live whatever life I had left. I met new people who I am grateful to have met and bonded with…but I never could marry another or have them move in with me. I will never be a whole person again. I'm afraid you won't either, Dawn. It happens to, I'd say, most people. They lose something in life and are never whole again without it.

"You will also think what-if about your ballet career if you hadn't ruptured that Achilles tendon. You will always feel a pang of jealousy about the younger dancers and the chance they have to make a career for themselves, unlike you. And yet, that hole left will shrink with time and the ability to taste ballet now and then. You will take classes with the adults and hate yourself for ending up here in the beginning, but after a while, the older dancers, stronger dancers, more technical dancers will fade away and you will learn to live moment by moment. I know that sounds too simple, but it is really the most refreshing experience you can give to yourself.

"Never forget the sunlight that streams in through that rose-looking window, or the spots where the oak floor creaks, or the smell of baby powder and new pointe shoes and rosin. Remember Madame Roberts showing you combinations and how young she looked doing it. Remember the piano, especially when we had a real pianist in class, and the soft notes guiding us along the path to rejuvenation. Allow your very bones to feel the *pliés* that woke up your body to the challenging work of ballet class. You used your whole body to express what you felt those mornings. And by the afternoon, your body was warm and at home with the idea of movement. Movement and you were in sync.

"Those are the memories I hold most dear to me now and they are ones I am grateful for every time I get to go to class. And I will *keep* going until I physically cannot any longer.

Madame Roberts will have to allow me to modify many of the steps for comfort as I age, but at least she will let me dance in the adult class. I will *always* dance, and even when I cannot physically, I can go back in my mind to that sunny spot and dance in there.

Both women shed fresh tears for what ballet had already done and was still doing for them—both young and old.

CHAPTER III

Sniffling, Dawn squeezed Natalie hard. "Teach me how to see life the way you do. I can't only feel that way in ballet class. There must be more. Right?"

"Yes, I did find other things in life to enjoy, but each experience brings with it a different kind of joy. For example, falling in love is not a joy I will be able to teach you. I'm sure you will find a young man someday to experience that with. But I can teach you to live slower and be grateful for more of the things around you. I'm not sure how successful I will be with a girl of your age. Believe me, when I say that slow living is easier the older you are, but I suppose it's never too early to start either. I wish I had learned it as a teenager," said Natalie, as she stood up slowly and stretched out her aching back.

Dawn got up swiftly, without pain in her back. She knew nothing of the aches and pains that lay ahead of her.

"Hey, I have an idea, but I'm not sure if you are ready for it," said Natalie.

"Oh, yeah? And what's that?"

"What if you and I be audience members for once? Let's go see a ballet performance. Perhaps that will give you a different perspective. I think the downtown theater is doing *Swan Lake*."

Dawn nearly tripped over herself as she turned around to

face Natalie. Didn't she know that being an audience member is like being a cuckolded man to a dancer? thought Dawn. Sitting there, watching other copycats follow the steps that she knew like they were second nature? To be ridiculed by those that still could over those who could no longer? Touching her warm cheeks, Dawn knew she was hot with anger.

Natalie watched the conflict unfolding in Dawn's mind, which she tried to assuage immediately. "Look Dawn, I'm sorry. Like I said, maybe it's too early—"

"Too early? Too early?!" cried Dawn, snatching up her sweater in a fit of pure rage. "When will I ever be able to watch other people doing what I love? How could I ever be okay with my love for every step in those classics being caressed and used by other dancers' feet?!"

"Shhh, shhh, shhh. Hush, dear." Natalie wrapped her arms around the weeping girl.

"We don't have to go if you don't want to. I just thought that maybe it would help you with your decision about whether or not to go back. I mean, if you still feel that strongly, then maybe taking a gap year isn't actually a good idea. Do you understand?"

For a moment, Dawn paused. She just prostrated herself in front of her art form, yet she had *no* desire to go back. What did all this mean? She felt more confused than before. She paced around the little living room in silence, while Natalie watched her with worry in her eyes. There was a rhythm made by Dawn's hobbling on her bad, booted-up leg and teetering back onto her good one. In a lull of contemplation, Dawn finally said: "What time does the ballet start?"

Natalie's features lifted, and she looked young again. "Well, there's a matinee in about fifteen minutes. Let's go!"

Both of them recklessly picked up the items that they thought they might need, dressed in their street clothes, and dashed to the car like two drug addicts heading for their next fix. They were addicted to ballet and every way that it touched their lives. It kept them vital. It was something to live for.

After barely stopping the car, Dawn threw her seat belt off and launched out the door. This theater was more modern, and it had much more efficient lights, a heating and cooling system, and newer wood that creaked less. The carpets, of course, were still of a deep, blood-red color that just tickled Dawn. There were certain things that a theater always had, and those carpets were one feature. It felt like home to both of the women. They breathed in deeply and sensed the tension building up before a performance given by real people who had real goals and dreams. They had emotions like Dawn, but her empathy with the other dancers stopped when the curtains opened and the trumpets boomed in the courtyard awaiting the arrival of Prince Siegfried and again when all the beautiful swans appeared.

I could easily have been one of those swans, seethed Dawn. *How could I be so ready and yet be so far away from my dream...or it was my dream?* For the next couple of hours, she spent the time looking at the person's head in front of her, the floor, and the stage. She could feel the movements at the moment and the pure physical geometry that their precise movements executed so well.

Odette was gorgeous in her white tutu and the crown atop her head. She moved her arms as gracefully as if she had real wings. It caused Dawn such miserable pain to know that she would not be seen nor captivate an audience the way this soloist was today. Her lines were gorgeous and long. All of her flighty steps felt like she really could rise up off the ground by herself.

The jealousy started in the pit of Dawn's stomach and crawled up to her neck. Swallowing hard, she tried to hold all the bitterness she felt down. But by the end of Act III when Prince Siegfried dances with Odile instead of Odette, tears were the only way she could pour out her mixed sorrows. Salty, bitter tears at losing his love and Dawn losing her dreams. She clenched her teeth and clawed at the theater chair. She knew how it would end. She knew that the two lovers would die for their love. So, must I die if I cannot dance? wondered Dawn. Was I right all along? Is another life for me simply a fantasy?

The sense of her error and optimism overwhelmed Dawn to the point she desired to scream. No, she *had* to scream. Stumbling up out of her seat, she ran to the back of the theater and out the closed doors into the sunshine.

***

It took a moment for her eyes to adjust to the blinding light, but as soon as she recovered, she hobbled out hastily. Dawn had no idea where she would go, but she was looking for somewhere to scream and hit and bite if she could.

Meanwhile, Natalie had kept her eye on Dawn the entire time, more interested in watching her reaction to the performance than watching the performance once more. As soon as Dawn left, so too did she.

Running in the direction Dawn took, Natalie pushed open the heavy wooden doors out into the light to watch as Dawn hobbled out across the street and toward the bluffs that surrounded the area. From the theater, she could hear Dawn screaming. She was worried that she may throw herself under a vehicle before she made it to the bluffs. Thankfully, she did not wait around on the street like a frightened squirrel. Dawn just kept going.

Natalie was in shape, but she was still out of breath when she reached Dawn, throwing her arms around her to keep her safe at last. But Dawn jerked herself away out of Natalie's arms, wrenching herself away from the only comfort she had left in a world devoid of ballet.

"Dawn, listen to me. Dawn!" Natalie shook her hard. "I'm so sorry. I didn't think you would have such a powerful reaction. We won't go back. We both know how it ends anyway..."

"That's right! We do know how it ends—in death! It ends in destruction for a glimpse of happiness again in another world but not this one! I have ruined my only chance at happiness here! Don't you see? I could have flown with the angels, but instead, I injured myself and damned myself to hell unless and until I end it all. There's no other way for me to be happy, Natalie. Can't you see that?!" shouted Dawn. Hysterically, she began to pull at the loose rocks on the side of the bluff, pulling out one after another, hoping that they were like teetering blocks that would fall on her if she just pulled out the right one.

"Stop! Stop!" Natalie cried. "This is not the strong young woman I saw yesterday who was full of hope and excitement at starting life over again!"

"Yeah, well, it took watching a performance of *Swan Lake* to prove to myself that I can't live without it."

Natalie bent down to Dawn's height in order to look her in the eyes. "Yes, you can. It will take time. You've only known ballet. All of your habits are built around ballet. But you will change those habits to let in new routines, new creative endeavors, new ambitions. You need time. Allow yourself that time, Dawn. I think one of the most miraculous things about human beings is their ability to adapt. There are people out there who have lost limbs and can no longer run or write or play an instrument, and those who do not succumb to their sorrows find new passions to enjoy. The emotions that you had around ballet are still there inside of you. You can still get that euphoric feeling with other things in life; not all is lost, my dear."

Sniffling, Dawn dabbed at her eyes and kept her focus on Natalie. Maybe she was right. Maybe I can still feel good again...even happy. "But Natalie, all of those years of practice. For what?!"

"I told you, dear. A majority of the children who start with ballet classes never actually go on to become professional dancers—only a tiny minority do. It happened to me, and did I find happiness again? Yes. Do I still use all I learned from ballet in my everyday life? Yes. Remember everything I told you yesterday? Ballet gives you grace and a true knowledge of your own body. Classical ballet taught me and many others the precision and etiquette that makes up a civil society. Every class has started with first position and ended with *reverence*, and every time those simple gestures allow for a meditation of sorts to happen. I am forced to focus on the moment. My mind stops thinking about what I want to eat for dinner or if the dishes need to be done or whether I should read this book before that book. No, I have to concentrate entirely on my body and my mind, on the combination, the music, and my body's precision—its lines. For a moment, time stops ticking away and I become immortal. You can still have that feeling, Dawn. Maybe you've heard about artists who can get into a 'flow state' while working. That act can produce the same outcomes. There are other things the mind and body can be totally indulgent in and you feel invincible. That is what is so wonderful about being human—as long as you have reason, you can find happiness in multiple ways."

Dawn sat down with her back against the bluffs and her head up toward the sky. "But I felt...feel so strongly about ballet. How could I betray it?"

Natalie joined Dawn on the ground, trying to avoid sitting on a tiny ant crawling aimlessly around the little patches of grass. "Ballet does not have feelings, only *you* do. *You* need to do what you are the best at and what fits you as you are now. You grew up and loved ballet and nothing was injured. Now, you have an injury that is severe enough to make you change direction. I've seen people who fight against change and it only ends up hurting them over a more prolonged period of time. For example, a student who desperately wants to be a classical ballerina cannot have a very wide bone structure. It just is not flattering to this specific art form. She will never become one of the greats because it is not naturally her strength. See? But if she fights the reality due to her love of ballet, then she will never make a name for herself when she could very well have done so in another field. Of course, learning ballet as a child can do wonders in a person's life, but it would not be a place where she, in particular, could shine career-wise. She is a person who will never be happy because she has doomed herself from the very beginning. You *must* find another passion to devote yourself to wholeheartedly, Dawn."

More tears burst from Dawn's tired eyes as she mourned the loss of her career...and her own childhood. If it took time, then perhaps she would live another day to find out. Dawn rested her head on Natalie's shoulder. She followed the path the sunlight made coming down through the tree branches above them into Natalie's hands.

Her hands appeared deflated near Dawn's own supple and fair-skinned hand. Natalie's skin was darker, ruddier, and looser, like the flesh merely draped itself over her bones and could choose to leave whenever it wished. Some sunspots showed up too, making their appearance more noticeable after all of these years of bathing out in the sun's warm rays. Only now has time caught up with her. The summers must have been so fun and free to have worn down her skin in such a way, thought Dawn. Her skin looked simply lived in, like a pair of shoes that are molded over time to fit your feet perfectly.

With looser skin, Natalie's veins were so prominent as opposed to Dawn's own hidden ones, as if Natalie proved to be more alive than her. She was made of flesh and bone and was of this earth. Whereas Dawn? She was new and pasty and flaky, still an unknown among many other unknowns.

Dawn rested her own hand on top of Natalie's and held it. Natalie's hand felt calloused and much courser than Dawn's own soft, plush hands. Her own hands had never known hard work, while Natalie's had scrubbed dishes and sewn and cooked and worked for years. Her hands had gripped and grabbed and scooped and pulled and tugged and strewn and lain and picked up and put down and thrown and held so many varying objects in her life—a life that now became clearly more unique and fulfilled than Dawn could even imagine.

Natalie's knuckles were more pronounced and Dawn had to wonder if she had ever punched or hit or knocked out another person in her lifetime. What other stories did she have to tell?

Little tiny white hairs blew in the wind from what seemed like black wells all over the skin on the back of Natalie's hand.

Dawn drew herself up close to her own hand to see the same little hairs and dots, but they were so much smaller and less noticeable.

Both of them shared short nails. Dawn knew that she kept them short to be able to feel the barre better and to avoid any inadvertent scratches while dancing. She thought about Natalie doing it for the same reasons.

Dawn watched Natalie's hand closely, staring at the veins to see if they moved with each pulse, but she could not see the blood pumping. Instead, she tried to envision Natalie's hand sans flesh, and she became queasy. Her skin told of so many experiences, but underneath that to be just muscle and blood and bone? How could those be animating what she saw from the outside? How could those parts of her be underneath Dawn's own skin?

The sunlight waned now, but it had exposed the fragility of the human being beside her as well as her own. If one thing collapses, then immediate intervention is needed, or else the entire organism stops. All of those experiences, all of that unending time, cease to exist.

Although Natalie was watching Dawn carefully, she left her alone to give her the space she needed to come to these little epiphanies, like a baby learning to walk for the first time.

Dawn reached down for her shoe and slid it off along with her sock. Laying her foot on the ground, she stared at her own foot. It was the only thing on her that was able to tell some of her story. There were scars from previous blisters still there. She remembered her bloodied point shoes when she was first forming the necessary callouses that would form in the proper places on her feet. Her toenails were always cut extremely short so that she would not suffer *en pointe* or have to cut them down constantly. The worst thing about her toes was the bunion and her crooked middle toe that was longer than the others. Growing up cramming her toes into pointe shoes for hours at a time, Dawn had caused her foot to grow in mysterious, unnatural ways.

She took pride before in her broken feet; she took it as a sign of discipline. Her ultimate goal was to transform her feet into the perfect servants of the pointe shoe since those are what made the ballerina special—the shoes are what made them fly.

Natalie saw the same story written on Dawn's foot that was bathing in what was left of the clouded-over sunlight. She could imagine Dawn pulling off her shoes in agony as the blood poured out from a newly opened blister. These were the growing pains that she never got far enough in the ballet world to experience much of herself...at least not to that extent.

In realizing that she did have a history in this world, Dawn gained a bit more confidence and spoke up for the first time in the last several minutes. "I devoted my life to ballet. Look, it's right there on my foot. That's my proof. I gave my body to my art. You'll just have to trust that I gave my mind to it as well. I can't ever fix my feet. How can I ever fix or change my career? Should I injure another part of myself for it?"

Natalie chuckled softly before saying: "No, of course not. Not all jobs put you at such risk of injury."

"Yeah, well, this is my story, though. I started it already. Those blister scars may never fully disappear. My crooked feet may never straighten out. These callouses may never become smooth. I already began molding myself into the person I wanted to grow up to be..."

"Dawn, sweetie, you are not going to stop shaping yourself. It will just be focused in a different spot. People are not animals. We are not forced to perform one action for our entire lives because of our instincts. And you will never, ever lose the lessons you learned from ballet. I will not lie to you and say that you won't lose your technical or skill-level over time, but you will never forget how it shaped your character, your mind, or the way it helped you learn how to interact in space with your body."

Dawn let out a long sigh, "But the time, Natalie, the time."

"You know, I keep forgetting that when I was a teenager, time was this momentary thing because I had no conception of what it was like to live even twenty years! It is a lot of your time right now that you devoted to ballet. But with respect to an entire lifetime? It is not such a long time, dear. You are certainly young enough to look for a new passion. Heck, most teenagers are just starting to figure out what they want to do with their lives and some people *never* find it."

"But I always felt behind…"

"You felt that way because ballet careers start and end so early in life. Our bodies are not made for that kind of rigor for years and years on end…at least not at the level that ballet nowadays demands. Perhaps that can change too over time. Not every dancer has to put their leg over their head in order to express joy," said Natalie, laughing.

"It is kind of crazy how much ballet requires of a dancer's body."

"You know, it wasn't *always* that way. In the courts of Louis XIV of France, it was more about aristocratic civility and positions that you could maintain in a public etiquette situation. You were mostly on both feet the entire time in shoes that may not have been quite comfortable, but they were at least not pointe shoes. Ballet was originally about using the

213

human body and its ability to create shapes that were pleasing to the eye and conveyed the utmost civility and culture. If classes were still taught that way, perhaps you would stay and many others along with you, Dawn. You would never feel inferior if you were not flexible or strong enough. You did not need to be in peak physical shape to dance ballet in the seventeenth century."

Now Dawn was boring through her boot in an effort to see what her tendon looked like in its current ruined state. It would never bump out of the skin correctly again. She would always have a scar from the surgery. How can I trust myself to dance again? wondered Dawn. The horrible snapping sound kept her from making any sudden movements while walking on her boot now. How could I forget such a sound? It was awful and so permanent, as if those vibrations will tickle my ears until I am no more.

She thought about being buried after all of this under the theater stage. Would I still do it? she thought. Dawn rested her head on her knees, letting the dim rays of light graze her neck like a guillotine. Her desire to be buried under the theater was still there, somewhere deep inside of her, but it felt further away. Maybe if she kept coming to the same theater for adult classes, then she could justify staying there forever. But who knows? Maybe Dawn would move on to devote her life to something else and some other dark basement would call to her. Either way, she wanted to rest in peace somewhere she was needed and longed to be always.

Dawn peered up at Natalie, who was watching the other little ants running around in chaotic circles around their feet.

"Natalie, where do you want to be buried when you die?"

Natalie gave a disquieted look at Dawn, but quickly recognized that losing a career could be like death to some. "Well, my husband is buried in a cemetery not too far from our...my house. I always thought it would be lovely to be buried right next to him, all snuggled up underneath the great oak tree that would keep us cool in its shade. I find it comforting to think that people could always find us in the same old spot if they ever wanted to reach us. I even thought about having our cat next to us too. All the same little family still together, just quieter." A single teardrop fell onto the ground and both women watched the ants circle around the pool and drink their fill before marching onward toward more important tasks.

Their heads leaned back against the bluff and raised to the sky where the sun and the breeze gave them fresh air to breathe. Time slowed to a halt. There was just the singing tune of birds and the breath in their lungs and the warmth radiating from the absorbent ground.

In a time of need, Dawn found a moment of silence to think in. In this precious bubble which she dared not pop with words, she allowed her mind to feel whole at the moment without the pressures of living affecting her feelings. Right now, she was fed, warm, and safe. She was in no pain. She was surrounded by the love of a friend. She had a body and mind that could do anything it wanted to. And at that moment, Dawn knew she could do it. She could shape her life in the way she wanted it to be as long as she remained honest with herself. Her ankle injury changed her trajectory in one way, but not in the fundamentals. Natalie had been telling her this the whole time. She was still in charge of how she reacted to her thoughts and emotions. She could still find the drive that comes with a passion. Her next job would just be to find that next passion and fall in love all over again.

CHAPTER IV

Meanwhile, the police had been knocking on doors, trying to track down Madame Angulaire after her little incident with Dawn was over. They asked all around the neighborhood, but no one had seen her in the past twenty-four hours.

Until a week later, an off-duty policeman saw a strangely dressed woman walk into the grocery store he was entering. She was wearing an obvious wig that was not fastened onto her head properly, and she was wearing a shirt that was much too large for a woman with arms that thin, and her pants were also too large for her skeletal body.

"Excuse me, ma'am," said the officer. "Ma'am. Wait!"

Madame Angulaire began running down the aisles, skirting around people and their carts, banging into the little racks that held sales and other goodies up. The officer ran right after her and it was an easy catch since he was much taller and, consequently, faster than her.

Catching up to her, he grabbed a hold of her tiny arm and with his other hand showed his badge.

Madame Angulaire just started laughing and held her head up high as she left the grocery store with the officer.

"What do you think I've done, officer?" asked Madame

Angulaire, when they passed the automatic doors.

The officer looked down at her and only said, "Kidnapping and assault…maybe even attempted murder."

Madame Angulaire gave a violent laugh. "Me? Do I look like I could *kill* a girl?"

"She was smaller than you, ma'am."

"Well, that does not mean I was going to *kill* her. I just wanted to teach her a lesson. That's all. Corporal punishment in an educational setting isn't illegal here, now is it?"

The officer stopped talking to her. He was not judge or jury. He simply arrested her and had her processed into the county jail, where she would await her first meeting with her attorney. When Madame Angulaire was initially deposited in that cold jail cell, she was still thinking about groceries and how hungry she was after all of these days of hiding out around town.

Now she was in a cell that had bricks painted over with white a million times and tacky-yellow bars. The toilet was a dark metal color and the sheet covering her crispy-thin-looking bed was a forest green. The only light came from the fake lights in the hallway, but there was no natural light in sight for her.

At least here, she would not have to worry about finding food or a place to sleep. She knew she would be discovered eventually, and maybe the judge would even agree with her side of the story. She was only teaching Dawn a stern lesson, a lesson that was needed if she was going to become a prima ballerina of *any* significance.

If I were doing anything illegal, thought Madame Angulaire, it would be letting that girl go on slowly killing herself by gaining weight she did not need.

She sat down in a huff on her bed, thinking about that day

over and over again. She watched herself grab Dawn and throw her violently into the trunk, slamming the lid on her, and finding the keys to keep her in there. She remembered the weight of the box digging into her thighs as she dragged the whole thing down beneath the theater and stormed out into the cool night air.

From there, she ran home to grab a few belongings and slept outside in an alleyway, shielded from the light of day and the police. She spent what little money she had in her wallet buying her lackluster disguise and food. She had not had a proper shower in a week since leaving her home…and now she was here trapped in her own costume box.

That insolent girl put me here, thought Madame Angulaire. It is her fault that I'm here. I was just trying to snap her out of her funk. She needed to grab onto the life preserver I was throwing to her of modern ballet. Only today's dance theory could help her overcome her struggles. But she failed me. Failed me!

Madame Angulaire smashed her hand against her bed, which creaked loudly as if in pain at her abuse.

"Hey! Settle down in there," shouted one officer from down the nebulous corridor.

"Hey! You! *Plié* for me, but with your knees tucked in!" Madame Angulaire shouted back. She laughed at herself for telling these large, burly men to dance. In fact, it made her giddy to choreograph a dance for the jailhouse guards. Yes, she thought, it would be more realistic than any set of trained dancers could pull off. I want raw magnetism! I want a masculine source of sexuality onstage that is perverted and twisted around my finger. I want men of great stature to get down on the floor and curl, curl up into the balls they are on

219

the inside, balls of fear! Sure, they look tough on the outside, but they have constant, nagging fears about their wives and children at home. They do not want to bring any of the filth of the jail cell home with them.

Well, I will show them what kind of art they have been missing. Everyone needs ballet. Everyone is helpless otherwise. Ballet can drive people to do crazy things with their bodies and their minds. I bet I could make them open these very bars with their own hands just to let me slip right through them. The power of modern ballet is all-inclusive and all-powerful. I am just its vessel. I am merely the messenger. I am only the humble executioner.

Madame Angulaire felt a sudden fatigue in her bones and she laid out on her bed, dreaming about how she would make her great escape using the power of ballet as her key to escaping. For the key would take some time, and she knew that convincing the guards of its power would be the hardest part. Tomorrow she would start fresh.

***

Tomorrow came faster than Madame Angulaire had expected, with a loud knock on the bars and a lukewarm meal of oatmeal and a slice of bread. Training must begin with me, thought Madame, as she ate and started stretching in her cell.

She had not stretched deeply for a week and her hips kept popping. But she knew that her body would soon warm up and the pops would tire eventually.

Her goal was to play the lead role in her new ballet with the guards as her entourage. Yes, it's perfect, she thought. I will have all of those unsophisticated workers stand around me, courting me, lifting me up high, and placing me down as gently as a flower, only to crush me in the end.

As an act of sacrifice for the dance gods, I will die at the hands of these guards in my last ballet. I will prove myself worthy to the Nijinsky's and the Stravinsky's of the past. I will worship at their feet in this tiny cell. The cold will not touch these bones.

I must dance for them without a self, without a soul…and maybe that way I can show all of those nonbelievers, like Dawn, that ballet goes beyond the individual. Ballet must be brought to the *right* side of history. The side of history that brings humanity *forward*. And like the yin and yang, it is moving forward while swinging backward to learn from our most primitive tribes.

I am part of the ballet tribe, part of the dancing cavemen who drew on walls and made love in the dirt. I am all those people before me and all the people after me. I am the vessel for the ballet gods!

Madame Angulaire was muttering most of these words while pacing around in her cell for hours at a time. In fact, most of the day had already passed when Madame wanted to start her first "morning" lesson.

"You! Tubby!" Madame Angulaire stuck her scrawny arm through the bars at the officer sitting in the corridor.

He grunted as he stood up, walking toward Madame's cell.

"What?" he asked.

"Turn in your feet, mister! We are going to start class at the barre now."

The officer stood looking confused for a minute before he chuckled and spit in front of Madame's cell. "Lady, you off your meds?" he said.

"N-no. How rude. That's no way to start class. My students never spit at me or refused to turn their feet in when I told

221

them to. You need to mend your ways, you."

Madame Angulaire scowled at the officer through her yellow-colored bars. She leered at him until he looked down at the ground and turned to leave.

"Wait! Officer, I am choreographing my final ballet. I need all of you men to be in it! I'm going to be the lead. By the way, where can I get my costumes and a stage?"

The officer continued to walk away, shaking his head. He had seen women going crazy like this before, but never so quickly...

Meanwhile, another officer came to relieve the current one and Madame Angulaire tried again.

"Hey! Mister Officer!" she shouted.

The fresh meat she saw walked over to her cell. "It's not dinnertime yet." He was thinner than the other man, but Madame found his gum-chewing rather annoying.

"Spit out your gum, young man! I want you to turn your feet in and then *plié*."

"Ma'am, this ain't no dance class. Leave me be," he said, as he walked back toward the uncomfortable black chair in the corridor.

"No! I need you officers to work with me. Forget your jobs, your status, and just follow my orders! You have no selves any longer. You must dance without thought entering in or else it will sully the emotions you are emitting."

"Yeah, whatever you ol' kook," said the new officer.

I can't believe these people. They must not see the dire need there is right now for modern ballet in the world. It's the only way to save our archaic and dying culture. "Don't you see?!" she yelled toward the officer.

They are ignorant fools...even though these are exactly the

kind of men my ballet needs. "Come on! It's my last ballet, *I promise*," she said.

The officer completely ignored her as he looked at his newspaper.

There must be some way to convince them that broken lines are necessary now for dance. There are no straight lines anymore. That's a thing of the past. The crooked and tense is beautiful now. In fact, my dancers will go to new heights with extreme extensions and their hips will be so askew they won't know how to relax them fully again.

My dancers will be a *new* breed, one that completely obeys and moves the way contortionists move in a circus. "I am an entertainer, damn it!" she said.

Her cell echoed, and another inmate punched their cell wall, trying to shut Madame Angulaire up. No one was listening to her, and it was enormously frustrating for someone who everyone always listened to. Her orders as the vessel meant almost life or death to the dancer. She held their future careers in her palm.

But the students were already elites; they were only acting as workers. They were not *real* workers like these men here in this jail. Madame Angulaire must break these proud men down and use them in her *final* work of art.

I promise to have complete control over these men by the end of my stay here, she thought. I must figure out their weaknesses and use them against them to make ballet mean something to the fools, and if orders won't work, maybe threats will.

They will work for me soon enough, like a machine. Groups of machines working for a better world where we all are on an equal footing and ballet will teach us all how to work together. For if one person falls out of line, then the whole thing collapses...

***

Madame Angulaire ate her dinner of cold peas, hard pasta, and runny applesauce. For some of the meal, she closed her eyes and nose to make sure she ate everything that was given to her. Even though she was skeletal, she required more food from having stretched and choreographed in her cell all day. Her stomach gave a low growl as she fed it some more peas.

When all the lights were shut off and Madame was alone with her thoughts that night, she fidgeted around in bed. Unable to fall asleep, she got up and did some *demi-pointe* exercises on the hard cement floor that made her knees ache. There was no one there to bark at, so she formulated the positions that her men would go by herself. She tried to look around in the dark for something to make *X*'s on the floor with, but everything was bolted down. The only option was to stick her finger in the toilet water and hope that the marks would stay there for her to at least finish her choreography for the night.

Dunking her finger in the cold, stench-ridden water made Madame Angulaire nauseous, but she would have felt even worse laying down on that bed with her own thoughts. She had never been cut off from stimulation like this before. She had always had class or the television or even a book at night to keep her thoughts at bay. But now they were creeping in like shadows, moving across the cold floors.

But Madame was in control, and she planned to *stay* in control of herself. She did a few jumping jacks and slapped her own head with her hands. Hitting out the demon thoughts was her best plan of action. Now, she thought, back to the dance! At this point, she stood in the middle of the room on top of the toilet-water X on the floor. In her mind, the woman was just as strong as the man and she must hover over him in the ballet to right the wrongs of the unequal past. Imagining the position for the man, she moved behind where she was initially standing, on her knees in the chivalric pose of yesteryear, only this time the man was behind the woman and grabbing at her head. The woman could lean back over him, but she was essentially walking away from his offer of permanent submission. True love between one man and one woman was a fantasy created by the elites, thought Madame. This ballet is about loving your fellow man as a whole. It looks different, inverted, opposite to the archaic ways of the past.

The next position was mimed by Madame as she played the woman kicking her leg out in front of her, like a march with her feet flexed. Pointed toes were for fairies that never existed, but humans walk flat-footed; therefore, they must flex their feet, decided Madame. She marched around her cell, humming the tune that worked with her steps, making it up as she went. Of course, she would either have to find music already created or, even better, a new composer to create the music for this masterpiece.

But she was getting ahead of herself. For now, Madame played the man wallowing at his unrequited love's feet, rocking like a wounded animal on the ground, weeping for his fate. "Shut up!" shouted one inmate, which startled Madame from her pitiful show of sadness. Feeling violated by the intrusive yell, she got down in a child's pose with her arms tucked in and her forehead touching the chilly floor. Her forehead muscles relaxed strangely enough because she had not noticed herself overheating. It felt so good to melt into a pool of ice on the floor. She played the puddle so well that she did not move until the sun came up and the fluorescent lights told her it was morning again.

The officer that morning walked by her cell and kicked the bars. "Hey! You okay?" asked the officer. Madame Angulaire, still half asleep, arose, but she had to uncurl carefully her painful knees and numb legs out from underneath herself. The officer saw she was still conscious and heard his question, which was enough for him. He walked along down the corridor without another thought as to her well-being.

Madame Angulaire was in agony as the pins and needles worked their way through her legs and feet. She tried not to move or else the pain was too much. The needles she felt were extremely sharp and dreadful. She was unsure about how she even managed to sleep upright all night like that. Her neck ached, but her back felt nice and stretched out. Then she remembered the shouting inmate and the late-night choreographing. She looked all around her for the toilet-water X, but it had evaporated by then, or Madame Angulaire had accidentally laid on top of it and soaked it all up with her uniform.

She patted herself down when she could finally stand up and her clothes were all dry. In an attempt to forget that she might be covered in toilet water, she began stretching—waking up the parts of her body that she had crushed last night. It was her form of apology. She would self-flagellate often when she felt she did something wrong, certainly anything that would upset the modernist movement.

Her breakfast was the same flavorless oatmeal mush, and it took most of the morning for her to swallow it down. The jail walls were starting to get to her already. She daydreamed for another few hours about what she would do with her students outside of the cell. She would teach them this new ballet and it would make the days and nights move infinitely faster than in this hellhole.

In order to force the thoughts back down, Madame tried to focus her entire attention on her ballet. She called out to the officers again, "Hey! Pretty boy! Bend your arms in toward your torso and knees toward each other. Then walk in such a fashion to me and I'll give you the next step!" But the officers all knew what she was about now and promptly chose to ignore her requests.

Madame Angulaire lost her audience, and now she realized she was also losing her students. There was no one there to order around but herself. She was forced to play all the roles in her own final ballet. How ridiculous, she thought, that I am alone for my finale.

A surge of anger brought her back to pacing her cell and shouting orders at anyone near enough to hear her. She imagined all the walls between the inmates were missing and she could see them following her commands.

"You! Left foot will be your standing leg and your right will be the working one. Place your right hand around your right foot while still standing. Do not fall over! Are we clear?" she shouted in the empty cell.

"Good! Now use your left heel to scoot yourself around like that as if you were on a pedestal and showcasing your body to the audience. No, no! Not like that, you buffoon! Like this." Madame Angulaire grabbed her foot and swung it around herself as her hips popped and her stiff back ached. But it was like she could not feel these things anymore. Now she was in her element.

The guards passed by her cell throughout the day, checking to see what strange pose she was going to contort herself into next. Some of them stood right in front of her and she pretended she didn't see them. All she kept doing was shouting and executing steps she was demonstrating to no one.

When meals came over the next several days, she barely ate them and barely slept, either. Her thoughts were all consumed by completing this final ballet of hers. Days and nights no longer mattered. She frequently collapsed with hunger and fatigue in her cell before waking up and repeating the same long cycle.

It appeared like this would be the longest ballet in the world, either that or her imaginary students were too dumb to grasp and maintain the choreography, so Madame had to show them repeatedly.

Her arraignment date was finally approaching, after it had been rescheduled once again due to her attorney begging the judge for continuances based on the erratic state his client was still in. But it no longer mattered to her. She lost track of the days after about a week of being in there. Who cares? she thought. I'm still able to choreograph from here. At least the cops can't take that away from me. Besides, I would never let them. I would rather take the death sentence if I could no longer dance. Anyway…enough about me; this is about art!

"Hey! Mister Officer, give me big outreaching arms and hop on both feet in *demi-pointe*. I then want you to skip around with your arms flailing like a lost bird with a broken wing. You are directionless in the opening scene until you find a group of other birds working on building a nest. You join their congregation and you suddenly feel whole. To show this, I want you to grovel at their collective feet. Allow them to squish your head into the ground, and you are to take it gratefully. Give me a big smile!" Madame Angulaire mimicked the most elastic grin she could fathom. Her thin skin wrapped around her bones so that her cheeks looked more wrinkled and yet still sunken in. She was truly a walking skeleton.

Her arms shook now from lack of strength. The guards had noticed that she was no longer finishing her meals. Today, they tried to remind her of her meal before taking it.

One of the more empathetic officers came over to her cell and said: "Look, lady, eat something. Your arms are shaking. You can barely lift your head up anymore. You want to keep dancing? Then you need to eat."

"I only eat, sleep, and breathe modern ballet, sir. I don't need your materialistic carbohydrates. You can take that and give it to one of the other lowlifes here who let themselves get fat…just like Dawn, the traitor. Madame Angulaire let out the loudest roar she was capable of in her state. She *hated* Dawn more with each passing day. Dawn was the one who got away, the one nonbeliever in her righteous fight toward saving ballet for good. She may very well be the downfall of ballet itself. It's people like her and Madame Roberts that keep ballet in the Dark Ages, thought Madame Angulaire.

She sat rocking on the floor with her hands wrapped around her knees. From that cold floor, she watched her food come in and leave untouched. She fell asleep locked in the position that she had sat in. Toward the end, she even relieved herself in the same spot. Her behind was numb and rotting now. The bones were practically touching the cement themselves.

Her final ballet was still being choreographed inside her own head. The somewhat alarmed officers sometimes heard her dried throat gurgling out the tune to the ballet she was still working on. Sitting there day and night, she literally did just eat, sleep, and breathe her progressive version of ballet.

She began hallucinating her *corps de ballet*, following behind her, while she whispered "finally" over and over again. Of course, she was the soloist, and she envisioned everyone crowding around her in their angled and obtuse way. The music hit so many extra, aimless notes that it was dizzying for the dancers. But that is exactly what she wanted—a dizzying sense of being alive between the plane of the living and the dead. Only a mixed and in-between state of life was the real.

"My dancers, my tireless workers, my warriors who eat, sleep, and breathe dance. Never stray from it, never think or question it, and you will be immortalized by the group. You nameless, faceless believers are the *real* heroes of humanity," murmured Madame.

It was only a couple weeks since she was put in this white-washed cell with the yellow bars. Madame Angulaire began to love the cell she was in because she thought she could be her authentic self inside its walls. She was finally freed from the materialistic world made by reasoning people, but she wanted a space where only feelings moved her. She got what she wanted in the cold, hollow cell. Her heart gave out on her with her head cradled on her knees and her arms circled around her tiny, bony legs.

She died in the shape of her art.

CHAPTER V

On the day that Madame Angulaire died in her jail cell, Madame Roberts opened up her next season of classes for adults. It was the very end of spring, right before the heat of summer took hold of the town. But this morning there was still a cool wind blowing Madame Roberts's hair around as she made her way to class.

She made her way up the same chandelier stairway that was covered in natural light from the windows. Madame Roberts loved when she taught her classes earlier in the day because the natural light refreshed her more than the darker, cozier atmosphere created in the evening. Taking a deep breath at the top of the stairs, she opened the door to the dressing room and stuck her bag and outer garments in her little locker. She smiled at seeing the little dancers' notebooks with their ballet vocabulary sticking out of the locker next to hers. Teaching the children was always fun, albeit a little wearisome, when one of them had too much sugar before class. It could be difficult to get children to listen to and learn from their instructor.

"Good morning, ladies and gentlemen," said Madame Roberts, as she wrapped her chiffon skirt around her waist and tied it in place over her leotard and tights.

"Good morning, Madame Roberts!" said the children.

Madame Roberts brought the basket of notebooks out from the locker where they were stored after every class. She passed them out to each child. Some had pointe shoe stickers on them, others unicorns, and some boys had race cars stuck to theirs.

The children were from three to six years old and completely oblivious to their own bodies. They were brand new to the world of ballet and yet they could absorb and mature so quickly at this impressionable age. The children were the most malleable now. When they grew into older dancers, they would have more control over their own bodies than most adults ever did. Their grace and fluidity of movement would become seamless by the age of ten.

"Today we are going to be learning about *chassé*, which means 'to chase' in French, said Madame. "It differs from *temps lié*, which we will learn about next week. They both involve transferring your weight in ballet. When you *chassé*, you always want to *plié* on both legs," said Madame Roberts as she *pliéd* for the class. "But then you will move your weight in an underturn from one leg to the other and then pull that following leg back into first position." Madame Roberts demonstrated the U-shaped weight shift with her hands on her hips. The students all watched her every move, breathless.

She was the most fascinating thing to look at in that studio. She was the envy of all the little girls and the dreams of all the little boys. The girls wanted to look like her when they grew up and they preferred it to be tomorrow that they filled the form of a real woman, while the boys wanted to grow into men quickly who could partner with Madame Roberts and show her all of his accomplishments.

The children all desired her and her ability to hold their attention with her movements. She was something to ogle over, and it was her feminine grace that made them come back repeatedly.

Madame Roberts walked over to the small whiteboard that was stuck to the wall. It creaked a bit every time she laid her hand down on it to write. She writes in large, pretty letters *chassé*. The children copied carefully the word down with their pencils and the youngest ones handed their notebooks to Madame Roberts to write in for them. She squatted down and helped them all spell out the word and what it meant in French. They all laughed at the little accent mark that needed to go over the *e* thinking that was the funniest-looking thing in the world. Everything was new and wonderful to them.

Madame Roberts felt her cup filling and overflowing with love for her little students. Her patience seemed to grow only for them because they did not mean to be so clumsy and slow, they were just new to it all. She rose and asked for the notebooks back. The classroom-studying portion of the class was over. Now, it was on to executing the step.

"Now, watch me first for a couple of times, and then I'll have *you* do it," said Madame Roberts. The children, of course, could not resist trying it along with her as soon as she began. But she had expected that and was waiting for them to all eventually join in. The group of children *pliéd* down in a U-shape together and got back up, teetering on their one leg only to help it with the other once they pointed it properly and brought it successfully back home to first position.

Madame Roberts remembered that first position was one of the very first lessons she taught these young ones. It was home. It was the beginning of a yearslong journey and it would stay with them for the rest of their lives. Ballet would course through their veins. It would save them from injuries and foolhearted decisions in the future. They would recover faster from both emotional and mental pain. They would learn to be resilient and get back up again after they fell. These children would never forget her if she taught them well. And years later, when she was old and gray, they might even come back to visit her and tell her about the lessons she *knew* she had already given to them, and she would just nod and smile with her wrinkled lips, much wiser than before. Classical ballet was an art form that brought the young and the old *together*.

Living in this world requires understanding our nature and the rules that dictate it and glorifying that existence is what art was made to do. Ballet, for Madame Roberts, was a way of celebrating life and the act of living. It respected the way we were anatomically built and accentuates the body's most beautiful features. We are on display as the model for what human beings are and what they are capable of, thought Madame Roberts.

Tears covered Madame Roberts's eyes and made them blurry for a moment. She blinked quickly to wipe them away and continued her class with the children. There was a little boy now jumping up and down as naturally as could be and another little girl trying to lift her leg to her ear, quite unsuccessfully. A few of the other children were still trying to conqueror the wiggliness of their bodies in performing a *chassé*. Unfortunately, for many of them, it was extremely difficult for their minds to tell their bodies what to do. They saw what Madame was doing, but when they tried to mimic her, everything just came out wrong. Some children even fell over for no reason other than they were moving in a space where gravity was not their friend. The youngest ones cried in frustration, while the older children grew stubborn and kept trying over and over again like an obsession. The entire class that day was spent on barre and then on this single movement until *reverence*.

The work that the children did was so pure and given with everything they could in that hour-long class. And when they laid their little heads down on their pillows at night, their minds would rewire and integrate all the movements and things they learned from class so that next time they would get better. Their growing bodies would morph into the future dancers and adults built to handle the world. They were all able and willing to participate on this great stage called life.

Madame Roberts curtsied back at her children and released them for the day. A few of them ran up to give their teacher a hug.

"Goodbye, Madame! *Au revoir!*" they said and giggled as they ran out of the studio, abandoning their notebooks and their thoughts about class for the day. The world was too new and exciting to focus just on one thing for too long. Madame and her class would be forgotten until the next time they showed up in the studio, but she knew that even that short time was enough to change them.

The minute weekly habits that the students incorporated into their lives compounded into a long string of memories and movements that became a part of who they were as adults. It happened to Madame Roberts when she was young, and it happened to countless others before her. She remembered her own mother taking her to the studio, and she sat in the corner on the floor, just mesmerized by all the older girls and how they could move so smoothly, as if it was second nature. She felt like a mouse, peeking out from its hole, and watching these dancers move with such ease like they were angels. Madame Roberts learned to be proud of her mother, who taught these students how to move, how to shift their weight, how to execute gracefully a combination in the face of reality. There was gravity holding them all down and the constant pull from one side of the body or the other to teeter off balance and land hard on the floor. The students had to not only fight those factors with constant, minute counterbalances, but they also had to make it all seem effortless. The length of their lines made with the body proved that not only could they push themselves to the edge, but that they could accomplish it without faltering. Ballet gave them wings. It used geometric shapes to create a beautiful image of what each body part contributed to Man as a whole.

Madame Roberts wanted to lead dancers like her mother did and help to guide them toward a life that held more meaning. A life where etiquette and grace were upheld was one where civilization could flourish and prosper. It was a world where Madame could live and learn in peace indefinitely, where nothing ceased being wonderful and exciting. The enthusiasm for living and learning that the children shared gave Madame Roberts the energy every single day to walk into the studio as if it was the first time: even though she knew where the floor creaked in places, even though she knew what time the sunlight would penetrate the rose-looking window, even though she knew the temperature that the studio needed to be in the different seasons, even though she knew how the barres were worn down in certain places, even though she knew how the white, floral lace curtain flickered as the air-conditioning came on and the music filled the air of the studio. She knew so much, as if the studio was a worn glove she had needed since her own childhood. Madame Roberts only grew to love the studio in the theater more.

With every passing year and every dancer's graduation from the studio, fresh faces appeared the next season. It was bittersweet every spring to watch her students, whom she may have been with since the age of three, leave for college or companies. But she reminisced with them about how much they had grown from the tottering little three-year-old, unsure of their place in the world, to the self-confident and elegant eighteen-year-old ready to head off to take on the wider world—one that was not just their parents' house or their school or their dance studio. They were going out into the unknown, but they were *ready*. Madame Roberts and all of their support system made sure of it.

Today, Madame Roberts upon hearing of Madame Angulaire's madness, starvation, and eventual death was feeling particularly good. She no longer had to fight a teacher who was opposed to the students finding their footing in life. She did not have to fear losing students to a cynical, nihilistic view of the world around them. After Dawn, she never wanted to see the light fade from her students' smiles nor watch them suffer under the wrath of an adult who was supposed to help and guide them on this journey through life. Madame Angulaire was the epitome of what happens when a person fights their nature and reality itself.

Today, Madame Roberts would say goodbye to the threat of Madame Angulaire and all that she represented and continue to teach her students well. There was such a thing as teaching properly and with standards as long as those standards were based on reality. Madame went to go eat a quick, healthy lunch of a salad and an apple. She needed to fuel her body for this evening's adult class. The adults needed just as much energy from her as the children, only for the adults, it required more of her knowledge about the subject and equally passionate energy for expressing it.

The evening class began as soon as Madame Roberts opened the studio doors to all the dancers.

"Welcome! *Bienvenue*! Come on in and take your places at the barre," said Madame. Today, she would teach the class similar to how she taught the children sans the notebooks and writing out the new vocabulary from the whiteboard. Instead, she went through barre which many of the adults had mastered, especially with the beginning *pliés*.

Natalie was in her regular tights and leotard. Her short hair was pulled off of her face by a headband that seemed like it was a leftover from the '80s. She occasionally wore her black legwarmers that had holes in the bottom for her heels. They certainly kept her calves and ankles warm and it served as a way to protect herself from injury. After last season, Natalie had to shell out money for a new pair of tights since her other ones began to get those awful runs. Her attire was a collection of the old and the new, and the new was only purchased at this point when she was unable to wear the tattered fabrics at all. As she grew older, having the latest leotard collection or shoe collection or skirt collection stopped mattering. Dancing was solely for her body and mind. It was not about looking better than the other dancers in the class or outshining them with something new. If anything, class in a group made her feel less lonely, feel a common sense of camaraderie about sharing a love for ballet, and a fun mood where everyone could laugh about mistakes made without worrying. After all, none of the adults were in the class for career purposes. They all had careers in other fields and some were even retired. Ballet was simply a joyous hobby for them.

Still, a sense of competition, as is human nature, was still there in the room. But it was a healthy and more awed sense of competition with whom could do more turns or jumps in the air. Even doing a split anymore was inspiring to see if someone could do it during the stretching section of the class. For Natalie, she watched her peers, for the most part, maintain themselves. Each year they grew a little wider or appeared with a few deeper wrinkles, but they slowed the aging process down much more than the other people she had seen at the grocery store. They were the few believers left in ballet and its ability to keep the mind and body vital, like a fountain of youth made to slow aging. Natalie made sure to drink from the fountain as many times as she could.

Madame Roberts was aging gracefully too. She was still only in her thirties, but she had a few flecks of gray in her hair, and when she smiled, the wrinkles of her future would appear more readily. But her slender wrists and gracefully long legs held up strong by her torso made her appear to be still a teenager. And her sense of humor and wit gave her the mind of someone just as youthful. Her laughter was bright and crisp; it was never loud and brutal.

"Now, class, I'd like to try something a little bit different in the center today. Please, all gather round behind me, facing the mirror."

The dancers walked slowly into place, all trained for years now to leave a "window" of space to their fellow dancers and staggered in such a way as to produce the most room for each person.

Madame Roberts stood in the front line by herself, facing the mirror, with her feet in first position. The rest of the class fell in line with her silently, awaiting her next direction. "Good. From first position, please lift your arms into fifth as I am doing now." She raised her arms up in a beautiful, symmetrical roundness that made her appear taller and even lighter on her feet. "Perfect. Now, open those arms as if you were releasing confetti into the air and were slowly ascending with the confetti." She released her large package of fun into the air and floated down. "But at the halfway point, I want you to lift your opened arms up slightly, turn your palms down to the ground, remember to keep your fingers light and delicate, and gently allow the arms to fall back down into a first position hold." Madame breathed in as she moved her arms up, turned her hands over, and breathed out on the descent. Her students followed along, some more gracefully than others.

All the dancers watched Madame and then switched their focus to themselves in the mirror once they got the idea down. Natalie had not felt so swan-like since rehearsing for ballets as a child. She loved watching her arms pick up and fall in the way something beautiful moved. Every moment she spent analyzing and tweaking little things about her breath was a series of little epiphanies about herself in the mirror. She noticed her wrinkled arm skin quivered more if she was too jerky with her movements and less if she took her time and imagined the wind beneath her arms. The next time she moved, Natalie focused on her scapula helping to hold her arms up with the strength required to maintain control while envisioning a string holding her from the center of her body out through the head. She tightened up her body more to appear looser and freer in her movements.

The more the dancers repeated this motion, the more energy they burned, muscles they built up, and grace they learned to attain. It was all working together to create a better person in the coming days. Natalie could sense it in her bones.

"In today's class and future classes," said Madame Roberts, "I want us to spend all of our center work on these slower, more analytical, and repeated movements to help you all improve and perhaps even learn something new. I no longer want us to move from one thing to the next just because that is how 'typical adult ballet classes are taught' and 'we have to get through all six days of ballet in one class.' I have realized that like my children dancers, the adults need just as much, if not more, of a slow-paced class that focuses on making tiny improvements over time. Practice, practice, practice! That's what you all really need."

A few claps and many smiles lit up the room as the adults took to this new, *slower* form of teaching. They never knew before what they felt was lacking in each class. But allowing them time to be with the music and watch themselves dance was a part of the joy they longed for since those childhood days of rehearsing the many hours required before a show. It was that kind of quality time on the floor and feeling their own bodies that made ballet a unique source of pleasure for the adults in the room.

"I'm glad to see that you all feel the same way about the direction these classes should go. Ballet, today, is stuck in its past triumphs, but we need a better culture to see what people today truly desire from dance. For the dancers, I think it is time to dance and improve their technique. It is not a race or a competition to see who can make the art form the most acrobatic it can be. For the audience, I don't believe they even know what to make of ballet anymore since it has turned into this mish-mash of abstract backgrounds and awkward physical shapes. There are no principles anymore for people to judge. Art is anything and everything people want to label it now." Madame Roberts clenched her fists as she paced back and forth in the front line she had created for herself before the mirrors. Her anger was deep-seated and all-encompassing and it needed at this moment to express itself. "For the teachers, it is our job to save the culture of classical ballet. We want to see a future for the boys and girls who enter our classrooms. We want to avoid pain and attract pleasure, and the only way we achieve that is by following the basic laws of nature. I want you all to dance without injury, which means knowing where to stop your turnouts; it means knowing where to stop hyperextending; it means knowing where to stop doing deep stretches before warming up your muscles first. And if you get injured, you must first and foremost *heal* from them. Take a rest. Do not dance through the pain and make things worse. It is practice things like these that allow for the longest and most pleasurable experience with the world of classical ballet."

By this point in the class, the center work was complete and *reverence* was about to take place. Madame Roberts faced herself head-on in front of the honest mirrors.

"Class, please just follow along with me as the music begins. *Merci*," Madame said.

The soft piano music came from the pianist's tired fingertips. It was slow and drunken in its lilt. Natalie felt a strange sensation of being completely drained of energy and yet full of inspiration. In her dizzying enthusiasm, she opened her arms like Madame and dramatically bowed to the mirrors, imaging the audience tossing roses onto the stage for her. What a *beautiful* way to end the evening, thought Natalie, like a warm glass of milk and a snuggly place to call home. The studio became everyone's home who chose to learn ballet.

After the final bows and curtsies, Natalie remembered the note that Dawn had handed her to give to Madame Roberts. Rifling through her sweater pockets, she found the carefully folded sheet of paper and gave it to Madame.

"Dawn wrote you this letter, Madame," said Natalie.

"Oh, do you know how she's doing with her ankle?" asked Madame, a worried look furrowing her brows.

"Yes, she's doing okay. Some days are better than others. She said that she won't be returning for a while. I'm trying to help her transition through this hard time. It's like she has lost her identity."

Madame Roberts lowered her head and opened the letter.

Dear Madame,

Please forgive me. I was angry and bitter about having to give up what I loved most when I got injured. I thought maybe I could take a shortcut to get what I wanted, but I was wrong. As a result, I was locked in a costume trunk under the theater for hours, growing cold and hungry and scared. I wanted to dance even at the expense of my health and well-being. But I was so unhappy. I miss being happy in your classes. I miss being on top. I have talked with Natalie a lot about my future and she's been kind enough to help me learn how to live without ballet...at least for now. I may not see you for a while, but I want you to know that I am not mad at you and I cannot quit ballet forever. I will return and I hope I will return a much stronger, happier version of myself.

Sincerely,
Dawn

Madame folded the letter back up, giving it a little squeeze, and hugged Natalie before saying: "This means so much to me, dear. Thank you. Do you think she will be okay if I write back to her?"

"I think she would like that very much," said Natalie, smiling.

CHAPTER VI

Natalie waited while Madame Roberts wrote a short note back. Ripping out a fresh sheet from her class lesson's notebook, Madame wrote:

Dear Dawn,

You don't have to ask for forgiveness. I understand. I also desired to be a professional, but I just did not find joy in the stressful world of being in a company, so I went to a regular college, majored in dance, and here I am now teaching. There are other paths out there made just for you. You simply have to keep searching for it. I will see you when you are ready to come back, as I will always be in this studio. Feel free to seek me out when and if you need me.

Heal quickly and take care,
Madame Roberts

"Here," said Madame, "take this back to her if you would, please." Handing over the folded notebook paper, Natalie curtsied once more to her teacher and turned around back toward the dressing room. All the other adult dancers had gone already for the day. Alone in the dressing room that was painted white with a rough blue carpet, strewn with tutus and hairspray bottles, and other costume accessories, Natalie took the time to wander just a bit longer. She touched the tulle of the tutus. Their rough netting kept the shape circular around the dancer's body. She took a deep breath to fill her lungs with the aroma of rosin and hardwood floors and new pointe shoes. She picked up her arms over her head to release what she was holding inside of herself and down her graceful arms came, only to be lifted by the wind and turned over to continue on their journey back down again. Natalie shared her own *reverence* with the room in a moment that could be utterly destroyed by the presence of another person or the sound of a human voice. The quiet time when all was asleep to be witnessed by a single soul was so beautiful that Natalie had to swallow the knot forming in her throat. In her dreams, it was like the quiet in *The Nutcracker* on Christmas Eve when the tree was still illuminated but the house was asleep. In a magical moment of silence, the memories and the smells that stayed the same came together to remind Natalie of the overwhelming, life-enhancing experiences ballet created for her.

Classical ballet was so much more than just a series of perfectly executed steps. It was an art form that made each moment, dancing or not, special. Natalie remembered when she saw her very first ballet live and how sad she was that not all of life behaved in the same way the dancers did onstage. Why couldn't everyone move and act the way these ballet dancers did? she wondered. For her, ballet died a violent death in her mind every time she walked outside of the theater. As Natalie witnessed obese men and women waddling to and fro, their bodies aching out loud. She watched boys on skateboards slump and walk funny with their pants too low. Her eyes traveled to the girls who wanted everyone to see everything, even the flaws of their bodies in risqué clothing instead of the modest dresses or skirts that the dancers wore. Being so young, Natalie even judged the older people as a pure affront to the dancers, simply because they had lost their youth. However, she would see a gentleman on occasion who walked upright with one foot delicately placed in front of the next, even if he was balancing with a cane. He brought Natalie back to the realm of ballet. Sometimes she would even hum a tune from class to his walking and there he was on a stage with all the rest of the dancers.

When Natalie became a teenager, she soon discovered that both the young and old had the capacity to be graceful. Her teachers, after all, were not all young and yet some of them had such *grace* in their manners. She began to rely on her mind and its tunes to start playing any time that the world of ballet could be seen in the everyday. The music helped guide her toward becoming a better person—one who had grace and etiquette and proportion, one who always tried to find the truth in problems, one who was always aiming to be integrated with both mind *and* body. Ballet created a *whole* person. No one could really dance without understanding the way their bodies turned or jumped or stood in space.

But then people like Madame Angulaire came and tried to dance by doing exactly that—dancing with no rules in a fragmented and compartmentalized fashion. She and many others like her were the younger generations trying to rebel against the rules. They screamed, "Whose rules?!" And they contorted their bodies in the most odious ways. The loudest group got the most attention, while the quieter one withered away. Today, thought Natalie, ballet is a confusing mess. Ballet has fallen into a dormant age where people no longer believe in it. Teachers, like Madame Roberts, are trying to reawaken the belief, but I'm afraid that only a few understand.

We need a better *culture*. We need a world where ballet brings back *harmony* to people. Ballet has transformed *my* life, thought Natalie, and I'm no one special. All people could use ballet's principles and apply them to their lives. They could all use Louis XIV's five positions of ballet. They could all look aristocratic in their postures and movements of grace and poise. Their minds and bodies would be inseparable when using their moderately turned-out feet and hips to convey a sense of ease and reason. The slower movements would allow the time for their reason to speak in a level-headed manner about problems that always arise in life. People could raise each other up. Civilization is only possible with the reasoning man who uses his manners to conduct himself accordingly.

Natalie lingered, stretching out her fingers over the costumes and walls of the dressing room. To Natalie, the light of the world came from ballet studios where habit, ritual, and routine transformed people into the ideal. Carrying that light with her as she did so many nights after class, Natalie turned off the light switch to the dressing room and headed down the stairwell.

***

Upon exiting the theater, Natalie walked back home with her head held up high and her feet barely touching the ground. Her emotions were going off inside of her like fireworks, exploding with light and then glittering away in the dark before the next set went off. She felt so elated. How lucky am I to have found something that is lost? thought Natalie. Ballet is performing its own dying swan solo in a culture that no longer values its gifts. I suppose I should really thank my parents who were of a different time. They put me in my first classes whether I liked it or not. I am not really sure I even had an opinion at that age.

Natalie watched as an elderly couple, holding hands, walked down the opposite sidewalk. A pang of envy and grief hit her in the very spot she desired to conceal from the world now. Her heart was open to these two people who encapsulated her own vision of what life could have been like had her husband lived longer. He did not have to live forever, she thought, just long enough for me to forget him.

She slowed her pace down and tried not to stare, but she could not help noticing their wedding rings shining on each hand. They were duller now in their shine, but anyone passing could tell what those pieces were, what they had meant, and what enormous value they mean now. Natalie rubbed her tired eyes. She would never replace her love. She promised him that at his burial. Life was sweet enough with ballet in it to fill her aching soul.

There were times when he had walked into the house with open arms. He held her when she was upset and said nothing else, as if he knew exactly what she needed when she needed it. He would have been such a wonderful father, she sobbed.

"Hey, Natalie. Are you okay?" It was Dawn walking up beside her in the dusk.

Hastily running her hands across her face, Natalie asked, "What are you doing here?"

"I remembered you had just gotten out of class and I wanted to see if you were home, so I just started walking."

"Well, what for? Why do you want to see an old lady like

me?" she smiled.

"You're my friend," said Dawn. It was the first time that she had admitted to being friends with Natalie, "old" and "wrinkly" Natalie.

Natalie's vulnerable soul tonight was happy to let Dawn fill as much of her heart as possible. Thank you, dear, she thought and looked up in the sky where she imagined her husband would be waiting for her. "What, my dear, did you want to discuss tonight? Does your mother know where you are? I'm sure she is extra worried about you being out when the sun is going down, especially after what happened to you."

Dawn rolled her eyes and tucked her hand into Natalie's own, saying, "Yeah, yeah, my mother knows. She trusts you and she is kind of disgustingly happy that I am taking a break from ballet and that you are helping me through the transition. She must feel like she owes you one now. I could probably stay over whenever I wanted at this point," giggled Dawn. Her laughter sounded lighter and her movements appeared more relaxed. The coil of competition and ever-present stress was unloosening.

Natalie closed her eyes and imagined her husband holding her hand at this moment and not the little girl's petite, soft one. She imagined his course, calloused, large hands taking hold of her hands. Only in his were her hands made to feel smaller and more feminine. He was the only one to make her rise and fall in safety, but then he took that away from her. She had to fend completely for herself now and guide others to a life worth living without the one she loved.

Dawn looked up after a while of walking together in silence. "Is it your husband again?"

Natalie stood still for a moment and the missed beat was

like a crater that formed and was impossible not to notice by anyone near.

"It is, isn't it?" asked Dawn. "You only look this sad when you are thinking about him. Oh, please don't cry, Natalie." Dawn turned around on Natalie and held her.

Again, Natalie imagined her husband holding her and making her feel small and safe. With her eyes closed, she could just about smell his musk and taste his salty chest. But then she opened her eyes and found a thin, young girl clinging to her and trying to imitate the being that she longed for the most. Natalie's heart softened more toward this child who only wanted to help, even though she was the one who was supposed to be the receiver of help. Drawing in her breath, Natalie squeezed Dawn one more time tight and then let her go, a smile hiding the doorway to her vulnerable heart again. Natalie would remain strong tonight for her student, her child.

"Listen, when we get home, then maybe we could talk and drink some hot chocolate. Does that sound nice?" asked Natalie.

"Oh, yes! I need to tell you more about how my parents are dealing with this whole thing and about all the professions I was looking into last week. Did you know librarians need a master's degree? I thought that was kind of disappointing. But paralegals only need an associate's degree. That's only two years of college! Then I could go to dance classes in the evening and do my job during the day. I did look into becoming a dance teacher, but it was too painful to research… I think it would feel like I never truly let go of my dream, like I was a failure if I chose to just become a teacher. Besides, no one knows yet how my ankle will perform once it is fully healed."

"I think it's a smart idea for you to follow your gut right now,

Dawn. There are also personality tests you can take, which may help you discover a field you would really enjoy," said Natalie.

"Yeah, I just learned about those in school. I think we are required to take one this year anyway," said Dawn.

"Look, I understand the drive to find a new passion quickly, but you are still young. There is no rush to figure it all out in a week—just remember that. Okay?"

"I know, Natalie. I just am not the kind of person who can sit around and do things aimlessly. I was not raised that way by the ballet world. You know that."

Natalie smiled down at the sidewalk as she kept strolling. "Yes, I know. I shouldn't even waste my breath about slowing down. You're at the age where all of that chaotic energy from childhood is being channeled in one direction, and I think that's healthy for a girl like you. I really do."

Dawn looked up at Natalie as they walked forward together toward a common destination. "Natalie, about earlier…do you still think about your husband daily?"

"Yes," she sighed. "But sometimes I don't really acknowledge the thoughts. They just come and go as they please. I still have dreams about him too…"

"I hope you don't take this the wrong way, but how come Madame Angulaire's modern dance doesn't appeal to you more if life is such a struggle without him?"

Thinking about the subject in silence for a while, Natalie finally said: "I guess I'm just not a nihilistic person. Pain brings you nothing in the end but more pain. A person with self-esteem carries on through life with their held always held high, even when times are rough. I will *never* be a person who becomes a victim that enjoys contorting around on the floor irrationally. It is like spitting in the face of everything that is still *good* about the world. Even though I lost my husband, I still can breathe and see the sunrise and watch the seasons change every year along with the other people around me. There are still birds singing in the sky and other people who could help and keep inspiring me. Of course, nothing comes close to touching my heart and soul the way he did, but it is all much better than nothingness. I live a grateful person. I enjoy new inventions people create and new ways I can push myself to be even better than yesterday as a human being."

"You are sure inspiring yourself, Natalie," said Dawn. "I have never really heard anyone talk like you, except for maybe Madame Roberts."

"That's because parents today wallow in their own struggles. They feel like there is no way out and the culture only magnifies that victimhood. It's people like me and even the young Madame Roberts who know or recognize a different way to approach life. Dancing is just another aspect of *celebrating* life, not cursing it. Classical ballet was meant to be a part of civilization—a visual representation of how far we had come as a species. But today people want to tear that representation down. They want us to no longer be civilized. They desire everyone to go back to the primitive state we started in. All knowledge, growth, and progress are anathema to the people who are upholding modern ballet. Rather, the strong urges they claim come from within, with emotions leading them by the nose like in the ancient days, are how they want us to live. Then I would have no inventions at my fingertips, no shelter with the amenities I have now, and I would be forced to continue working to grow my own food which could easily be stolen from me without an ordered civilization around to keep me and my goods safe. I would still be able to breathe and see the sunrise and the birds, but I would have no time, space, or energy to even care about those things in a victim-ridden, primitive world. Does that make sense?"

It was difficult for Dawn to wrap her head around these big ideas, but she still felt in her gut that Natalie was a role model. She was someone to look up to and guidance from her was the only way that Dawn would find the ground beneath her feet and not on top of her head, crushing her to bits. As someone who showed no wrinkles or gray hairs or saggy skin yet, she had time to learn from someone else who was more knowledgeable about life than she was. And as she grew to know Natalie, the wrinkles and other time-worn features seemed to fade. Only a youthful Natalie, full of life and experience, spoke to her now. She could no longer make fun or feel sick when watching the adult class because they each had their own stories to tell. Their worn appearance was from a life *lived* which was long enough where when they were her age they thought the same way—I will never grow old. But aging was a slow and subtle process, one where the owner barely noticed the changes, but the person meeting them for the first time imagined they always looked the way they were—old. It was only when Dawn grew to know Natalie that she realized she was more than just "old." She was a *person*. A person who learned to live in the world on *her* terms no matter what changes occurred.

"Natalie, I may not understand everything you said, but I can feel that you are right. I will try to concretize the lessons you have given me for myself so that maybe one day I can sit with you over a cup of tea as an equal. You make me feel like living is such a wonderful gift. Thank you."

Natalie cried on the last leg of the trip home. She had always wanted a daughter who was as mature as Dawn was, and she knew that ballet had opened her up to become such a mature and graceful young lady. A lady who, thought Natalie, would grow up learning that life and its joys are all about subtlety. In order for a ballet dancer to appear as though they are gliding along the stage, it takes the subtle lengthening of the fingers and looseness of the hold, the long legs pointing in the direction of flight, and the strong torso holding all the moving parts together. These are micro-adjustments that only come from the hours of strength and stamina built up over time at the barre. To Natalie, ballet helped the dancer hone in on the tiny adjustments that make major differences. Discovering those differences in the way one walks upright without slouching or holds weights firmly without losing hold to cause injury or shifts the angle of their pen to write more legibly, all of those seemingly minor changes made people into healthy individuals, better weightlifters, more adept writers.

"Dawn, this may sound like an odd question, but I'll explain after I ask it. What is wrong with a line?" asked Natalie.

Dawn screwed up her face before answering: "Nothing. Madame Roberts was always telling us to remember our lines. It's the foundation of classical ballet."

Natalie smiled. "Exactly. The human form from head to toe is essentially a line. The creators of such movements were focused on the geometry of the human body. Standing upright forms a line, and when we splay ourselves out with our hands and our feet, we can create new lines at varying angles. That is why the head can only point to or away from the direction of the arms and legs. It loses its grace and precision when the

255

head is caught anywhere in between."

"Yes, I can still remember being scolded for not getting to the proper position in time with the music. I was frequently caught somewhere in between, but I learned quickly that the in-between was wrong. It was not even sort of the position. It was just not the correct position period—like math. I was often frustrated by those corrections. When I looked in the mirror, I always thought I was about where I needed to be, but Madame Roberts could tell in a second whether or not I was off."

"Yes, excellent teachers have the amazing ability to see the subtle shifts in the body that signify the correct or incorrect positioning. It becomes important for the dancer especially when they need to move and not lose balance. They have to be in a line on top of their standing leg before they can successfully execute a turn, for example. If they are askew at all, then the movement will not work. The teachers are the scientists of ballet," said Natalie.

"I suppose so. I never thought of it like that. Ballet was always just an art form to me."

"Well, it takes *science* to understand the physics of how you get dozens of *pirouettes* out of one preparation. The dancer executes like a soldier. Only when the dancer accomplishes the step, do they feel this overwhelming sense of ecstasy. Dancers are really *worshiping* the line. The line gives them the symmetry and grace required to produce a harmony visible to an audience. Anyone who walks near a dancer sees a bit of the divine. They see the clearer form of Man as he could be every day—not stuck in the in-between, the not really, the kinda-sorta, the wishy-washy, the gray mush that people like Madame Angulaire work under. The line is *real*, and it *exists*.

Ballet helps remind us of its existence in reality."

Dawn had never felt so drawn back to ballet before. She had no conscious reason before for lugging her shoes and tying up her hair and squeezing herself into a leotard and tights every day. Classes had seemed like a drag after a while and everyone was merely in competition with Dawn. She judged the young and the old for their outward appearances instead of their own stories and what they were personally trying to accomplish. She never slowed down to listen really to the music or her body. It was solely about executing the steps like an automaton. What was the reason for doing so? Dawn just obeyed the teacher and never asked why. If the teacher told her to slouch, she would slouch; if the teacher told her to stop sickling her foot, she would stop sickling; if the teacher told her to turn her feet inward, she turned them inward. She followed these orders indiscriminately until the desire and love for ballet withered, and it no longer felt worth it to even pull her hair up into a bun anymore. Her passion had been killed by a teacher with the wrong philosophy.

"I...I never realized how important the line was. I feel kind of foolish for believing that ballet always was and always will be. I had no idea how *fragile* it really was. Can you believe it entirely relies on other people to keep it going?" asked Dawn.

"It is kind of frightening and I am afraid that the line right now is waning from ballet. The line is being spat on by the modern dancers and after the hateful smears, it might fall away until a new, better culture picks it up again. Only those who understand the line can carry it forth and make people's lives meaningful once more. I'm afraid that only a few of us left still share my sentiment. I can only hope that someday, people will awake from this dormant age and, through reason, find the harmonious line," said Natalie.

Dawn fell a little behind Natalie as they approached her house. Visions of the studio and its smells of sweat and rosin filled her senses as she watched Natalie walk. Natalie stood up tall like there was a string holding her up by the head. Her legs carried her forward gracefully, yet without any hesitancy. Her feet pointed out in front of her until they went through a *demi-pointe* and onto the flat soles of her feet, moving through that process with every single step. Her arms swung lightly, opposing the weight of her legs. Her hands, her beautiful, lived-in hands, loosely curved with each finger, delicately given a space of their own. She was a *true* dancer.

THE END

About the Author

Kaitlyn Bankson (born Kaitlyn Marie Quis in New York, January 3, 1994) is an American writer. She studied literature and philosophy throughout her education, which shaped her creative voice. She is the author of the novel *The Paper Pusher*. Kaitlyn's unique perspective and raw prose bring light to matters that are often left untouched. She lives in Dubuque, Iowa, with her husband. Readers can see more of Kaitlyn's work at www.kaitlynbankson.com.

You can connect with me on:
- 🌐 https://kaitlynbankson.com
- 🐦 https://x.com/kaitlynbankson
- 🔗 https://linkedin.com/in/kaitlynbankson

Subscribe to my newsletter:
- ✉ http://eepurl.com/glJhKf